Fuzzy Socks

and

MIDNIGHT CLOCKS

Fuzzy Socks
and
MIDNIGHT
CLOCKS

SHERRIE MACKELPRANG

SWEETWATER BOOKS
An imprint of Cedar Fort, Inc.
Springville, Utah

ISBN 13: 978-1-4621-3980-4

Published by Sweetwater Books, an imprint of Cedar Fort, Inc.
2373 W. 700 S., Springville, UT 84663
Distributed by Cedar Fort, Inc., www.cedarfort.com

Library of Congress Control Number: 2021932752

Cover design by Courtney Proby
Cover design © 2021 Cedar Fort, Inc.
Edited and typeset by Valene Wood and Hali Bird

Printed in the United States of America

10 9 8 7 6 5 4 3 2 1

Printed on acid-free paper

For Mom
Thanks

November 1st, Sunday

"Just give her the roast." Mom pushed the frozen package into my hands without giving me a chance to consider whether or not I should take it. Then turning on my sister, she snipped, "Annie, do something."

Mom was unstoppable. I had made the cardinal mistake of mentioning how much I enjoyed being single. Her long eyelashes framed her feisty blue eyes. Dad had vacated the room with my brothers-in-law, but not before giving me that look that said, *Hang in there, kid.*

Knowing that it was best to just let her say her piece, I held my opinions securely inside my head. "Teach your sister what it takes to get not just any man . . . but a husband," Mom clarified, as if it were needed. I suppose from her perspective, the clarification was essential. "A good man." She reemphasized waving her arms as though she were flagging down the last ship to save her sinking daughter.

Annie failed miserably at hiding the it-stinks-to-be-you grin on her face. Then her snarky demeanor dissolved into a faint smile. She had plenty of reasons to smile. Her tall, dark, and handsome husband worships the ground she walks on. Not only does he earn a nice living, he also does the dishes every night.

Mom turned sharply as if reading my thoughts. She doesn't have a lot of patience when she feels that she is being excluded from our nonverbal, sisterly glances. She always thinks we're formulating plans of wicked defiance. Hardly.

Finger aimed at me, she announced, "Lindsey, you have got to get a husband. Stop frittering around in silly little romances, and stop being yourself." With her last comment still painting the air, maybe I could use a little defiance.

Annie snorted.

My other sister, Susy, reclined easily on the leather sofa cradling her perfect, angel baby. She was clearly out of the crosshairs. Her gaze was a pitying one.

I shrugged it off. "Mom, I don't need the roast." Casting my eyes around the room, and bracing for the backlash that would undoubtedly follow, I opted for the truth to free me from this stacked up menagerie of motherly emotions. "I don't know how to cook a roast."

This was not earth-shattering news. Everyone was fully aware of my lack of interest in the kitchen. I quickly added, "And . . . I don't see myself eating an entire roast." I dumped the frozen brick onto the table, massaging blood back into my fingers.

"You are missing the point," Mom bit. "The roast isn't for you. It is for you to manipulate a boy over to eat it with you." Her arms flew into the air with a huff. Then, with her finger cocked and pointed squarely at me, she gave me the to-do list. "*You* make the roast, and *you* tell that pin-headed boy you've been gawking at to come over and help you eat it." Her eyes pinned me like a bug under glass. She studied me hard to see if I was getting the message. Unconvinced, she turned and pointed her motherly finger in Susy's direction. "You can practice the dinner invite on your little sister." Then she swooped back to me. "It isn't difficult. Just tell the boy you've got a roast. He'll come running."

I wondered how Isaac (he is the *silly little romance* that Mom so pointedly despises), who is busy working on his master's degree, would feel about being referred to as a *pin-headed boy*. I also wondered how he would feel about being invited over to eat a massive slab of beef since he declared himself vegan two months ago.

"Mom," Annie chimed in, "Lindsey will probably have to have him come over to cook it."

Okay, so it was a little late, but there it was, the jab I had been anticipating. Good one, Annie.

Annie's pointed criticism caught Mom off guard. Hooray. Her mouth twitched. I didn't wonder what was next. It began with the twitch at the corners of her mouth. Next, her eyes scrunched up as she tried to hold it in. First, just a snort, then a big, hearty laugh. Susy and Annie swapped glances and burst out laughing.

Susy immediately caught herself and hushed as her little one stirred. Mom roared. I shrugged. What can I say? I would rather clean a bathroom than cook a meal.

Susy, who also has a perfect husband, put a finger to her lips. We all quieted.

Whispering, Susy did not miss out on taking an opportunity for a good sisterly jab. "Whatever you do, just don't show him your weird feet."

Ah, my feet. Perfect. Let's lay all my weaknesses out in the open. I knew someone would bring them into the conversation eventually.

Mom turned her shocked face toward Susy. Then she gave me an *almost* sympathetic glance before erupting with laughter once again. Annie's face turned pink as she tried to muffle her giggles behind her hands. Susy's eyes danced as she cradled Michael.

Ugh, let me explain.

It is a vicious challenge. I have ugly . . . very ugly . . . toes. As a kid, I didn't know anything was different. Toes are toes, right? Then I started catching stares when I would go to the swimming pool. The comments followed.

"What did you do? Did you put your feet in a blender?"

"When my dad lost his marbles, they all stuck to the ends of your feet."

"You *really* need a pedicure."

This is the reason closed-toe shoes are my friends in every season. Afterall, feet hiding is a delicate skill.

My sisters and mother regained their composure when Michael started to fuss.

Such was the grand finale of my weekend visit to see my parents and sisters. And, as you can see, there are reasons that some things should be kept hidden, especially from family.

Oh, and in case you were wondering, I did bring home the frozen roast. Dad convinced me that it was a sensible food item to have on hand. I'm sure I can find a blog for a yummy way to cook a roast, or I can always gift it to one of my neighbors. Possibilities.

Until next time . . . Me

November 4th, Wednesday

I had better explain some things here, for my future posterity. I am an elementary school teacher. I teach fourth grade. I am five foot eight. I am half African American. My eyes are deep brown. My hair is black and curly. I am currently finishing my master's degree. You also need to know that I paid off all my debt from my bachelor's degree before starting the master's program. (Silent applause!) The finish line is now in sight.

You should also know that I did see Isaac today, the famous *pin-headed* boy. We crossed paths on the commons lawn as I was hurrying to my night class. No, I didn't mention the roast. However, he did invite me to dinner on Friday.

Isaac and I have known each other for the better part of a year. We met at a crowded lecture where he offered me his chair. I gratefully accepted and, as Mom would say, have been "gawking at the pin-headed boy" ever since. He and I have been seeing each other a lot lately. I thought it best to keep Mom out of the loop. I'm sure you understand.

It was sweet really, how he asked me out. With his hand on my arm, my skin sizzled, he lowered his head just slightly, and asked. "Lindsey, do you have plans for this Friday?" The outdoor lights reflected on his hair.

Smiling, I shook my head. "Nothing that can't be changed." Lifting his head, he smiled warmly back at me. "Have dinner with me?"

Something jumped and twirled in my middle. With a small nod, I said, "Yes."

There's one for Mom to digest. I have another date with Isaac, no roast required. I suspect that I will put Mom in the hospital if I do not marry before the next winter Olympics. Thank goodness that's her worry and not mine.

Until next time . . . Me.

November 6th, Friday

I like teaching. I do. Lately though, I just keep feeling that something's off. I catch myself considering doing other things. Other careers. Or . . . keeping the career but moving somewhere else. I don't know what it is. Mom would say I need a husband, a family, the stable things in life, or something like that. I don't know. Maybe I'm just restless.

Now, let me tell you about this evening's dinner with Isaac.

I wore my black dress. Yes, the cute one with the slender silver belt. I love that dress! With my ankle boots, closed toe of course. I couldn't miss.

Isaac picked me up late, but with an extravagant bouquet of pink roses. "You look amazing," he gushed as he held the door of his SUV open for me. His dark eyes sparkled. "We need to do this more often."

I smiled and slid myself onto the leather seat.

Mom may call him a pin-headed boy, because she thinks he's skinny, but I've gotta say he is hot. Don't judge me harshly. I do spend my days with nine- and ten-year-olds. "Hot" is a perfectly acceptable adjective to describe the man. Isaac is tall and fit. His dark eyes are an exquisite match for his dark, perfectly placed hair.

Braving the Las Vegas traffic, we ate downtown at *Le Chateau*. Walking into a restaurant with him is like walking into a classroom with ice cream bars. Heads turn.

We sat at a private table, as per his reservations. His conversation was riveting as we discussed everything from our career dreams to world events.

"I like being with you," Isaac spoke as he softly lifted my hand. His smile simmered.

I smiled back, and my cheeks got hot.

He slowly lifted my fingers to his lips and kissed them lightly. Butterflies ice-skated inside me. I shivered.

"Can I see you again this week?" He lowered my hand to the table but did not let it go, his fingers wrapped neatly around mine.

I nodded like a fool. Smiling up at him, I asked, "What day?"

Releasing my hand for a quick minute, he reached into the inner pocket of his blazer and produced two tickets to *Michael Jackson ONE*—The *Cirque du Soleil* show—I had been dying to see. Even though Michael Jackson was from my parents' generation, I wanted to go to the show for ages now. Isaac cleverly knew that. With his eyes twinkling, he asked, "How about tomorrow night?"

My smile stretched halfway across the restaurant.

Sliding the tickets to me, he added, "And you keep the tickets. That way if you get a better offer, you can kick me to the curb and still go to the show." Leaning back with a smile and a sigh, his white teeth put the flickering candle on the table to shame.

I laughed and scooped the tickets up from the table. My eyes bulged. He had purchased expensive seats. I tucked them into the front pouch of my purse.

I can't wait for tomorrow.

Dropping me off at my apartment, Isaac politely, softly, and with just a hint of lingering, kissed me goodnight.

Sweet dreams . . . Me

November 8th, Sunday

I am exhausted.

Isaac picked me up thirty minutes late yesterday. Poor guy. Instead of flowers, he showered me with compliments.

"You are pure perfection. How do you do it?"

I soaked it up.

We had planned on having dinner before the show, but due to Isaac's tardiness, there just wasn't time. We did manage to steal a few minutes to walk a little and drink Italian sodas before the show. He made me laugh.

It felt good to be with him.

Our seats were perfect. Three rows back, dead center. It was like nothing I have ever seen, or heard, or experienced. I loved it. I am pretty certain that Isaac and I were the youngest people in the audience.

After the show, Isaac was sweet and bought me a souvenir t-shirt. Next, he took me to *Lupo*, an Italian restaurant where I stuffed my face with the most amazing pasta. After dinner, we walked and talked. He told me about his work, his family, and his dreams. It was easy to walk and listen.

Stopping at a beautiful, tiled fountain, we sat on its edge and ate ice cream. Isaac polished off his ice cream then bent over and began unlacing his leather oxfords.

"What are you doing?" I asked, nearly choking.

He grinned mischievously, cocking his head sideways to see me. "I might get arrested, but I have always wanted to wade in a fountain." He surveyed the surroundings. Sitting up, he bobbed his head in either direction, "There aren't too many people. I might get away with it." Stooping, he tugged off his shoes and paused. "But probably not." He winked at me and pulled off his navy-blue socks that were covered with yellow pineapples. Kicking his shoes and socks against the base of the enormous fountain, he stood and offered me his hand. "Join me in the fountain, my princess?"

"What?" I panicked. All the blood drained from my face. "No. No way!" No way was I taking my shoes off for anyone. Not Isaac. *Especially* Isaac. What if he saw my weird, misshapen toes and ran away crying, like I was a circus freak? I was physically shaken at the thought.

"No problem." With a flourish, he was on his knees heading for my shoes. I jumped up. He couldn't get them off of me if I was standing. I held my position like a statue at Easter Island. He gave a few jovial tugs at my feet. I was rock solid.

"My princess . . ." he pleaded with his arms open wide.

A few people filed past us. Most glanced our way.

Shaking my head vehemently, he finally gave up on me.

With a look of gloomy defeat, Isaac sat back down on the edge of the fountain. He replaced his socks and his shoes. "Maybe some other time," Isaac smiled back up at me. All was forgiven. Relief . . .

Offering me his hand, we stood together. A security guard magically appeared and watched us. Too late. There was nothing to patrol here now.

We walked on. My jitters melted like cotton candy on the tongue. I was safe again.

Leaving the glittering lights, Isaac took me home. As he pulled to a stop in the parking lot of my apartment, I said. "You really surprised me."

Isaac laughed, a warm easy laugh. He inhaled deeply and replied, "Sometimes I surprise myself. I guess it's the kid in me. Sometimes it just wants to get out." He leaned over, touched my face, and kissed me sweetly. I climbed out of the SUV and floated home. I pondered on what could be.

Morning came, as morning does. I wasn't ready for it. Thankfully, I was still on time to church.

For posterity, I should mention that I attend a family ward. I like it.

You should also know that Sundays tend to cause me to wax a little poetic, or long winded, in my journal writing. But hey, it is all for posterity. The future and rising generations deserve a shot at deciphering the intricacies of my brain. Ha ha!

To enlighten the masses, I am going to tell how I came to be me. That was a good line. Laying biology aside, and stepping into an almost soap-opera storyline, let me give you the scoop. I am the daughter of Janet and John Jones. I am their only daughter.

Anyway, my parents met in Las Vegas. My mother was working part-time at a restaurant called *Pie A La Mode*. Dad was a mechanic for a car dealership. They met in a classic romance sort of style. Mom was newly divorced and a single mom. It was just she and a two-year-old, Annie. Dad would eat at the restaurant, leave extravagant tips, and always ask for a date. After two months of coaxing, Mom went out with Dad. It was all the dreamy magic that any romance should be—chocolates, roses, and expensive shows. Annie even tagged along. After a dreamy courtship of about two months, they married at the Chapel of Love.

Great story, so far, huh? Keep reading. It gets better. Turns out that my dad had just the tiniest bit of a gambling problem. Well, that's a complete lie. Forgive me, posterity. I will tell it to you like it was—or as I have been told. Dad was hooked on gambling. He was one of those sad cases you hear about. He could spend an entire night in front of a slot machine. He didn't need to eat, drink, or sleep when he was in front of the machines or playing at the tables. It was chronic. Just prior to meeting Mom, he had checked himself into a rehab clinic for gamblers. Serious addiction. He was on the mend when he and my mother crossed paths. After the marriage, however, he went downhill in a blink. The stress of a wife, a daughter, and a baby on the way (me) was more than he could manage. As fast as the paychecks came in, they were devoured by the slot machines and gaming tables. Mom picked up a second job and prayed he would change. She was really a trooper.

Regrettably, he did not change. Gambling was like a noose around his neck.

My parents ended their brief marriage shortly before I was born. So, I never really knew my dad. I just heard the stories as I was growing up. I am not completely sure that he ever even knew about me. Mom has always been a little vague about that.

As a child, I used to wonder about him. I would make grand plans to run into the nearest casino and rescue him from the clanking machines. I never did.

Now, don't think that my history ends there. It doesn't. There is more.

Like the miracle that it was, my mom reconnected with her first husband. Oddly, he came to find her at *Pie A La Mode*. He was devastated without her. He regretted the divorce and the mess he had made. They were in love again.

At only a few weeks old, I was dolled up in a ruffly, pink dress, and I was passed from one relative to another at the wedding reception as the parents that I know got married.

Confused? Hang in there.

Two years later, they gave me a little sister, Susy. That is the true story of how I came to be the only child of John and Janet. It also explains why I look nothing like either of my sisters. Mom, Annie, and Susy are all blue eyed and blonde. I am the only African American in my family. I am thankful my parents gave me such beautiful genetics.

Good night . . . Me

november 11th, Wednesday

First thing, an update on my education. This is my second to last semester of classes. Then I will be the proud earner of an MED degree. That's a Master's in Education. I can't wait! I won't be rolling in the dough, but I will get a raise and that is nothing to sniff at.

I received an impromptu surprise. Isaac caught me after school and took me to a play. It was on campus. The title was *The Sound of Violets*. Weird title. Weirder story. I really do not know what it was about. However, with Isaac, it was lovely. He smelled good, and I got to breathe him in for two and a half hours. Just lovely.

I can easily list all the things I like about him. I love his attention. I love the attention of being seen with him. I like how he smells. I even like the flair that he adds to all of our dates: flowers, chocolates, or something fun. Once, shortly after we met, he brought me a frisbee. We were going to a convocation on Mistaken Beliefs in Educational Practices. The frisbee was the promise of another date—something a little lighter than educational practices. That's Isaac.

Sleep well . . . Me

november 13th, Friday

They say that if you want to have a better day, go and do something for someone else. Well, I had a whopper of a day.

One of my colleagues, Tammy Bradley, broke out in a horrible case of hives. I spent my prep, and all of my lunch, trying to help cover her class. There was some miscommunication with getting a sub. For the last hour of school, I taught a combined class. We got through it, but I'm beat.

To combat my self-pity, I am going to make cookies for my neighbor. (Yes, I bought the cookie dough.) My self-centered, tired brain is rebelling, but I am determined. My neighbor is a sweet, kindly soul that leaves treats at my door from time to time. Besides, I could also use some of her goodness to rub off on me.

Because my neighbor keeps a "Shoes Off" sign by the door, I'll be sure to wear socks when I take the cookies.

Isaac just texted!

> *Hi Gorgeous, I can't stop thinking of you. Will you go to a party with me? It's tonight, after the basketball game. It won't be as fun if you're not there.*

> *Hmmm . . . a party. That sounds fabulous. I even have new shoes. I would love to go with you.*

Isaac picked me up at 8:30. He handed me a foam finger. "Here, I bought one for each of us. It'll make us look like real fans."

I laughed. "We'll need that, especially since we'll miss the game."

He put the foam finger to his lips. "No one will know . . . Besides, I think we'll make the last fifteen minutes if we hurry."

The stadium was crowded with screaming fans. We stood close together, as the final seconds of the game ticked down. At the buzzer, a UNLV player took a shot. It was a perfect basket. The crowd erupted. We waved our foam fingers. Air horns blared. Balloons dropped from the ceiling. Isaac wrapped his arm tightly around my waist as if protecting me from the wave of fans that rushed out onto the floor. I savored his touch.

We left the stadium and drove to a house in a nice neighborhood. The house pulsed with people and music. Isaac held my hand as we walked up the drive. Leaning into me he said, "Thank you for coming tonight."

I smiled and squeezed his hand.

The door to the home flew open as we approached and a half dozen people spilled out. We walked into the grand house. Isaac spoke into my ear. "One of the guys at work owns this house. I think he just wanted to show it off."

I laughed as the crowd absorbed us.

Isaac waved and nodded his head at dozens of people.

Unfortunately, at that moment, my feet started to complain. After the long day, my new shoes were a bad choice.

"Hey, Lindsey." A girl from one of my night classes shouted above the noise and waved.

Surprised to see anyone I knew, I smiled and waved.

Noisy conversations about the game competed with the music.

Isaac found my waist and steered me into the backyard. He spun me under his arm and we joined a dancing crowd on the lawn. The music slowed and Isaac pulled me close. I loved his touch, but my feet were throbbing. Evil new shoes.

As soon as the song ended, a friend of Isaac's stepped up and slapped him playfully on the shoulder. Isaac introduced me, but all I could hear was the thump of the next song. The two talked with their heads together.

Slipping from Isaac's grip, I knelt to loosen the laces on my shoes. My feet thanked me for the relief. It was actually a blessing for Isaac's friend to be there. Knowing Isaac, he would have offered to rub my feet, and there was no way I was going down that road.

Before I stood, I caught a glimpse of Isaac's friend's tattoo as he passed something into Isaac's hand. I chuckled inside. A cartoon seal . . . people do strange things. I'm glad Isaac isn't tattooed.

The man left. Isaac lifted my hands in his. "Sorry about that." His smile melted over me. I forgot my aching feet for the moment.

We danced.

He kissed me lightly on my front steps when he brought me home. I'm glad I went to the party.

Smiling . . . Me

November 14th, Saturday

Isaac invited me to lunch. A very important lunch. Read on.

Isaac picked me up, his SUV gleaming with a recent detail job. I wore my new jeans and cream-colored sweater. My gray booties were perfect. (Thankfully I had had enough time to shower and clean up after helping my neighbor clean out her spare bedroom. When I took over the cookies, she asked if I could come back and help today.)

Isaac was in his element. Holding the door for me, we entered an elegant Chinese restaurant. The atmosphere was mysterious, dim lighting, golden dragons, all the servers dressed in black. Isaac impressed our server by ordering in Mandarin as we sat side by side in a corner booth. Then all his attention was on me. His black eyes sparkled in the low light. He reached across the red satin tablecloth and took my hand. It was warm and thrilling to sit there holding his hand.

I smiled and blushed as he stroked the back of my hand with his thumb. This must be right. We make the perfect pair.

He leaned in close.

"Tell me your thoughts," Isaac spoke low, his breath tickling my ear. I couldn't resist rubbing the sensation from my ear. I may have looked a little childish rubbing my ear, but I am okay with that.

I whispered back to him, "I think I should have ordered chow mein instead of trusting you to order for me." I turned and met his sparkling eyes with a smile.

"You're beautiful, you know." He gave my hand a little squeeze.

A ripple of happy emotions danced up from my troubling toes.

His lips found my face and he kissed me gently on the cheek. With my heart gliding, I smiled. Tilting his head, he kissed my eyelids sweetly.

I turned away, not wanting to encourage him.

Thankfully, our food arrived. I can't tell you what I ate, but It was amazing.

All through the meal, Isaac barely ate. His attention was fixed on me. I loved it, but it confused me.

Between bites, I managed to ask, "What are you up to?"

My question seemed to catch him off guard. A shadow briefly darkened his features. His smile illuminated again. "Lindsey . . ." He set his fork on his plate. He picked up my hand in both of his. "I've decided to be honest with you . . . and with myself."

I lowered my fork. "Honest?" a strange sensation swept through me. "What do you mean?" I quirked an eyebrow and smiled. "Do you have some demons in your life that I need to know about?"

That same troubled look flitted across his face before dissolving into another one of his picture-perfect smiles. "You think you're funny."

I smiled and shrugged.

Sliding closer, he softly spoke. "I want you to know that I feel for you things that I didn't expect to feel. Good things." He studied my gaze to see if I was catching his meaning. The corners of my mouth turned up into a smile. He appeared to breathe a little easier. "What I mean is, I don't want to be a simple or casual part of your life. The truth is, I want to be a permanent part of your life." His fingers wrapped a little tighter.

Permanent? "What do you mean, permanent?"

He flashed me a smile, kissed my hand, and flagged down our waiter. With a healthy tip left on the table, Isaac stood and reached for my hand. "Come on. There's something I want you to see." He held my hand tight as we exited the restaurant.

The late afternoon sun brushed the city in yellow gold. This is my favorite time of year. The Las Vegas heat lifts and the soft desert winter starts to nudge in.

"Where are we going?" I asked as Isaac motioned me to his car. Isaac held up a finger. "Wait and see," he said with a boyish grin spreading across his flawless face.

We drove west until the city was behind us. With his sunglasses on, he pulled into a parking lot. Red Rock Canyon. As I climbed out, he snatched a small backpack from the back seat. He had planned this.

I followed along dutifully as Isaac headed for the red rocks. "I am really not dressed for a hike. These boots will kill me on the rocks."

He flashed me another grin, took my hand and led me up a shallow sandstone incline to a spot where it leveled off, facing the city.

Digging in his backpack, he produced a small fleece blanket. Spreading it on the rock, he motioned for me to sit down. I looked at him with my best fishy smirk and obeyed. "What is this all about?" I asked as my insides danced and played tug-o-war.

Kneeling in front of me, he produced a slightly bruised rose from the bag and handed it to me. I couldn't keep from laughing. A wisp of hurt dimmed his face. "I'm sorry. I'm not laughing at this," I said holding up the rose by the little vial of water that held the stem. "I'm laughing because you have obviously planned for this for some time. I seriously just thought we were going for a hike. What's going on?"

His grin reignited to its full brilliance. Holding up a finger, he signaled for me to wait. My insides fluttered with delight. I soaked up the happy.

Pulling two silver forks and two ceramic plates from his bag, he set them neatly on the blanket in front of me. Two crystal candlesticks with electric candles followed. He turned on the flames, though they were barely visible in the late afternoon sun. Next, he produced a black Styrofoam container with two slightly melted raspberry cupcakes inside. Laughing again I blurted, "You brought me out here for dessert?"

He served up the cupcakes and looked me steadily in the eyes. "Not just for dessert . . ." He finally spoke. Lowering his voice, he added, ". . . but for this." Sliding onto one knee, he produced a red velvet ring box from his pocket. My heart thudded like a thousand running stallions.

Opening the box to reveal a fabulous diamond ring, he said, "Lindsey, I can't imagine my life without you." Without breaking his gaze, he asked, "Will you be my wife?"

It was perfect, everything about this moment was like a fairytale dream come true. Prince Charming, nervous and on one knee, the thought-out plan, and the setting. I had thought about this possibility, marrying him, more than I had ever admitted to myself or anyone. Now here it was. He could love me despite my feet. Couldn't he? It must be right. All of these thoughts swirled and crashed into my answer to him.

"Yes, you silly boy. I will happily be your wife," I exclaimed.

He sucked in a breath and about knocked me over as he gripped me tight and kissed me once. He slid the ring on my finger, it was *nearly* a perfect fit. We'll get it sized.

What a life-changing day!

I want to call Susy and Annie. I want to tell Mom, but Isaac and I thought it was better to wait to let our families know our plans. I know Annie will flip. Susy will be excited. Mom will undoubtedly launch into some frenzy of wound-up motherly emotions. There will be no peace once she knows. Goodness.

I'm excited to be Isaac's wife, and I am nervous. It's a lot to think about. I know he earns a good living. He is patient and kind to everyone. I think we will have a good life together. We plan to stay in Las Vegas. He wants to buy a condominium. I don't really care where we live, but I think it will be exhilarating to sort out the details of our lives together, day by day.

Wonderful . . . Me

November 5th, Sunday

I decided not to drive home, well back to St. George, for the weekend. I will continue to enjoy the quiet happiness of being engaged for a few more days. Besides, Isaac and I talked and Thanksgiving is just around the bend. That's soon enough to tell the family.

I must add, though, there is something exciting about a ring on my finger and Isaac's hand in mine. My nerves seem to be getting used to the idea of being his wife.

Until next time . . . Me

November 19th, Thursday

One week until Thanksgiving!

My students cheered over my new ring and my name soon to be changing to Mrs. Samuels. It was fun.

Isaac sent me a sweet bouquet of red roses today. It caused quite a stir in the office. When I went to pick up the flowers, the secretary grabbed my hand and took a long look at my ring. The nurse leaned in to have a look, and the principal gave me a thumbs up. Then came the flood of marital advice. I will share just a small portion of the advice I received:

The school secretary, Mrs. Milridge: "Keep him fed. That'll keep him quiet."

The nurse, Ms. Nethbie, was a little more serious: "All I want to tell you is that you marry that boy as he is. You take him as he is. You keep loving him as he is."

The principal asked how soon she would need to change my name plate in the hall.

Isaac and I are struggling to pick a date. We talked for an hour and considered every option. He is eager to get on with our lives together.

It's funny. I didn't tell him, but I'm feeling a little hesitant. I don't know what it is. It's probably just nerves. I mean, I know it's silly but at some point he is going to lay eyes on my feet. That thought stirs my insides. Maybe that's all I'm feeling? Or, maybe it's the stress of trying to plan a wedding and balance classes and work. I don't know.

Before we said goodbye, I told Isaac that I would be okay with any wedding date.

Oh, I received a strange letter in the mail from an attorney's office. It was from Craig and Associates. I tore it open without thinking as I was going through my mail. It said something about setting up an appointment to meet with them regarding an estate, or something. I threw it away. It must be a scam.

Gotta study . . . Me

November 26th, Thanksgiving!

Okay, so we did it! I am at my parents' house. Isaac came too, and my parents know that we are getting married. Mom is on the phone, as I write, telling as many family members, friends, and random strangers as possible about her daughter *finally* getting married. Isaac, and the rest of the family, are lounging in front of the football game in the basement. I kind of hate football. (Please do not slam my journal shut. I apologize if any of you are football fanatics.)

I will say though that the game gives me some time to be alone and an opportunity to write.

I thought it would be fun to show up at the door with Isaac and surprise my family. Isaac agreed. Just like a scene from a Hallmark movie, Mom was thrilled. My sisters both hovered around him and asked him all kinds of probing questions. Annie jumped up and down at the sight of my ring, and Susy gave Isaac an approving nod. Dad grinned and hugged us both. Victor and John, my brothers-in-law, slapped Isaac's back, hugged me, and wished us well.

Isaac was full of charm and ease with all of my family. He was the perfect conversationalist. He sealed things with Mom when he volunteered to mash the potatoes and stir the gravy. He won Dad's approval when he borrowed the drill and repaired the wobbly table leg. Dad always approves of anyone that can handle power tools. (Frankly, I had no idea that Isaac could do the job. He impressed me as well.)

It has been a perfect afternoon. I just wish those pestering feelings of doubt, and my insecurities, would leave me alone.

Isaac called his parents. I was a little nervous about how they might react. They knew he was spending Thanksgiving with *a friend*. They just didn't know that this *friend* is his fiancée. He spoke privately with them.

Isaac found me in the kitchen and kissed me on the cheek after his call. "They're thrilled."

"Really?" I searched his face for any hint that he was lying.

"Really." He lifted my hand and kissed it. "They are eager to meet you."

Relief washed down to my toes.

Isaac knows something of the *get married* pressure I have been feeling. His parents are not terribly different from mine, it seems.

Still no feet sharing . . . Me

Later

Annie and Susy left with their families. Isaac is settled in the guest room upstairs. We had an opportunity to sit on the porch earlier and just talk, after the tryptophan and food coma had sent both of my parents to bed.

"You look nothing like your sisters," Isaac said the words cautiously.

I smiled. With a little laugh, I explained. "They are my half-sisters." I couldn't believe I had never told my story to Isaac. It never came up. Silly me. I have shared more with invisible posterity than with the man I am planning to marry.

"What does that mean?" Isaac asked, wrapping his arm around my shoulders.

Breathing him in, I explained about my dad.

Nodding, Isaac asked the blunt question. "Was your dad white?"

"My dad, my biological-gene-pool-sharing-dad, had a dark complexion, dark eyes, and thick, curly, black hair. Also, he was very muscular and tall." I paused for effect. "No, he was not white. He was African American."

Because of my unexpected appearances, all my life I have lived the classic "things are not what they seem" scenario. It went something like this:

Random well-meaning lady: "Oh, are these your daughters?" pointing to Susy and Annie.

Mom: Proudly speaking: "Yes."

Random lady: "They are lovely. What pretty girls."

Mom: Beaming.

I step into the conversation.

Random lady: "Oh, is this your daughter too?"

Mom: "Yes."

Random lady: Struggling to save face over her surprise, "Well, (awkward pause) . . . she is lovely, too. Very pretty."

Mom: Beams and nods.

Simply stated, I catch people by surprise. No one is going to expect such a dark complected *beauty*, my descriptive word of choice, to be sandwiched between two wide eyed blondes with flowing straight hair. It's kind of fun, though. I have to admit I get a kick out of the look of consternation that crosses people's faces when they try to make sense of the family dynamic. Most assume I was adopted. I just let them think it. It's easier than trying to explain the truth.

Isaac puzzled over what I told him. "You never met your dad?"

"No, but it's okay. I have a dad." This always seemed to bother other people more than it troubled me. "I have a loving, happy family."

He leaned his head on mine. "Do you ever get curious? Have you ever tried to find him?"

"No . . . well . . . when I was little, I would think about finding him."

"You don't think about it anymore?" He stroked my hand.

"Not really. I am pretty happy with my life."

"That's good."

It is good. I saved my feet to be revealed another day.

Talking with Isaac stirred something. Now, lying in bed, my thoughts drift. Where is my biological father? I wonder if I should look for him. I mean, I am getting married. Would he want to know?

With questions . . . Me

December 2ⁿᵈ, Wednesday

Busy week. I've hardly seen Isaac. He is deep into his graduate project. Poor guy. I keep getting sweet little text messages from him.

> *Missing you.*
>
> *You are my forever and always.*
>
> *I can't think of a more beautiful and inspiring person than you.*

We still haven't set a date. My parents, well Mom, is getting a little bent about it. Isaac's work has him all over the place right now. He goes to Mexico next week. I am pea green with envy. He assured me that he will not be spending any time at resorts or beaches. It is all business . . . so he said.

His work is in marketing. From what I understand, he represents an insurance company. Isaac likes to keep aloof when it comes to discussing his work. It's part of his charm. He thinks it's in poor taste to mix work and social time. I was a little surprised when he mentioned this trip to Mexico. I thought the company was only in the US, but, like I said, Isaac is aloof. Regardless, he seems to do okay. He has a townhome in a cute, gated community. He wears nice clothes. His SUV is all but new. He never scrimps on our dates. I guess I can live with not fully understanding the details of his work for now. We will have all our lives for me to figure it out.

Isaac's mom is putting some pressure for us to set a date, as well. I still have not met his parents. That will happen over Christmas vacation, just two-and-a-half weeks away. I hope I make the cut. I'm really nervous to meet his sister.

With jitters . . . Me

December 4th, Friday

Ah, Friday!

Full weekend of homework for me.

Isaac's in Mexico. He flew out two days early. I didn't get to see him before he left. All he sent was a brief text:

> *Flying out today. So sorry. Unexpected. Love you. Talk*
> *soon. What do you think about January?*

January? I like it. Early January, at the change of the semester, might be perfect. My heart flipped and tumbled. January.

A second letter arrived today from the Craig and Associates law office. I opened it. Scanning the page, my eyes stopped at my name and my biological dad's name. If it is a scam, it's a new one. I have never had any correspondence that links me to my biological dad. The only place that I am aware of that links me to him is my birth certificate.

He really disappeared.

This is pretty weird.

My homework is waiting . . . Me

December 10th, Thursday

Another short text from Isaac.

Back in the States. Can't wait to see you.

I tried calling his phone while he was in Mexico. It was like he had it turned off the entire time. I was disappointed, but I will get to see him soon.

Missing him . . . Me

December 15th, Tuesday

The school Christmas sing-along was a success. Three more days till the break. I am also happy to announce that I have officially completed all the requirements for my graduate degree! The research project was a bear. I am so happy that it is through. Months and months of work are now behind me.

Isaac is picking me up for dinner tonight. I can't wait. I didn't realize I could miss seeing him so much. I volunteered for all kinds of little tasks at work this past week, just so I could stay extra busy while he was away. My emotions ping ponged as I swatted back the uneasy twistings in my gut. Goodness, he was not even gone a full week. If his being away hits me like this, I just might have to get a puppy. I wonder what the landlord would think?

Bought a new outfit for tonight. I hope he likes it . . . Me

Later

Isaac was a little off tonight. I don't know if it was just me reading into things, but he was a little weird. First of all, he was unkempt. I don't know that his face had seen a razor in a week. His car still had his bags in it from his trip. He looked at his phone about a hundred times through dinner. I even quit talking, and he didn't notice.

Sadly, the pangs of longing to see Isaac have evolved into a tight knot of uneasy emotions planted in the bottom of my gut. Maybe this is normal relationship struggles? I am so inexperienced, I really don't know. But I do know that I don't feel at peace right now. Not at all.

Struggling . . . Me

December 20th, Sunday

Church was great today. I needed it.

I reminded myself that Isaac is allowed to have bad days. I am so silly and such a romantic. I read too much into things.

He is coming for dinner tonight. (Remember the roast? Yep. He gave up on being vegan.) One Black Friday crockpot and I have single handedly made my first Sunday dinner for myself and my fiancé.

Maybe tonight will be the reveal of my feet? Maybe? Then again, I think I would rather cook a thousand roasts and walk ten miles over hot coals.

Good luck . . . Me

December 21st, Monday

Okay, things are getting a little out of hand. That attorney's office has somehow gotten my number. I had a three-minute voicemail on my phone. Three seconds into the message, I deleted it.

I am breathing a little easier about Isaac. Last night's dinner was a dream. I cooked again tonight. Look at me go. This time we ate chicken enchiladas. The food turned out better than I expected. Isaac brought chocolate mousse for dessert. We played card games. We talked about the future. I conveniently avoided making any conversations about my feet. I just couldn't do it. My feet will have to wait until after we are married, I think.

But we talked about important things tonight.

"I don't want to wait any longer. I say January 4th." Isaac's eagerness thrilled me. "Will you be happy with a winter anniversary?" Isaac poured his eyes over me as the words tumbled satisfyingly from his lips.

"A winter anniversary for the rest of our lives?" Exciting. "Sounds like it could be fun." I laid down a card, smiling like crazy back at him.

"Then, should we tell our parents?" His face glowed.

"Absolutely, let's spread the good news."

Isaac kissed me tenderly. Little did he know that I was just about to call "Uno."

Pleasant dreams . . . Me

December 24th, Thursday

The moment of truth arrived today when I met Isaac's family. Isaac's parents live in Henderson. We decided to spend Christmas Eve dinner with his family and then drive to St. George for Christmas day.

"Come in. Come in." Isaac's mother whisked him right through the front door, leaving me standing on the sidewalk. I followed behind them as they walked into the house. Donning my best smile, I hoped to make a good impression.

His mother fawned all over Isaac as we stepped into the entryway of their elegant two-story home. Granite floors and sparkling chandeliers made the home feel like a resort. Thankfully, everyone wore their shoes.

An expensively dressed young woman stepped up beside me. I figured it had to be Jane, Isaac's sister. She wore a classy black sweater, designer slacks, and pretty, open-toe heels. I felt a pang of envy at her pretty pedicured toes that she could show off. Her hair was dark like Isaac's. The shape of her mouth and eyes were also like his.

"You must be Lindsey." She spoke looking at me across her thick eyelash extensions.

"I am." I extended my hand. "Hi. You must be Jane?"

She looked at my hand but didn't take it. I lowered my arm as though I was smitten with the plague.

"So, have you two set a date?" Jane wasted no time. Her flawless features made no effort to turn out a smile. I saw more enthusiasm in the guy behind the counter at the Chevron station when I prepaid for my gas.

"Yes." I smiled then turned it off to match her cool tone.

"When?" Jane's eyes went to her brother who was now in a big bear hug from his father.

"January fourth." A nervous twist in my gut made the words sound more like a question than a happy declaration.

Jane was completely unreadable. She reminded me of a glamorous mannequin. Her mouth and eyes were flawlessly still, not a twitch or a wrinkle. Then she spoke. "Mom will not be happy." She walked away and into the kitchen where a caterer was plating our Christmas Eve dinner.

Isaac peeled away from the hugs of his parents long enough to reach out his hand for me. I took it gladly and stepped up beside him. "Mom. Dad. I want you to meet Lindsey." Isaac smiled warmly at me, "The love of my life."

I thought I saw a little twitch at the corner of Isaac's dad's mouth. Was he laughing? I brushed it aside. Extending my hand, I looked each of his parents in the eye and shook their hands in turn.

"It's time for dinner." Isaac's mom's eyes barely skimmed over me before she stepped away to lead us all into the dining room. A tall man was already seated at the table. Before I could even think to sit down, Jane took a seat beside Isaac, and his mom took the other. I ended up sandwiched between Isaac's dad and the tall man, who I learned is Isaac's uncle, Eddie. Uncle Eddie is in the mining industry, and he let me know.

I pushed and poked at my food so that I would not be the first one finished while Isaac's dad and Uncle Eddie bantered about ore prices, machinery, and shipping. So fun.

Throughout dinner I tried to catch Isaac's attention. I failed. He was dedicated to his conversation with his mom and Jane. Filled to the brim with the topic of mining, I couldn't take any more. I politely excused myself from the table.

I slipped into the bathroom. The same elegant grandeur graced the "guest bathroom," as Isaac's mom called it. I stood at the mirror. My feelings clawed. Was I making a mistake? I shook it off. Afterall, I wasn't marrying his family. I was marrying Isaac. Since I had only been gone a minute, I decided to take the opportunity to do a quick internet search on mining. That way I might at least join in the conversation. It was fruitless. I returned to the table just in time to hear Uncle Eddie recite the price per train car of raw material.

After a slice of pie, everyone moved from the table to the living room. Uncle Eddie was still going strong. Jane was still expressionless. She met my eyes twice. Each time I looked away quickly as though I was listening to Uncle Eddie.

Isaac broke free from his mom and sister when they went to check on the caterer.

"Hey," Isaac said softly as he sat down beside me. "I'm sorry."

"It's okay," I assured him. I changed the subject. "Your parents have a beautiful home."

He flashed a dazzling smile. "Thank you."

Isaac's mother returned to the living room, and Isaac stood up. He cleared his throat softly, then opened his hands. "Mom. Dad. Uncle Eddie . . ." Jane walked into the room. ". . . Jane . . ." Isaac rubbed his hands nervously on his thighs. ". . . Lindsey and I have set a date."

Uncle Eddie perked up at this and grinned. I searched the faces of Isaac's parents for any indication that they approved. They both appeared as though they were getting a root canal.

Isaac motioned with his arm to me. "Lindsey and I will get married January fourth."

"What?" his mother gasped.

"January fourth?" his father questioned.

Jane showed the greatest expression of emotion that I had seen from her all night. She arched an eyebrow a nanometer. The message was clear. *I told you Mom would not be happy.*

Uncle Eddie jumped up, slapped Isaac on the back, and gripped my hand with a tug. Shaking it, he declared, "Well, congratulations you two."

"Thank you," Isaac and I replied in unison. I smiled through my jumbled nerves.

"Isaac . . ." His mother moved across the room to stand next to his father. She beckoned him with her extended hand. ". . . may we see you for just a minute?"

"Sure." Isaac gave me a nod and a squeeze of my hand. Then he left the room with his parents. Awkward.

Jane announced, "I'm going home." With a twist of her open-toed, high-heeled shoes, she was out the door.

"Well," Uncle Eddie began, "you two are digging into something. I had no idea you were Isaac's fiancée."

"Yep." I smiled. I was grateful that someone was happy about the news.

"Well, you are a pretty one." Uncle Eddie sat on the couch and picked up a magazine.

"Thanks." I wanted this day to end.

By the time Isaac returned, Uncle Eddie and I were both buried up to our noses in traveling magazines. The only difference was Uncle Eddie was actually reading an article about the Canadian Islands that are for sale, and I was stewing.

When Isaac returned, he was sandwiched between his parents. He must have convinced them that I was about to become family because they each approached and hugged me stiffly.

"Welcome to the family." His dad bobbed his head and awkwardly patted my back.

"We are so happy for you," his mom sniffed. I wondered if her sudden display of emotion was brought on because she was truly happy, or she was mourning the fact that I was about to become her daughter in law. I didn't want to know.

Isaac offered me his arm. I rushed to his side. I am grateful that Isaac is a very independent person. I don't think I will have to worry about too many family reunions. But if so, I will stick with Uncle Eddie.

What a horrible evening.

We exited with some pie wrapped up by the caterers. Isaac touched my chin and lifted my face to look into his eyes. "I'm sorry," Isaac gently offered as he opened the car door. "They can be a little abrupt."

"No problem," I lied.

"I love you." He smiled.

His words did little to quiet my tumbling insides.

Fretful . . . Me

December 25th, Friday, Christmas Day

"January fourth!" Mom's eyes torched holes of indignation through me. "You are only giving me *ten* days!"

With vibrant charm, Isaac reached across the table and gently placed his hand on Mom's arm. "Mrs. Maximus, I can only say that any time away from your daughter is pure torture. My work schedule has turned upside down. I will be in and out of the country for a while, and January fourth is the best day. My boss keeps a tight leash on me. If we marry on the fourth, we can still have a two-day honeymoon. Then he smiled and said, "I can only imagine how wonderful it will be to come home from each trip to your darling daughter . . . my wife. I don't want to wait a minute longer than we have to." He sealed it with a light squeeze to her arm. Only he could pull it off.

Mom's gaze darted between me and her future son-in-law.

I have to say. I drank his words. My heart did little flips when Isaac said, "My wife." Then, a small sinking feeling pushed in, trying to quash my joy. I've been feeling this troubling sensation more and more. I chalk it up to my nerves about his family. Maybe I'm overreacting? It's probably nothing.

Mom broke the spell. "But a Monday? Who gets married on a Monday, for Pete's sake?" Pointing her finger at me she barked, "What about your class? You can't just take off and leave your class. You'll get canned." Mom's blue eyes stormed almost black.

"Mom, it will be okay. I have a couple of personal days that I haven't used. I can get a substitute for two days."

Mom appeared to digest this.

"What about a reception? Everyone does a reception." Mom bore deep into my soul again with her probing eyes.

"Well . . ." I paused, weighing the possibilities. "Isaac and I were planning to go out for dinner with all the family." Mom's eyebrows slammed together. "But . . . we could probably do something small, if you wanted."

Mom snapped. "That would require invitations so that people would know what and when and where to attend." She exhaled loudly. "And with only ten days to prepare . . ." She shook her head.

Dad piped up and diffused the drama. "Wow you two, I think this is great news. A new year, and a new life together. What could be more exciting?" Dad's freshly whitened teeth radiated from his tanned face. He wrapped one of his massive arms around Mom, smiling at Isaac and me. He squeezed Mom's shoulder, causing her face to pucker in frustration. She hated when he didn't take her side in a matter, and she made no secret of that with her expression. "Let's make the most of this." Always quick to find the bright side, Dad announced, "I will get us some pie. Let's all have a celebratory slice of pie." He grinned with pride and went to work on slicing us some "celebratory" pie. I love Dad.

Mom was still in a fit. "What about a dress? Have you thought about that?"

"Mom, I live in Vegas. I am sure that I can find a dress."

Isaac smiled and squeezed my hand.

"What about your sisters?" (Annie and Susy had each committed to spend Christmas with their in-laws. Otherwise, they would be here in the fray to speak for themselves. They were missing out on some great family drama. Lucky for them.) "They can't go out and buy substitutes, you know. They have busy lives," Mom fumed. I could almost smell the smoke. It was thick and smelled like burnt wedding dresses.

"Mom, don't worry." I tried coaxing her out of her angst. "Annie and Susy can figure things out." I went to her side. "Isaac and I want to keep things simple. We were hoping to get married in St. George. That will make things easier on everyone. We will be the ones to travel. That way, no one else has to. Well . . . except his family." (Isaac had already dropped that bomb for his family.)

Mom's face loosened a little at that.

Dad served up the pie. Pumpkin. My favorite. A small comfort.

Mom fired off more questions as Dad ate pie. "What about invitations? You haven't answered me on that."

Isaac took this one. "We'll announce the wedding on Facebook, but we are only going to invite immediate family members. We want to keep it small." He threw Mom another winning smile.

Dad, seeing the smolder, cut in. "Dinner with the family is a smart idea. I will contact my client that owns the *Italian Noodle* on Main Street. We'll book the place for that night. What do you think?" He stroked Mom's shoulder. She caught his eye with a glint of irritation. He nodded between us with soothing assurance.

Mom's resignation was visible. Lowering her shoulders, she replied, "I think that will work." Another forceful stare was fired at me. "But I want to see your dress before you buy it."

"Great." I smiled. Weddings really are about mom's and daughters. "I can text you pictures while I shop." I grinned wider.

Mom shook her head. "And make sure you get some closed toe shoes."

I flinched. My eyes darted to Isaac. He showed no signs of concern. I had to deter Mom before she said anything more about my feet. "I will be fine, Mom. I can shop for a dress."

"You'll need my help. My mind is made up. I am coming back to Las Vegas with you." I knew better than to try and dispute the point.

Isaac and I exchanged glances. With an almost imperceptible shrug, Isaac nodded his approval of the arrangement. I can't say that I was overly thrilled to have my mom camped in my apartment until the wedding. I hoped her stay wouldn't interfere with my spending time with Isaac. Yet, catastrophe averted. No more fuming—or mentioning of my feet.

I hugged Mom tight and said, "That sounds great."

The rest of Christmas dinner went off without a hitch.

Joyeux Noel . . . Me

December 28th, Monday

Modesty and Las Vegas? Goodness. I thought we would have better success. Finding a dress has proven to be a little more difficult than I expected.

Mom has settled in. I have given her my bedroom for her stay. I am camping on my couch in the living room. It is nice, however, because the TV is in the living room. I am a picky TV watcher.

Isaac has been absent since the day after Christmas. He said it was a work thing. I don't know where he is or what he is doing. Should I? Because after the thrills, butterflies, and drama of announcing our plans to my family, I have to admit that the panic that churns in my gut doesn't let up. Maybe it's a normal bride-to-be syndrome? I don't know. I tell myself it's normal. I mean, getting married is a big deal. There has to be some amount of normal nerves.

Mom just ran out of the bedroom, wearing pink pajamas and waving her cell phone.

"We don't have to look anywhere else tomorrow! I just spoke to your Aunt Mildred. She looked it up and there is a modest bridal shop just west on Decatur Boulevard. They specialize in modest gowns. I would never have guessed we could find such a place. We won't have to go anywhere else." Mom held the phone to her chest. She stopped and looked at me. I sat wrapped in the soft flannel quilt that she made me when I first graduated from college. She smiled. Her tone was wistful as she sat down beside me and patted my arm and lifted up one corner of the quilt. "You will be a beautiful bride, even if you have to wear this blanket to dinner that night." Leaning her head against mine. We sat silent for a moment. Just mom and daughter. Those moments don't come often, nor do they last very long. The knot in my gut dissolved. A little.

Until next time . . . Me

December 29th, Tuesday

"That is the one," the sales lady gushed as I stood on a princess-like platform with mirrors on three sides.

The dress was perfect. The sleeves were elegant. The satin, like nothing I have ever felt. The train was just long enough to draw attention to the delicate details down the back of the dress.

I also found the perfect pair of shoes, strappy at the back and around the ankle but completely closed over the toes. Perfect.

Back at the apartment, Mom plopped her skinny self onto the couch. I raised my eyebrows. On her lap she held a large bag. It was cream colored with huge purple roses on it. The handles on the bag were big wooden beads. Mom unsnapped the bag and revealed a wad of white satin. "Go get your dress. We don't have much time to do this."

A smile curled up the corners of my lips. Like a third grader going to a birthday party, I fetched my dress.

Mom smoothed out the satin mess from her bag. "I need your iron, ironing board, and some good light. Hang your dress on the door casing there, and let's see what we can do here."

I went to the hall closet for the requested supplies, except the lighting. Taking the shade off of my bedside lamp, I positioned it beside Mom.

This was tradition. Now it was my turn to take part in it. A happy shiver danced through me. I bit back a little nervous tug. This will prove I am okay. This has to be right. Doesn't it?

Let me explain. Mom sets a great store in traditions. Her dream *was* to have all her daughters wear her wedding dress. (The dress she wore to marry Gerald. I'm not sure about the dress she wore to marry John. I never asked. I don't really worry about those kinds of things, anyway. I leave that to my Mom. She worries over enough details for all of us.) Since none of her daughters are five foot two and an even one-hundred two pounds, she came up with a unique and beautiful way for each of her daughters to wear her dress. Mom is an expert seamstress. I know she would have made me a dress if she would have had enough time. She made her own clothes for years: tailored suits, pleated skirts, formals . . . Mom can do it all. So, with each wedding, Mom creates something amazing from the fabric of her wedding dress and sews it onto the new wedding dress. For Annie, Mom handmade gorgeous flowers. Each one was a work of art. Susy insisted on having flowers made for her headpiece. Mom made it happen. Like a fairy tale crown, the satin flowers highlighted Susy's amazing blond hair. Mom also made a few flowers that trailed from the bodice of Susy's dress to the skirt, tying the whole image together. Again, the look was incredible. Now, it is my turn. I confess I have daydreamed about this. I wonder what she will determine for my dress. I have no strong opinions about it. I know it will be grand. No wonder Mom was stressed about getting a dress in time. These details are a lot of work. But so worth it.

Watching Mom plan, excitement bubbled. Then a trickle of nerves washed down my spine. I pushed it aside and focused on the dress.

I knew the source of my nerves tonight. Isaac didn't text. I don't know what to think. Ugh. I need to get out of my own head. Maybe I should bake some cookies? Maybe I should eat some cookie dough? I'm worried.

Side note: I showed Mom my most recent letter. It came today from the attorney's office. She thinks it is real.

"Lindsey, don't toss this out. You need to contact these people and see what this is all about. I don't see anything in this letter that looks like a scam. Have you called them?"

"No, they called me, though."

"What did they say?"

"I don't know. I deleted the message." I braced for Mom's reaction.

"You what?" Mom worked up a huff then changed her mind. "Oh, never mind. You need to find out what this has to do with you and your father. I don't like this, but I don't think that it is a scam."

"Do you think my dad is trying to find me?"

Mom placed the letter onto the coffee table. Her eyes took on a new faraway look. "I don't know, Lindsey." Her voice was soft.

I nodded, careful not to say anything more. I didn't want to uncan a bunch of unsavory memories for her.

"But you call them. Okay?" She patted my hand.

"Okay . . . I will. After the wedding."

Mom nodded, her eyes still reflecting that faraway look.

Lost in thoughts . . . Me

December 31st, Thursday

"Don't you know that it is bad luck for the groom to see the dress before the wedding?" Mom sat at the kitchen table busily adding beads to what will soon be another set of delicate satin flowers.

"I thought it was bad luck for the groom to see the bride in the dress," I said as I clutched my phone.

Isaac had finally called! He was on his way over. He and I devised a plan to hide from the downtown masses and ring in the new year peacefully over a late dinner at my place. I asked why I hadn't heard from him and he said he would explain over dinner. Was this the prelude to a breakup? I mentally kicked myself for thinking anything negative about Isaac and our wedding. I was just being foolish.

Mom was less than enthusiastic about Isaac coming over for dinner. I know she didn't want to spoil the big reveal of me in my dress on our wedding day, but I didn't love the idea of going out on New Year's Eve.

Mom closed one eye and poked the end of her thread through the needle before speaking. "Either way, do you want to take the risk?"

There were some things that were better avoided. "We'll go out. Can we bring you something?"

Pointing the needle in my direction, there was no hesitation as she quipped off her order, "Yes. I want one of those sandwiches. You know the one. Like we had the other night."

"The turkey, avocado, spinach wrap?"

Mom nodded, with her eye following the needle. I grabbed my purse.

I always keep a hundred-dollar bill in the zip up pocket for emergencies, not that a sandwich was an emergency, but I double checked that it was still there. It was.

Mom cemented her focus onto her sewing.

Watching her work, thoughts tumbled through my mind. Was I as dedicated to my future life with Isaac as Mom is to those flowers? I tried to feel that I am. I reached inside for a happy flutter to assure me that it was all going to be the joyful adventure I have dreamed about. Maybe after I see Isaac all these confusing feelings will settle into one happy comfortable emotion. Maybe. I asked Mom. "Did you ever feel nervous about marrying Dad?"

Lifting her eyes, she studied me. "Of course. Why? Are you feeling nervous?"

I nodded. It felt good to share a little of what I had been feeling.

Mom patted the couch beside her and motioned for me to sit down. I sat. "Are you having second thoughts?"

"No . . . I don't know . . . sometimes . . . I just feel like I'm about to jump into a pit of snakes."

Mom's eyebrows pushed together. She nodded. Then meeting my eyes, she said, "I think you need to study those feelings and find out what they really mean to you." She patted my arm. "You need to follow what you feel. I do believe that."

I nodded. What she said made sense. But how? I stood. Isaac would be knocking on the door any second. I needed to focus on him. The wrestle inside of me would have to wait.

Time for dinner . . . Me

Later

Isaac swept me up into an "everything's okay" hug when I opened the door. He held me tighter and longer than I expected. My heart beat a little easier as he touched my face and held me close. He seemed especially grateful to see me.

With a smile and a wave at Mom, we left and drove the short distance to a small cafe, far from the center of town. I wanted to ask where he had been, but he'd said we would talk over dinner. I chose to wait. Before we got out of the car, he turned, squeezed my hand, and said, "Lindsey, I've let you down. I'm so sorry. It's been crazy with work. I literally did not go home for two days. I didn't want you to worry." He looked a strange mixture of confident and alarmed as he added, "It shouldn't happen again."

My heart relaxed. I met his eyes. His face held a lovely smile, just for me. I waited, thinking he might say more, but he climbed out and waited for me beside the car.

I held his hand as we crossed the parking lot into the restaurant. I pushed all the reasons that I love him to the front of my thoughts. It was a fight. Over and over doubts crashed. I swatted them back.

Over some artichoke chicken pasta, I peered into his dark eyes. His smiles drew me in. Then, the longer sat, I felt a strange distracted, fearful tension radiating from him. I put my thoughts aside.

"Four more days." I swirled pasta onto my fork, hoping to lighten his mood with thoughts of our upcoming nuptials.

With a light laugh that sounded a little forced, he glanced sideways and replied, "Yeah . . . it will be here before we know it." Tossing me another token smile, he turned to his plate, vigorously sawing his steak.

Watching him tear apart his steak, I asked the obvious question. "Are you okay?"

Isaac abruptly lifted his head. His fork and knife paused, still embedded in the meat. He locked on my eyes. Tension flashed across his face like a spark of static then vanished as quickly.

"Yeah . . ." His dark brown eyes warmed ever so slightly. "Of course . . ." A smile. "I'm with you. How could I be anything but perfect?" His features cooled though he held a smile on his lips. "I am fantastic." Isaac reached and took my hand. I studied him. A dead pause, that was a little too long, hung between us. He rescued the moment by saying, "I am marrying the most amazing girl on the planet in just four days."

I loaned him a cheesy smile as a reply to his cheesy comment. A wrenching tug in my gut forced me to lower my eyes and stare at the patterns on the tablecloth. I had to get my emotions in check. Leaving my purse on the bench, I slid out of the booth. I excused myself to visit the restroom. With every step, I tried to quickly bury the sinking feeling. I know Mom said to study it, but it didn't make sense. Why do I feel this way? Isaac is a wonderful guy. Digging deeper, I pushed again to focus on why Isaac matters to me.

It helped. A little.

As I crossed the room back to our table, Isaac's head was lowered. I breathed deeply and let out a sigh. Lifting his head, Isaac met my eyes and held on. I sat back down. Taking my hand in his, he rubbed his thumb across the back of my knuckles, he explained, "I'm sorry if I seem a little distracted. I am just trying to get some financial things tightened up. You know, before the wedding."

"Oh?" I pulled my hand from his and picked up a bite of chicken with my fork. "Like what?" That would explain the long days at work.

Pushing his food around his plate, Isaac spoke. "It's not a big deal. Just some things I thought would be cleared up before we got married." He flashed another one of those forced smiles that was meant to reassure me. With Isaac charm, he continued, "But that's life, right? What goes according to plan?" Again, the nervous laugh.

I leaned back suddenly feeling a little defensive and heated. I don't know why, but something about his last comment stung a nerve. Even though he didn't require a response, I felt pressed to give him one. "Our wedding . . ."

The words came out rather snippy. He turned his face to me. Isaac dropped his Hollywood smile. I bit each word and spat them at him, "*It* will go according to plan."

Isaac shook his head and raised his eyebrows in attempted amusement as deep lines creased his typically smooth forehead.

I studied him. He resumed pushing his food around his plate. At last he seemed to reach a decision about something. Dropping his utensils and rubbing his hands over his thighs, he leaned in and spoke low. "You don't happen to have eighty thousand dollars that I could borrow?"

A healthy guffaw burst from my mouth. A couple at the table next to ours turned.

Isaac shook his head as if to say, "We're okay here." Color rushed into my cheeks. I looked away. He launched a winning smile at the head-turned couple. They resumed eating.

I studied him hard. "Are you serious?" I asked, leaning close and whispering fiercely.

He back-pedaled vigorously. "It's no big deal." He waved his hands in apology. "Sorry . . . I've just . . . well . . . some things have come up." He clasped my hands in his and kissed them. "Really, it's nothing."

Now I was nervous. "What kinds of things?"

"Nothing that will change any of our plans." He held my hands all the tighter.

Suspicious, I squinted my eyes at Isaac. He smiled. He then paid for our meal with a hundred-dollar bill, leaving our server a generous tip.

The night ended quickly after that. We didn't even make it into the new year together. He had some "things" that needed his attention, or so he said, so we ended the night a little before midnight. The dead-weight is heavy in my gut. *Eighty thousand dollars?* What is happening?

Back at my apartment, Mom happily ate the sandwich I brought and sewed the rest of the flowers.

Wearing fuzzy, pink socks, I twisted the diamond ring on my finger and tried to distract my discomfort with a Hallmark original movie.

From the inside of a man-eating snake . . . Me

January 1st, Friday

I woke with a headache, still reeling from Isaac's asking me for eighty thousand. I feel sick. I wanted to talk to Mom, but she seemed so happy.

Isaac texted:

> I'm so sorry. I've got to work this weekend. I miss you
> every minute.

I clicked off my phone without texting a reply.

Dad knocked on the door a little after breakfast. He came here to pick up Mom.

While Mom was taking a shower. I unloaded some of my worries on him. I explained my feelings, Isaac's two days of no contact, and the eighty thousand. "I don't know what to think. I don't want to make a huge mistake either way."

Dad listened patiently. Wrapping an arm around me, he said. "I remember the financial mess I had gotten myself into." He looked at my face as if deciding whether or not to continue. He must have decided to go ahead because he said, "I may have been like Isaac . . . I don't know . . . but I had made some bad investments. I had acquired a lot of debt. I was in over my head."

I nodded. I had never heard Dad open up about this before.

"The truth is, it was my financial messes that caused our divorce."

"What did you do? I mean, how did you know to go forward?" I wanted this to apply and help me with Isaac. I just didn't know . . .

"It was rough. First, I had to do a lot of soul searching, a lot of changing. Then, I had to meet with financial planners and find a way to sort out the messes that I had made." He met my eyes. "It wasn't easy. My problems didn't disappear overnight. It took years to set me back on my feet. But what I want you to see is that we did overcome those hurdles."

"You don't think I should give up on Isaac?"

"I think you have a level head, and I can't tell you what to do." Studying my face, Dad squeezed my shoulders. With a fatherly smile, he remarked, "I just want you to have a shot at happiness. With or without Isaac."

Nodding, I leaned on his shoulder as he hugged me with one arm. "I understand." Dad was right. Isaac was a good man. He might have some problems, but we could work through them.

Sitting there with Dad, I silently prayed to be strong. I glanced at my ring. I remembered his proposal. Everything had been perfect that day. Why should I let it all slip away? Afterall, wasn't marriage about working through things together? Closing my eyes, I leaned against Dad. If Mom hadn't been willing to see past Dad's faults and marry him again, she would have missed out on all the happiness that they shared. I wanted happiness.

Mom walked into the living room. Dad stood and wrapped her in a hug. Watching the two of them, I understood their relationship on a new level. In that moment, I could see them as more than just my parents. They were two people facing the world a day at a time. I made up my mind to move forward.

I stood by while Mom packed up her things. Dad stepped up beside me and placed his hand on my shoulder. "Are you going to be okay?" he asked.

With a reassuring nod, I breathed deeply and said, "I'll be fine."

Dad left with Mom. They are going back to St. George. She took my wedding dress, decked with flowers, with her. She insisted on giving them one more stitch. The thought of any of them falling off kept her up most of the night.

I saw the finished effect before she left. Her work was magical. The flowers were sewn discreetly along the hem of the gown. They will play hide and seek as I walk. Just a subtle, beautiful detail and a continuance of tradition. I don't want to toss that aside.

With new resolve, I picked up my phone and texted Isaac:

I miss you. Wishing you a great day at work. Can't wait to see you.

With my parents gone, the apartment seemed so empty. I stood in the living room. My thoughts rolled around and around. In three days, Isaac and I would be sharing this place. I needed today to get ready.

Then, I suddenly felt very tired. All the anxiety and worrying had worn me to the bone. I sat on the couch with my head in my hands and prayed.

Picking myself up, I set to work making space for Isaac. The work was slow. I kept getting distracted. I found myself reliving the past few days over and over. I shook it off and took a sack of donations to a thrift store.

By a quarter after eight, I was starving. I had forgotten to eat lunch. I ordered takeout. I opened my purse. The zip up pocket was open, and my emergency money was missing. Strange.

I've been robbed . . . Me

January 2ⁿᵈ, Saturday

I am packed and ready to get on the road. I will be driving to St. George to stay with my parents until the wedding. Everything is ready for Isaac and I to launch into life together. It took some careful strategizing to make room for his things in the closet, but I think I've done it. He should be proud.

I haven't heard from Isaac today. I texted him, he didn't reply.

I still haven't shared my feet with Isaac. I'm strangely okay with that. I'm okay if he never sees my feet.

Sadly, I also wonder if he took the hundred from my purse, besides Mom, he is the only person who had any contact with my purse.

I don't know what to think. I keep replaying what Dad said. I keep replaying the proposal, the happy dates, and the way he spoiled me.

Well, happy times await. Right? Why do I still feel like I am heading blindfolded into a pit full of man-eating snakes?

See you in St. George . . . Me

January 3ʳᵈ, Sunday

It's over. I think you saw it coming. The thing is . . . I didn't think it'd turn out this way. This bad. I could have never imagined this. Ever.

My "wedding day" is minutes away. I am back in Las Vegas, in my apartment. It is after 11 p.m. My head is in a scramble. Broken emotions. Stirred up trauma. Insanity.

No one died. Nothing like that.

Aaaaagh! What a mess!

I've got to get this all down. Maybe then I can sort it all out. Where to begin?

Here goes:

I went to stay with my parents yesterday in St. George, all according to plan. This morning I went to church with them, as planned. During the meeting, I got a call from an unknown number. I thought it was nothing. Spam. But an urgent feeling wrapped up around me like the bindings on a mummy. I needed to check that message.

I took a quick trip to the restroom before the closing hymn, so I could listen to the message. The message was brief. Just a number for me to call back. It was the Las Vegas Metro Police Department. My body turned to ice. *What on Earth?* Why would I have the police calling me? Did I have an unpaid traffic ticket? I know there are traffic cams everywhere. Did I break a law and not know it? Was I due in court?

If only . . .

I dodged all the well-wishers for my upcoming marriage as they poured out of the chapel and made their way through the foyer. Mom was in full swing telling everyone she knew about Isaac and me. I skirted out and around the crowd. Before I could be whisked off to Sunday School, I sneaked out the double glass doors to the parking lot.

Tucking myself against a tree, I called the number. Shivering against the cold, the call went through.

After two transfers, and a verification of identity, I was connected with a Detective Jade. As he spoke, every drop of blood drained from my face and must have slipped into the soil beneath me. My muscles threatened to give out as I shivered uncontrollably. My heart pounded inside my chest, each pulse seeming to leave a dent in my body.

I was informed that I was needed in Las Vegas for questioning in a case regarding Isaac Samuels. The words illegal, trafficking, drugs, thousands of dollars . . . clung to my brain. Isaac was in the custody of the Las Vegas Metropolitan Police for the trafficking of prescription drugs. *What? How? No!* The call ended. I can only assume that I responded with the correct "Uh-huh's" and "Okay's." I don't remember.

I stood frozen.

I had no choice. I had to go to Las Vegas. Me? . . . A day before my wedding, I was needed for questioning about the criminal acts of my fiancé. How was this even possible? This was the stuff TV shows were made of. Not my life. Not to me . . .

With legs shaking, I walked as a zoned out zombie to find my parents. With my head swimming, I tried to make it make sense. I couldn't. Isaac in jail? It would explain why I hadn't heard from him, but jail? Isaac? Catching Dad's eye as I peered into the Sunday School classroom, the blunt force trauma of the call ripped through me. Tears threatened and stung at the corners of my eyes. Motioning with my head, I beckoned him to come.

Tapping Mom on the arm, Dad closed his scriptures. Mom grabbed her bag and with apologetic glances toward the teacher, they met me in the hall.

With Mom's best attempt at a whisper, she asked, "What's going on?"

A few tears spilled. I couldn't help it. I weakly tried to hold them back.

Dad rested a hand on my shoulder. "I think we had better go." With his arm around me, he steered us toward the door.

I nodded, not trusting my voice.

During the car ride home, I stumbled to retell the information from the detective.

With Mom gasping at every other word, she shook her head violently. "This is too bizarre. They have got the wrong guy."

Dad was stumped. "This just seems completely out of character. It doesn't seem like the sort of thing Isaac would be mixed up in. He's smarter than that."

I took comfort in their words. They were right. They had to be. Isaac wouldn't be mixed up in something like this. Crime, detectives, and drama always seem so fascinating when it involves someone else, but this is horrible.

Little did I know, it was about to get much worse.

Without changing out of my church dress, I sped to Las Vegas. I drove alone. Mom had insisted on going, but Dad thought I'd better face this without her interfering. I think he was right. Whatever I am about to face, it is mine to face. My thoughts plagued and tormented me with all the implications and possibilities that would greet me as I met with the detective. It got so bad inside my own head I started to suffocate. I barked at my phone to play some church songs. Technology came through. I shouted as many of the lyrics as I could, to force my focus, as I blazed a trail across the Mojave Desert.

Detective Jade was straight out of a Traci Hunter Abramson novel. Six-foot-two, dark curly hair, steely eyes. His build was thick, to say the least. His black dress shirt and tan slacks were creased and pressed to precision.

A male police officer and another lady sat with us. I don't remember who the lady was, nor could I tell you the name of the police officer.

Detective Jade led the questions. "I appreciate you coming so quickly to meet with us. I know the timing is less than sublime." He lowered his large frame into a leather chair across the table. I nodded, eyes wide. "Given you came over from St. George," he glanced at his watch, "I won't ask about your driving speed." He and the police officer chuckled. I guess I made good time. I don't even remember telling anyone that I was in St. George. Either I had forgotten, maybe they just knew, or maybe Isaac had told them.

Detective Jade spoke again. "Let's get down to the nuts and bolts of why you are here. I understand you are engaged to Isaac Samuels."

"Yes," I replied, even though it wasn't a question.

The detective nodded. "How well do you know your fiancé, Miss Jones?"

There it was. The question I had asked myself a million times. Now I *had* to answer it, and truthfully. "I think I know him fairly well." I chewed the inside of my lip nervously.

He continued. "Are you aware that he has been making frequent trips to Mexico and back?"

I dumbly nodded. The detective raised his eyebrows and stared at me for an answer. "Yes," I answered. With a quiver in my voice, I added, "I mean, I knew he went a couple of times. For his job."

"What is his job?"

I met eyes with the detective. "Well, he works for Barnest Incorporated. He does marketing research . . ." I paused. *Was that what he does?* ". . . I guess." I paused again. I remembered. "They are an insurance company." I lifted my shoulders and shrugged. Embarrassed by my lack of knowledge. The detective leaned back in his rolling chair.

The male police officer spoke up. "What did he tell you he was doing in Mexico?"

"He didn't tell me. And I didn't ask." I flipped my keys over in my lap then gripped them tightly.

The officer spoke again. "Did he ever mention any names? People he worked with?"

I shook my head. "No." My voice was barely above a whisper.

"Did you ever go with him, to Mexico?" The detective spoke from his chair.

"No."

"Miss Jones, have you ever had any contact with any of Isaac's colleagues."

"No. I never met anyone from his work. He didn't like to talk about work when we were together."

The detective leaned forward. He and the officer exchanged glances. The officer spoke. "Any information would be helpful."

"I only know what I told you." My heart hammered. "I am so confused right now. Isaac has never done anything illegal."

The detective spoke again. "When was the last time you spoke with Isaac?"

"Friday . . . well, he texted."

"So, you didn't talk to him?"

"No, just a text."

"What time on Friday?"

"In the morning some time." I fished for my phone. "I can show you the message." Swiping the screen, I passed my phone.

The detective glanced at the message and passed it to the others. They each took a glance in turn and returned my phone.

"Did you know where Isaac was on Friday?" The woman spoke up for the first time since I entered the room.

"No, he told me he was at work." Small tremors shook my legs. "You said he was arrested for trafficking prescription drugs. I don't understand."

The woman spoke again. "Barnest Incorporated is a pharmaceutical distributor. They are not an insurance company. They purchase pharmaceuticals directly from the manufacturers and distribute to federally licensed providers, pharmacies and whatnot."

"Okay?" I answered lamely. My head swam. I looked at the faces in the room. "I'm confused. Isaac doesn't work with pharmaceuticals. There has to be a mistake."

The male officer spoke. "We're wasting our time." He met eyes with the woman.

The woman leaned forward. "Miss Jones, Isaac Samuels has been illegally running prescription medications across the border for roughly three years. We need to understand your level of involvement."

"What?" My level of involvement . . . blood drained from my face. They thought I was a criminal?

"Where were you Friday night?"

I closed my eyes, took a breath, and reopened my eyes. "I was at home."

"Was anyone with you?"

I shook my head. My nerves fired, causing uncoordinated tremblings. I wanted to cry.

The woman nodded at Detective Jade.

The detective spoke. "Is there anyone who can confirm that you were at home Friday night?"

"No. I . . ." My voice trailed. My head was spinning. I was being accused. What *was* I doing on Friday night? I fought through the turbulence in my head. *What was I doing?* I shouted in my thoughts. Takeout. I had ordered takeout. The delivery driver had seen me at the door. "I did see someone. Friday night."

The woman sat back. Her eyes steady on me. "Who did you see?"

"I ordered takeout. I saw the driver."

The male officer spoke. "At what time?"

"I don't know?" Fumbling, I found the order confirmation on my phone. I pushed it across the table.

Taking my phone, the woman stood and exited the room.

My heart heaved. My hands turned cold.

Leaning forward, Detective Jade rested his forearms on the table and drummed his fingers. "Let me throw some light on your fiancé. Isaac Samuels has been keeping some pretty big secrets from you. He is a key player in a kind of corporate gang, or crime ring, if you will. Skimming off corporate funds, Isaac, and his colleagues, would go out of the country for work . . ." The detective framed the word "work" with air quotes. ". . . but while out of the country, they would purchase prescription medications at a fraction of the price. Because of their low-profile positions, they could often slip through security carrying thousands of dollars' worth of meds in their luggage. Once back in the states, they would sell the meds to whatever dealer, or gang, that will give them the price they want. Everyone gets their cut, and the cycle continues. Like I said, we've been after these guys for three years. Because of employee turnover, and changes in dealers, we've had a tough time pinning them down. Your boy Isaac helped us out though. See, Friday night we got a domestic disturbance call. There was some commotion going on at a nice house out in The Lakes area. Our guys showed up just after Isaac had had the snot beat out of him by a couple of his colleagues. Unfortunately, his colleagues took off before we got there." The detective studied me hard, assessing how I was processing everything. I must have appeared to be taking it in because he went on. "We brought him in, and he started confessing faster than we could keep up." Eyes directly on me, he added, "Some people do that, you know. They surrender themselves to being arrested and spit it all out."

I asked the question that had been gnawing. "What does this have to do with me?"

"I'd say it has plenty to do with you, if you are planning to marry this guy, but that's your choice."

Realization flashed. "Eighty thousand dollars. He asked the other day if I had eighty thousand dollars. . ." I looked up from my fisted keys, ". . . but then he told me not to worry about it."

"Did you give him any money?"

"No," I said. My stomach contracted and my hands shook. "If I had, would I be arrested?"

The detective shook his head. "Depends." He rocked back in the leather chair.

The pallor of my face and the fidgeting of my fingers must have inspired him to tell me more.

"Miss Jones, Isaac picked up a delivery of meds just over a week ago. At some point after picking them up, his better self kicked in, and he decided that he wanted out of the business. He flushed, literally, more than eighty thousand dollars worth of meds. He went to his buddies at The Lakes and told them. They were not as thrilled about his sudden growth of a conscience. They were going to take the flushed profits out of his skin, so to speak." Back on his forearms, he leaned across the table toward me. "Your fiancé will be doing some time in prison."

At that moment, the woman returned with my phone. "It checks out," she said.

She handed back my phone. With my eyes wide, I looked up at her.

She met my puzzled stare and replied, "The delivery driver confirmed the delivery at 8:45, with a full description of Miss Jones."

At those words, the earth dropped. I pressed all ten of my fingers against my forehead as if I could steady my thinking. Tremors coursed and shook more violently. Isaac was going to prison, and my takeout order had become my alibi!

Stunned with shock, I finished the interview. I answered their questions. I was fingerprinted. Ultimately, what did it matter? The man I had chosen for a husband was in custody awaiting trial so that we could all find out just how many years he would get to spend in prison.

Detective Jade did mention that because Isaac named all the Barnest workers that were involved, the judge might smile on that.

Sitting here, right now in my apartment, reliving this ordeal in my head, I simply feel nothing. I don't hurt. I can't even feel proper anger.

I did call Mom and Dad. Thankfully, Mom took on the mission of letting everyone know the wedding was off.

Hurt . . . Me

January 7th, Thursday

I'm sorry that I haven't written sooner. I've been kind of a mess.

My whole family descended on my apartment Monday morning. Everyone had taken time off for the wedding, so they came to console and comfort me. Once the story was told, I became an idle witness as I watched and listened to everyone hash and rehash the events of my life.

Dad was still stunned. My sisters, along with their husbands, were angry. Mom stormed and stomped, saying she always knew he wasn't good enough for me and what a pain it had been informing friends and relatives about the canceled wedding for the better part of the night. The conversations circled around and around. I was spent, drained. I didn't want to rake through it anymore.

Susy caught my eyes, and sensing my need for respite, suggested, "Hey, let's go downtown. We can celebrate Lindsey's freedom."

Mom put both her hands on her hips. "Susy, what do you think your sister feels?"

I stood up. "I think it's a great idea. Let's go."

We found a buffet and ate lunch. Then we all walked through the aquarium.

Though the apartment felt extra empty once they left, I was ready for the quiet. I curled up on the couch, and the tears that wouldn't fall yesterday fell in rivers, soaking the sleeves of my shirt as I lay with my head nestled between my arms.

That night, I texted the principal. I told her that I didn't need the extra days off for my wedding after all. She was relieved to have me back. Thankfully, she didn't ask too many questions.

Work is a welcome respite right now. For six and a half hours of the day, I can escape the battleground of thoughts in my head.

I believe in forgiveness. I do. I believe I can forgive Isaac for his stupid choices. The next question is, however, how long will it take me?

I have an appointment to go and see him at the jail in an hour. I wonder what my feelings will be then?

Signing off . . . Me

Later

Well, I did it. I spoke with Isaac.

After passing through security, I was escorted to a booth to wait. An old-style telephone receiver hung on the wall. A small screen was mounted on the wall of the booth, facing me. My heart hammered in my throat. I didn't have to wait long before Isaac, dressed in an orange jumpsuit, appeared on the screen in front of me. I picked up the phone receiver, just like I had been instructed.

All the words and scenarios I had played out in my head failed me as I looked at him on the screen. I simply said, "Hi, Isaac."

Isaac was not having the same difficulty at finding words that I was. Like flood waters breaking, he commenced apologizing over and over. "I am so sorry, Lindsey. Please forgive me. I'm sorry. I was stupid. Just forgive me. We can get past this. I need you, Lindsey. Please . . ." He continued on like this for some time.

Suddenly sick of his tear-filled ramblings, I cut him off. "Isaac . . ."

I was impressed with how calm I felt. There was not a single tremor in my voice. All my wondering and searching for answers unfolded in that moment. I did not know this man. Once more, I could not honestly say that I knew me. All my life I have rolled along just going through the motions of what I wanted to do. I have a great life. I have a family, a job, an apartment, a car. I have everything I have ever really wanted. But, like with Isaac, maybe I have been misleading myself. Am I really living, or am I simply going through the motions? Do I *like* my job? Do I *like* my apartment and car? Do I really *love* Isaac? Did I ever really love him?

What does that even mean? We are cute together. We have fun. He makes me feel like a princess the way he flatters me. Is that love? I don't even know his shoe size. Does that matter? Are marriages built on shoe size? He has never even seen my scary feet. Have I seen *his*? Something inside was pushing me on. Pushing me to see beyond my shallow exterior and turn a mirror to look inside. I was fluff. This relationship was built on fluff.

"Isaac, don't . . ."

He paused and blew his nose into a tissue provided by a guard at his side.

I continued, "Don't apologize." I was surprised how easy it was to say the next words. "I forgive you."

He ducked his head. He sucked in deep breaths. Tears coursed down his chiseled cheeks. Between sobs, he burst, "Lindsey, thank you. I will make this up to you. I promise. I will set things right."

I cut him off again. "Isaac, it's not me you need to get right with."

"Yes. Yes, it is, Lindsey. I stole money from you. I did. Lindsey, I took money from your purse, and that's not all." He was visibly trembling now. "Lindsey, I was dating someone else, as well."

My eyes widened at this revelation. His words were torrential. I understood what Detective Jade had meant about him confessing all. He kept on as I tried to determine if what he was revealing even mattered.

"Her name is Melissa. I've known her since high school. When I didn't come to see you, it was because I was visiting her. I wanted to break things off completely with Melissa before you and I got married. It was wrong of me to keep seeing her, I know. It was just a foolish thing. Really. We dated years ago. We just never ended it. I guess I was keeping a back door. We were just friends, though. Really. I'm not lying. I've never lied to you, Lindsey. I just hid things. But I never told you an out-and-out lie. I wouldn't do that. You've got to believe me." His deep eyes were difficult to behold. He was torn in two. He was a broken man.

I pitied him.

Letting go of a deep breath, I replied as calmly as still water. "Isaac, it doesn't matter. I don't care about the money . . . or Melissa." I paused to gather my thoughts. Was I really this calm? I searched deep. I was.

"Isaac, these past few days have taught me some things. Part of me wants to thank you for opening my eyes, Isaac. We nearly got married. We don't even know each other. Our marriage would have been a more serious mistake than this mess you've gotten into." Yep, still waters. Not even a quiver. What a blessing to be so calm in the face of a disaster.

"What? Wait, Lindsey. Don't do this. I am in love with you," Isaac sobbed.

A deep sense of pity tugged the corners of my mouth slightly downward. I stood and slipped my arm through the straps of my purse. I spoke again into the phone. "I think we were both in love with the idea of being in love. You'll be okay, Isaac. I have faith. Just do what you need to do."

His body shook with sobs. All I could hear through the receiver were little gasps. What kind of stone heart do I have to see a man so broken, and all I can feel is a peaceful ending? No. I don't think this is what love should feel like. Fluff was not a secure bond. "Goodbye, Isaac. I truly wish you well. It is time for us both to move on." My eyes were steady on the screen as the fingers on my right hand worked to twist the sparkling ring from my left. I made little show of leaving the ring on the counter in the booth.

Back in my apartment, the dam broke for the second time. Tears washed my face. I thought of my mom carefully stitching the handmade flowers onto my wedding dress. I thought of the picture-perfect proposal. I thought of his thoughtful little gifts and the flowers that he so often sent. Why am I such a mess?

Why do I always kiss too soon? . . . Me

January 20ᵗʰ, Wednesday

I took a personal leave day from my class. It wasn't my idea.

You see, Isaac's sentencing was passed today and, because Dad said it would give me closure, I attended his hearing.

Isaac confessed to every crime he had committed since birth. I think this made the judge a little sympathetic. Maybe? The judge was an iron-faced, imposing sort of man. He reminded me of Isaac's sister, Jane. Jane and Isaac's parents were all in attendance. Not one of them even looked at me. Thankfully, we were seated on opposite sides of the courtroom. Isaac was sentenced to five years in the Nevada State Prison. He was the perfect model of stoicism through the whole ordeal.

After his sentencing, Isaac turned to me, and our eyes met briefly. He mouthed the words, "Thank you," and bobbed his head in a kind of fare-well. I tossed him a half smile to say, "It is what it is," in a happy trails kind of way. My face was dry. I was at peace.

Melissa, Isaac's other romance, was there as well. She was lovely. Petite. Blonde. Wide-set blue eyes. Pretty toes in strappy shoes. She reminds me of Annie. Not the character in the play but my sister. I could see from the mascara streaks running down her lightly freckled cheeks that she was deeply, emotionally invested in Isaac. More than just a "friend" like Isaac had said. Everyone in the room could see the tears that filled Isaac's face as he extended both his arms toward her before he was escorted out of the room. Hmmm . . . Yep, that is definitely closure on any lingering feelings I may have harbored.

Curiosity had me wondering if Isaac had spilled everything to Melissa about me. I decided to drop the bomb in case he had not. Afterall, she had a right to know. I introduced myself to her after Isaac was escorted from the room. (A little snarky of me, I know.) I stuck out my hand and said, "Hi, I'm

Lindsey . . . the other woman." Oddly, she wrapped her arms around me and hugged me like I was her long-lost cousin. Unexpected. Her mascara streaked my blouse. I awkwardly patted her back.

"Sorry . . ." Melissa said through her tears and wet sniffles as she let go of me. Then she gripped my forearms tightly. She studied my eyes. "Isaac told me all about you and how you forgave him," she gushed. So, he did tell her about me. "He told me how you handled finding out about me." She rubbed a tissue under her nose. The twinkle of a strangely familiar sparkly ring caught my eye as she dabbed and blew. (I wonder how he got it to her? He sure didn't waste any time at getting engaged again.) Wadding the tissue nervously in her hands, she continued, "I think it's nice that you came to support Isaac today."

Maybe I should have told her the real reason I came was for closure and that she had just sealed it.

It was a surreal experience. Standing face to face with the high school sweetheart of my former, prison-bound, fiancé. This is the makings of a lifetime of therapy sessions. Yet, there I was. Me. No one else. This was my reality.

I went out for a hot dog. Mustard. Sauerkraut. Sometimes, when life gets thick, a hot dog just makes sense. Simple processed meat and not too many fixings. I wonder if Isaac knew that about me. I'm a closet hot-dog consumer.

Maybe I should get a puppy now that Isaac's nothing more than a page . . . or fifty-five pages . . . in my life. Hmmm?

I'll stick with my hot dog habit for now. And it's cheaper than therapy.

Please pass the mustard, and get me out of this mess . . . Me

February 8th, Monday

Annie, Susy, and their kids came to visit today for an impromptu girl's night. They left the husbands at home and spent the day shopping. They were all waiting at my apartment as I got home from school. I should mention, because I failed to before, Annie has two daughters. Mindy, who is four and into anything and everything that has to do with ponies. Alice, her other daughter, is two-and-a-half and is just into everything. Susy, as I mentioned before, has a four-month-old son, Michael. He is full of energy these days. Susy is sleep deprived.

Me too.

When I attempt to sleep, Isaac comes running into my thoughts. All the indicators that I missed. I should have paid full attention to all those awful feelings that hovered over my thoughts of our life together. Next time, if there ever is a next time, I will.

After dropping my bag of schoolwork onto the kitchen counter, and wiping melted chocolate off two little faces, we all went out for dinner at my favorite Mexican restaurant. I am officially a "regular" at the restaurant. I wonder what that indicates about my social life, or my eating habits, or my cholesterol levels.

I should get the puppy.

Alice happily ripped apart a chicken quesadilla while Mindy colored her paper placemat. Michael drooled and grinned almost the entire time. Susy nibbled at a fajita then fired off the question that she had danced around for the last hour. "Okay, Lindsey, when are you going to start dating?"

With my mouth full of veggie burrito, I shrugged.

Annie took the opportunity to pipe in on the subject. With a broad smile, she pulled quesadilla bits from Alice's fingers. "There is a guy in our ward that just got home from his mission." Alice shrieked as Annie pulled a gob of cheese from her fisted hand.

Nearly choking, I slurped some water. Taking a breath, I said, "Just home from his mission? That means he is like twenty. No way." I stuffed in another bite of burrito. "I don't want to babysit."

"He is really cute. I could set you up."

Susy pulled melted cheese strings from between Michael's fingers. Alice had shared. "That's only five years." She wiped the cheese on the cloth napkin. "Five years is nothing. Look at Grandma and Grandpa, they were thirteen years apart."

"Yeah," I said. "He was thirteen years *older* than her. That is completely different. I can't date someone that much younger than me."

Annie lit on a new idea. She nudged my arm with her elbow. "What about our server?"

"Charlie?" I mumbled around my food.

"Yes, Charlie," Susy whispered across the table. "He's good looking."

"Seriously," I said. "He has gray hair. He probably has a wife and six kids at home."

"Well, he's older."

Annie was hilarious.

Charlie returned to fill our water glasses.

Susy's eyes danced. "Charlie," she blurted, "do you know any attractive young men for my sister to date?"

Perfect.

He gave me a sly wink. Charlie dutifully listed any *young* man he could think of, including his cousin who was recently divorced, for the fourth time.

I think he sensed my pain.

"Well, it was worth a shot." Susy smiled.

Before the night was over, with the little ones all tucked into various sleeping arrangements in my apartment, we sat down to binge watch the last three episodes of *Forgotten Territory*.

Annie reopened the subject of my relationship status. "You ought to at least get on one of those dating websites."

"Yeah," Susy added. "I think that would be a lot of fun."

I pondered all the different types of fun a dating site could bring: frequent random messages from strangers that I did not want to meet, photos of male models that turn out to be men that strongly resemble a sun-dried raisin with hair . . .

I broke from my fun thoughts and spoke up. "I think what I really need is a change."

They both nodded.

Susy plopped down beside me. "After the ordeal with Isaac, I think you are absolutely right."

Annie pushed a bowl of popcorn onto the coffee table. "You'll know what's right." She grinned, turned the volume up two clicks, and added, "By the way, Mom is still determined that the whole world will know all about how you were wronged. I think she has already informed the better part of the continent and all without the aid of social media."

"I know." I sighed. "That's why I haven't been home."

"It's probably for the best," my sisters said in unison and laughed out loud. I laughed too.

Later as I brushed my teeth, Annie ducked into the bathroom waving an envelope. "What are these letters? Is it stuff to do with Isaac? Everyone knows you had nothing to do with his crimes."

I spit bluish-white foam into the sink and rinsed my mouth. "I don't really know. It's something about my dad."

"Your dad?" Annie's eyebrows arched skyward.

Throughout the years, we have never really talked about my dad. Even though I am strikingly different in appearances, I grew up in a family. My family. I grew up as Gerald's middle daughter. As far as I was concerned, he is my dad and Annie and Susy are my sisters, not just half-sisters.

"Weird, huh?"

Annie looked down at the envelopes and nodded. "You need to find out what they want."

"I know. I will. With all the Isaac drama, I guess I forgot."

She didn't bring up the subject again for the rest of the visit.

It was a boon to see my sisters. I am so glad they came. I am ready to get back to work tomorrow, though. An exciting day of equivalent fractions awaits my fourth graders.

Find your least common denominator . . . Me

March 1st, Monday

Today felt like summer. I gave the class an extra recess this afternoon because the classroom was too hot.

Maybe it is the weather. Maybe I am finally growing up. Today, I feel different. I no longer replay all the events surrounding Isaac in my head. I believe I have finally, *honestly*, forgiven him.

During the extra afternoon recess, one of my students (Kathy) asked me what I want to be when I grow up. *Good question.* I told her I was doing exactly what I wanted to do when I grew up.

For my future progeny, I will now expound on something other than my failed attempt at marriage. I have previously enlightened you all that I am a fourth grade schoolteacher. Let me share some of what my work entails. I work at South Bend Elementary. It is a charter school. We are a K-8 school. All of our students are admitted through a process of qualification. The academics are rigorous. Students are also trained in the arts. My specialties are math, language arts, and social studies.

I really do enjoy what I do. I am blessed to be a teacher.

This year we taught the students about the "Hero's Journey." The students write their own hero's journey. Many of them choose to write about their own experiences in facing and overcoming adversity.

After reading their papers, I am inspired to consider my hero's journey. Every hero has adversity to overcome. I have faced the bearded dragon of Isaac's choices. I have conquered. I have changed. I have faced impossible circumstances, and I am still standing.

I wonder at some of the characters of the hero's journey. Every hero seems to have his funny sidekick. Harry Potter has Ron. Luke Skywalker has Han. Who is my witty sidekick in this life story? Susy? Annie?

There is also a mentor to lead the hero with wisdom. Who is the wise Obi Wan or Dumbledore in my story? I suppose there are many. Dad (Gerald) is the first who comes to mind.

I wonder where my hero's journey will lead. Tonight, I will be the hero of vacuuming and finishing the laundry.

Oh, I submitted an article for the Review Journal about parental impact on a child's education. I was asked to write the piece by the school board president. The Review Journal will run the article next week. The governor's initiative to increase parental involvement has sparked the newspaper, radio shows, and a few billboard ads to inspire parents to "Be Involved." I am the school's rep for the initiative and will go to Reno in June for a conference.

Looking up . . . Me

March 23rd, Tuesday

I was surprised to find a letter from Isaac in my mailbox today. I can't remember if I have ever received an actual handwritten letter before. This might be the first. He began the letter with the same apologies as from the jail. Skimming through, I was pleased to see his optimism and his determination for growth and change. He hopes to write a book when he gets out. He also mentioned pursuing a degree in sociology. I hope it works out for him. There was no mention of Melissa or of any romantic implications. I tossed the letter in the trash.

Under his letter was yet another from the law office of Craig and Associates. I held it over the trash can. Something urged me to open it. Inside was a typed personal letter, not the form letter like I had received before. It was signed by Camille Noelle Saylor.

I stuffed the letter under my arm and climbed the steps to my apartment. I decided I would sit down, after a quick swim in the complex pool, and read it while I finished my laundry.

Active . . . Me

Later

Relaxed from a fast shower, and cozy in warm-from-the dryer pj's, I sipped a cup of blueberry lemonade and digested the letter.

> Dear Lindsey Jones,
>
> I hope this letter finds you well. We have made several attempts to make contact with you over the past few months. I regret that we have not yet been able to meet or visit in person. I am hoping that this letter will reach you, and that you will take the time to read what I have to say.
>
> Without going into great detail, I wish to express that your father, John Jones, played a significant role in saving my life. He may have very well saved the life of my father, as well. As a result of your father's selfless acts, we would like to meet with you.
>
> Please respond by calling us at the listed number. We look forward to meeting you.
>
> Warm regards,
>
> Camille Noelle Saylor

I've avoided this for so long. Now, I'm nervous. What are these comments about my dad? They must have the wrong person. There have got to be a thousand men with the name of John Jones in the world. It's funny, though, after everything with Isaac, I can no longer believe that life changing events only happen to other people. I'll call them in the morning and see if I can figure out what this is all about.

Curious . . . Me

March 24ᵗʰ, Wednesday

After drinking a protein shake for breakfast, I made the call from the kitchen table. After three rings, a female voice answered. "Craig and Associates, how may I direct your call?"

"Hello, I have a letter from Camille Saylor. Is she available?" I tapped the letter with my forefinger.

"One moment. I will put you through."

A new female voice answered. "Hello, this is Camille."

A flutter of nerves spun in my chest. "Hello, my name is Lindsey Jones, and—"

She cut me off. "Lindsey Jones? I'm so glad that you called. We have been trying to contact you for months. I am so happy to hear from you. Did you receive the letters that we sent?"

"Yes, I did," I replied, surprised by the enthusiasm on the other end of the call.

"Well, then, I won't waste your time. I would like to set up a time that we could meet."

Meet? Wait. What was this about? "I'm sorry. I'm not really sure that I understood the letters. You mentioned John Jones and how he saved your life."

"Oh, yes. Did you read about the estate?"

"I read something about an estate, but I have to admit that I didn't read it that carefully." I pulled the letter in front of me to quickly scan it again for any details I may have missed. I didn't see anything that I hadn't read the first time.

"Lindsey, we really need to meet and discuss this with you. I have an appointment in thirty minutes that I can't change, but before we end this call, I would like to know a time that my brother and I could meet with you. It will be better to discuss this matter in person."

I looked down at the handwritten letter again. With curiosity winning, I replied. "I could meet any day after school."

Camille gave a little laugh. "You're in Las Vegas?"

I thought the question was silly. She had sent the letters to my address. "Yes."

"Here is what I would like to do. I am in Pennsylvania . . ."

My eyebrows lifted.

"My brother and I would like to fly out and meet with you. I've got my hands tied for a couple of days here, and I know Spencer needs to be in Salt Lake City in a week. So, I . . ."

An idea worked its way into my head when she mentioned Salt Lake. With spring break just around the corner, I could use a vacation. A chance to get out of Las Vegas and leave all the craziness behind. Cutting her off, I blurted, "I could meet with you in Salt Lake?"

She paused then said, "That is a long way for you. Too long. I am happy to fly into Las Vegas and set up a time to meet with you there. If you would rather . . ."

"Salt Lake would be fine. I don't mind the drive."

"Okay, then . . . Let me look at Spencer's schedule . . ."

I mentally made vacation plans while I waited for the attorney's reply. A trip to Salt Lake was perfect.

"Could you meet Saturday, the 3rd?"

"Yes."

I booked my hotel as soon as school got out for the day.

My vacation awaits . . . Me

april 2nd, Friday

The Salt Lake Valley glittered with lights as I drove into the city. I had booked myself a tower room at the Little America Hotel, very luxurious. It worked out to be very practical, as well. The law office is just a few blocks from here.

I am here all alone. I kind of wish I would have brought one of my sisters. I was not sure that I should involve them. I didn't want them to feel awkward about this since it is about my dad, not theirs. Family matters can be interesting, can't they? I purposefully hid this trip from Mom. I don't know what tomorrow holds, and I didn't want to turn her into a tornado of ranting outbursts. I also considered inviting a friend, but since all my friends are married with children, it just seemed easier to come alone. Honestly, ever since Isaac has been out of the picture, I find that I don't mind being alone.

Maybe that is my huge character flaw. Every hero has one, right? Mine is being too wrapped up in me. Oh sure, I have faced and tackled life's challenges, especially the one named Isaac, but I have always had a safety net and the support of family as a protection. Sure, I went to college. Yep, I am the proud bearer of a master's degree. This shows that I can tackle hard things, right? But who am I?

If I were to meet my dad tomorrow, what would I tell him about myself? I'll take a stab at it.

Lindsey Jones:
- Likes dogs but will never own one. Too much work. Or is it too much of a commitment?
- Likes TV dramas about people who have grit.
- Likes the city life. Great for anonymity.
- Owns a ridiculous amount of clothing and shoes (all with closed toes).

What a ridiculous list . . .

I am anxious about tomorrow. To say anything else would be a lie. I know so little of my dad.

Introspective in Salt Lake City . . . Me

april 3rd, Saturday

This day has shaped and altered my perspective forever. It is as though I have been viewing life through just one lens. Tonight, I see through newly discovered lenses.

I was so stymied about what to wear to the appointment today that I packed six outfit choices. A little overboard, but I needed to make a positive, and even professional, first impression.

I decided on a pencil skirt and a black top. I wore flats so that I wouldn't be too overdressed.

Camille met me at the front door of *Craig and Associates Law Firm*. She was warm and bright and full of smiles. Her curly strawberry blonde hair bounced and shone, yet she was the model of professionalism in her silk top and tailored slacks.

Inside the office, I met Spencer Craig. Camille introduced him as her brother. He was tall and fit. It was easy to see the two were related. Spencer wore an expensive tie and a designer suit. The office was furnished in burgundies, golds, and richly stained woods. Expensive art hung on all of the walls. If I had ever imagined the inside of a law office, this was it.

I followed the brother and sister into a large conference room on the first floor. Leather chairs were tucked neatly around a wide mahogany table. Spencer pulled out a chair and motioned for me to take a seat. Two file folders rested on the table. Both looked substantial.

I sat. My heart danced like a hive of bees. This was a lot of splendor and ceremony for a girl they didn't know. Spencer circled the table and sat directly across from me. Camille took the chair beside me. Since my arrival, she had not taken her eyes off of me. I looked to her to initiate the conversation.

"You'll have to forgive me if I stare," she smiled, "but I feel like I've known you my entire life."

That was unexpected.

Camille put her hand on my forearm. Her eyes shone. Sliding one of the files directly in front of me, she opened the cover. There, staring back at me, was an eight-by-ten photograph of my dad. It was a picture I had never seen before. He looked strong and handsome. He was holding a guitar. He was young, maybe my age. His smile was broad and genuine. He seemed to be smiling right at me. His dark hair and the shape of his eyes were so like mine. It was easy to see me in him.

I stared.

Sensing Camille and Spencer watching me, I said, "I've never seen this picture before." I lifted it, holding it carefully at the edges. I studied it more closely. It was definitely my father. I could see that plainly.

Camille lowered her arm. Looking intently into my eyes she asked, "How much do you know about your dad?"

"Not much, really." The face smiling back in the photograph was a stranger. "He had some habits that broke him and my mom apart. I understood that he died when I was really young. I grew up with my mom's first husband as my dad."

"That must have been hard on you." Spencer spoke up from across the table.

"Not really." I returned the photograph to the folder. "I grew up surrounded by love. I was cared for. I had everything I needed." Or so I thought.

Spencer straightened the sleeve of his suit. "I think you will be interested in what my sister and I have to tell you. Well . . . we hope you will be interested."

I absently traced the edge of the photograph with my finger. Camille took a breath as if preparing to speak. Turning to face her, I said, "You mentioned in your letter that my father saved your life?"

Camille's smile brightened. She evidently forgave me for interrupting her. "Yes." Camille reached for the file from under my dad's photograph. "May I?" she asked politely.

I nodded. Keeping the photo, I slid the file toward her.

"Thank you." Turning the file so the contents faced her, she lifted a few sheets of official-looking printed pages.

She looked at me and said, "This is an account of all our father's interactions with your dad. I think it would be best if I read it, unless you would like to read it for yourself?"

Shaking my head, I replied, "No, go ahead. Please."

She pushed the pages between us. I followed along as she read.

> To the lawful heir of John Jones:
>
> Here below, you will find a detailed account of all of my interactions with John Jones. I have taken this account from my memory and my journal pages. In doing so I hope that I can share a portion of my feeling and perhaps shed a glimmer of goodness on difficult events, namely the death of John Jones. The events are as follows:
>
> At three months old, my daughter, Camille, became very sick with Human Respiratory Syncytial Virus. This RSV, compounded with bronchitis, left our daughter sick and weak.
>
> My wife and I were scared. Then, late one night, Camille took a turn for the worse. My wife and I sat up with her, doing all we could think to do for our precious daughter. At one point, little Camille became so congested that she stopped breathing and started to turn blue. As you can imagine, we were frantic. We were struggling college students at the time, living in the cheapest housing we could find in Las Vegas. It was in a scary neighborhood. We had no medical insurance. There were no neighbors, or family members, that we could turn to for help.
>
> In our poor state, the only vehicle that we owned was an old Buick Skylark that had belonged to one of my grandparents.
>
> Desperate to get Camille to the hospital, we woke up Spencer. He was three at the time. I loaded us all into

the Buick, but we were dealt another blow.

With Camille turning blue and fighting for breath, the car failed to start. I can vividly recall the awful click of a dead battery. There we were in the middle of the night surrounded by strangers with a baby who was, at this point, starting to go limp. Her little body was giving up the fight. We did what we should have done from the start. We turned to the only one who could really help us in our situation. We prayed.

I choked out a prayer to our Heavenly Father as I pounded the steering wheel with my fists. My beautiful wife was beside herself, cradling our daughter. Spencer howled with fear and confusion.

It was nothing short of torture, feeling so helpless.

That is the moment an answer came. Like an angel of mercy, John Jones showed up. We didn't know him very well. He lived in the neighboring apartment and mostly kept to himself. He was always quick to lend a tool or give me a hand if he saw me struggling to repair the old car. We took him cookies more than once to express our thanks to him for his help, but beyond casual greetings, we did not know him at all. Busy with college life and a small family, we were simply trying to survive.

Spencer interrupted, "And to be quite honest, with your dad's stature and appearances, I think they may have been a little intimidated by him."

I laughed softly. Glancing at the photograph again, I could just imagine him, a six foot something, well built, African American man approaching the broken car of a little family in the middle of the night. "What happened?"

Camille went on with the letter.

He was walking to his car, but I believe it was the noise of Spencer's crying that must have drawn his attention. John Jones approached.

Shaken with desperation, I opened the door. John Jones calmly asked, "Are you having some trouble?"

He must have taken in our situation in an instant. Before I could offer him an explanation, he thrust the keys of his own vehicle into my hands. John Jones then rushed around the car to where Camille and my wife were sitting. He opened the door for them and helped them out. I was dazed by it all as I witnessed this man next take Spencer's hand and lead him from the back seat of our car to the back seat of his car. In a blink, I was behind the wheel of this man's car. So grateful, I stuck my hand out to shake his.

John Jones shook his head, pointed down the road, and said, "Go. Just go. I have a daughter, too. Now you go and get your daughter to the hospital." Regaining my senses at that point, that is exactly what I did.

I was fully engrossed in the story. This was my dad? An angel of mercy in the night? "I never knew anything about this."

"We know."

Spencer cleared his throat. "Nobody knew. Except our parents. Dad said it was around three a.m. What are the odds?"

"Is this why you wanted to see me? So I could learn something about my dad?" I asked.

Spencer shook his head. "No, and yes. First, let me tell you the rest of the story. See, that was the last time my parents saw your dad."

"Really?" I wondered softly.

Spencer shifted uncomfortably. He tugged his tie. Releasing a quick breath, he said, "This is harder than I thought." He looked across the table at Camille for rescue.

I followed the exchange with my eyes. Camille pinched her lips into a sympathetic smile. Now, I was becoming uncomfortable. "What?" I pressed.

Camille piped up. "It's here in Dad's papers." She pointed at the stack in front of her. "If you would rather, I can keep reading."

"No. I think I should tell her." Spencer reached for the file. Camille slid the pages to her brother. He cleared his throat, glanced briefly down at the table, and spoke, "Your father was murdered that night."

"What?" My heart jolted. A little tremor shook my hands. "My dad was murdered?" This was wild. Never had anyone said that my father was murdered. He was a gambler. "Are you certain? When?" I asked.

Camille looked deep into my face. "Are you sure you're okay to hear this?"

"Yes. I am." I steeled myself against the waves of shock. "I want to know everything. Please, go on."

Spencer glanced down at the pages before he continued. "Our dad left the hospital as soon as Camille was stabilized. He wanted to return your dad's car. It was later in the morning by then. Our dad made one quick stop at an auto parts store for a new battery, purchased on credit." Spencer tapped the edge of the table. Shaking his head, he went on, "Our dad knocked on your dad's apartment several times, but no one answered."

His words filled my mind with images and sounds from another time. I witnessed it all, like a fly on the wall of a faded memory. Within my imagination, I could see all the colors, feel the sunshine, and hear the tenor of the voices now long gone. I watched it all like an old movie on a reel-to-reel projector.

Spencer's voice trickled back in through my thoughts. "An older man in a different apartment heard our dad knocking. The old guy opened his door and asked, 'You looking for him?'

"'Yes,' our dad responded.

"'He ain't here.'

"'When will he be back? I have his car.'

"The older man explained it all to our dad. 'He ain't coming back. He got jumped last night by a pack of hoodlums. He was walking home from the convenience store. Guess a gallon of milk cost him his life.' The old man spat on the concrete sidewalk. 'Stupid fool for walking to the store in the middle of the night. What was he thinking? I liked John. He was smarter than that. Cops were here just a while ago. Asking everybody questions. Was he a buddy of yours?'"

Spencer paused, took a breath, and looked steadily into my eyes. "My dad said he dropped to his knees right there on the spot. Right in front of your dad's apartment and sobbed. Then he went back and banged on the door of the old man. He handed the old man the keys to your dad's car. He did what he could to explain about your dad letting us use the car. The old man wouldn't take the keys. He told our dad to take it to the cops. Our dad was desperate to do something. He shook the keys at the old man and said, 'I don't even know his name.'

"'John Jones,' the old man told him. That was the only information our father could get about your dad." Spencer finished.

Without realizing it, I started to cry. Something I didn't know within me was burning and aching like a river of hurt that ran forever deep, penetrating my heart.

Camille wiped at her eyes with a tissue. She passed a polished, brass tissue box my way. I took two. The black mascara that smeared the white tissue paper jolted my sorrow. I would never know this man of whom they spoke. I had invested all my thoughts into thinking of my father as nothing more than a hopeless gaming addict. What was wrong with me? I cannot think of a time that I ever stopped to really consider him as a man with thoughts and feelings and dreams of his own. The fact that he was thinking of me when he loaned out his car . . . my tears streaked unashamedly down my cheeks. Swallowing the lump that bobbed in my throat, I managed to ask, "How did you know that John was my dad?"

Spencer straightened in his chair as though eager to share. He smiled kindly and lightly tapped the pages with his pen. "You've been a big part of my dad's work."

"What do you mean?" I asked, wiping away the rest of the mascara.

He met my gaze squarely. "The way your dad saved Camille's life, and the way it cost him his own, was a tipping point for our father." He paused and leaned toward me. "So, our dad worked like crazy. He said your father's passing drummed into him a fever to live every day with intention. And I can tell you, he did. He changed his major. He was nearly finished with an engineering degree, but he changed his major to law. He was determined to protect the innocent and get criminals like the ones that killed your dad off the street. They never did catch the guys that killed your dad, but our dad was ruthless in the courtroom. He was bent on seeing justice done."

"Our dad was determined to honor your father in whatever way he could." He leaned back. "Now, he only knew two things about your dad. The police were tight lipped when he later took them the keys and the car, but he knew your father was John Jones and that he had a daughter."

I didn't even know what to say. My thoughts fought to sort through these new revelations. I confided, "I feel so strange about all of this. I don't know what to think or even feel. I'm overwhelmed." I stared down at the table and studied the photograph of my dad again, wishing I could ask him the questions that began to take shape in my mind. Pangs of guilt for all my negative thoughts and feelings about him through the years tugged on my heart. He was gone. I should have considered him as more than a gambler.

"We really wanted an opportunity to express our gratitude to you and . . . through you . . . to your father."

I looked between them. "But how did you find me?"

Spencer took this one. "We hired a detective. Social media, and the fact that you are a teacher made it easier."

"Well . . . thank you for telling me about my dad," I said, my voice husky. "I appreciate knowing that he helped your family. Thank you."

"Lindsey, before you think this is all there is to our meeting, I need to tell you that there is another reason we needed to meet."

I wiped my eyes and let her continue.

"Our father passed just over six months ago."

My words sounded as mechanical as they felt. "I'm sorry for your loss." A knee jerk reaction. Listening to them talk all this time, I had assumed their father had passed some time ago. Now I felt completely stupid for not having asked them anything about their dad as they divulged about my father. Feeling dumb, I quickly met eyes with each of them and said, "From what you have said, he sounds like a wonderful man. I would have liked to have had the chance to meet him." I nodded soberly.

They each nodded and smiled warmly at me.

Camille said, "Thank you. He was a great dad." Spencer lifted his hand from the table and motioned for her to continue. She obeyed her brother's gesture, saying, "Lindsey, you are listed in our father's will. You have an inheritance, and as attorneys . . . and as his children . . . it is our obligation to fulfill the terms of our father's will."

I tugged at the tissues in my lap. "What does that mean?"

Spencer spoke directly. "You have been left a portion of our father's estate."

"What?" My head felt like a swimming pool. "I didn't even know your dad. Whatever it is, you two can have it. It belongs to you." A brotherly-sisterly half-nod half-smile passed between them. I continued my protest. "You've given me so much to think about, with the story of my dad. I think I should get going. I need to get back to my hotel."

"In a minute." Spencer held up a finger.

I wonder if he did that in the courtroom. It seemed fitting. It was a very authoritative finger . . . much like Mom's.

"Lindsey . . ." His eyes met my eyes dead on. "A will is a legally binding document. And our father's is rock solid. It is our responsibility, and our legal obligation, to fulfill his wishes . . . down to the last detail." He uttered those last words slowly, so I was certain to get the point.

I shook my head. My temples throbbed. "No." Knowing about my dad is all I could ever want. "I have enough to consider with everything you have shared."

Spinning the second file toward himself, Spencer left me no room to argue. Lawyers.

"Once again, Miss Jones," he grinned at his own formality, "this is not about what you, or I, or my sister want. This is about fulfilling a legal obligation that we owe to our father. Even if he were not our dad, this will is binding."

Spencer was definitely the pushy one. He could use a share of his sister's compassion. His voice ordered me from my childish stupor.

"So, let's not argue any points of the matter. Let's honor both fathers and fulfill his wishes." Spencer flipped the file open.

Camille squeezed my arm. She smiled enthusiastically.

It seemed my only choice was to stay and let them continue. I cast a glance at the door. I longed to march right through it.

Spencer slid a pair of reading glasses from the front pocket of his suit coat. Sitting up taller, he adjusted the glasses onto his face and twirled the pen across his fingers. Then he purposefully recounted all the legal jargon of the will. Most of it was Greek to me. My face must have betrayed my confusion. Spencer peered over the top of his glasses and looked me squarely in the eye. After a pause, and what must have been his silent assessment of my understanding, he broke it down for me. "Essentially, Lindsey, you have inherited two hundred acres and a home in Southern Utah."

He could have said I had inherited a herd of elephants and a yurt. My shock would have felt the same. It was like a mislabeled Christmas gift. What were they talking about? Acres? A home? It wasn't mine. It was theirs.

Camille held up her hand to silence her brother. "There are contingencies in the will. If you do not want the land, or the home, you will be given the full sale price of the properties and all the amenities." She looked at me for a response. "You have two months to decide whether you would like to keep the property or have it sold."

A tidal wave would have been less troubling. I replied, "That is a lot of land. A house . . .? Southern Utah . . .? I . . . ." My words got stuck in the confusion in my brain.

Spencer spun the folder so that I could see and pointed at the will. There were some numbers indicating plots or parcels of land. I am really not sure what it all was supposed to mean. I read the words, "Iron County, ten miles west of Cedar City, Utah," aloud from one of the diagrams in the folder. I looked between Spencer and Camille. I felt like I had been handed a fairy godmother. I know that is an odd figure of speech, but I felt as though I had been handed a million wishes . . . like I had all the wishes . . . but they were not my wishes. They were theirs. Why push it on me? I shook my head to realign my thinking, so I could tell them I wanted none of it.

Spencer gave no indication that he was troubled by my consternation. He thumped down that thick, attorney finger onto a satellite image of some land. Land that was ready for me to take over. "That is where the house is located." His voice was unanimated. He tapped it twice. The rectangle of a house was easy to pick out. I spotted a second house rectangle, a smaller one, a short distance away. The impulse to inquire what it was, was put out of mind as Spencer drummed forcefully onward with his recounting of the estate. I didn't have a chance to speak.

"The majority of the acreage is mountain land. For pasture. The house sits on a pretty piece." He slid some photographs out from under the map. I lowered my eyes as if to look at them, but my gaze drifted to the face of my father, still resting on the table. *Dad . . .?*

Spencer detailed and itemized every speck of the images, of the land, and of the home. His voice buzzed in my ears. I attempted to nod at the appropriate times, but honestly, it was all a blur of words and maps and a face. My dad's face.

Camille fidgeted, her hands now twisting in her lap. Almost before Spencer finished his last word, she butted in, "Lindsey, can I say something?"

I looked at her.

"I'm sure you must be feeling somewhat overwhelmed." She read my thoughts so plainly. They must have been stamped on my forehead. "I can only imagine how this has been a lot to process. I wish our dad were still here so that you could hear it directly from him. Please forgive us that we are secondhand accounts, but he wanted it this way. He didn't want to interfere in your life, but he wanted to repay kindness. I may be overstepping here, but I think it would be valuable for you to see the land, and the house . . ." Her face turned apprehensive. ". . . before you decide whether or not you will keep it."

Spencer scolded, "Camille, let her think for herself." Then turning to me, he said, "Don't let her influence you. She is a little sentimental about the house." He looked back to his sister. "This is about business as much as it is about family."

Camille graciously absorbed her brother's reprimand. With gentle eyes, she said, "Please, come with me to the house. If you decide to sell, at least you will have a full perspective."

Nodding dumbly, I measured it all out as best I could in such a brief moment. The whole situation was completely surreal. I was lost somewhere in the middle of all of this. Somewhere inside of me resided those familiar responses, my little quirks, and all the things that make me *me*. What was wrong with me? I should be celebrating and happy dancing all over the room or storming out of the door to escape. Looking again at my dad's face, I settled on one thing. I was too overwhelmed to think rationally about anything. Frustrated, I chose to take Camille's advice. "I will look at it." The words felt like tin falling out of my mouth. I didn't even say *thank you*.

Camille clasped her hands in joy. "Wonderful. Does Wednesday work for you? I blocked out all my appointments on Wednesday in the selfish hope that you would agree to go with me. I wish it could be sooner."

Good thing next week is spring break. So much for my little vacation. "Yes. I can meet you there Wednesday," I replied flatly.

So that is how we left things. And that is how my day unfolded before me.

I can't think right, so I just ordered dinner from room service. I've never done that before. A day of firsts.

I have a lot to consider . . . Me

april 7th, Wednesday

I wish I could live at the Little America. They were very kind and canceled the rest of my reservation without any fees. It was nice to be the princess in the tower for a while. I had so much rolling around in my head. It is providential that spring break landed when it did. I needed this time. More than I could have ever known.

I called Dad. He put me on speaker, and I told them I was on my way to Cedar City.

"Are you going to stop by?" Mom asked.

"No. I'm actually in Salt Lake right now."

"What are you doing in Salt Lake?" Mom quizzed.

"I was hoping for a little vacation, but it didn't turn out that way."

"Alone?" Mom was always good at pointing out the obvious. "Why didn't you call one of your sisters? You know they would love a vacation, too."

"I know." I hesitated to go on with what I had intended to say. I decided to wait. I would see the property first, then I could tell them more. I wasn't sure how hearing about my dad would hit Mom, anyway. "Well, I have a couple of stops to make in Cedar City. I just wanted to let you know where I am."

"That's a good thing," Mom blurted.

"Let us know if you need anything," Dad added.

The call ended with my parents still in the dark. I paused and considered calling one of my sisters. Then tossing my phone on the passenger seat, I decided to get on the road.

Camille met me at the Love's truck stop just off of the freeway exit in Cedar City. Living in St. George for so many years, I am no stranger to Cedar City, Utah, but I have spent very little time here.

Camille offered for me to ride with her, but I chose to take my own car in case I decided to leave before her.

I tailed her as she drove northwest on back roads until we were past all the homes and neighborhoods of rural Iron County. Continuing west, miles of sagebrush stretched out on either side of the road. We cruised up and down the low rolling hills, with a slow, but steady, ascent. The sagebrush mingled with scrappy looking cedar and juniper trees. We were out in the sticks of nowhere. I was surprised by how many cars passed us in the opposite lane. There must be some life out here. Then again, those cars were all driving back to Cedar City. The road ahead of me was . . . not surprisingly . . . empty. Snow still clung to the ground on the north sides of all the bushes, inclines, and trees. The thermometer in my car read forty-two degrees outside. Good thing I brought my coat.

Cresting the highest of the hills, a beautiful green valley opened up below us to the left. The sun streamed down. Camille signaled left. I followed her off of the two-laned highway onto a gravel road. At twenty miles an hour, the dust swirled. The ride was a bumpy one. I was surprised that she drove a BMW out here. After a mile or two on the gravel road, an impressive home came slowly into view. It took my breath away.

Nestled among the sage and junipers, it was a giant, two-story house. It was tasteful and beautiful. The grounds around the home were a continuation of the sage and junipers with a small lawn and a few flowers caressing the walkway. A porch big enough to park on stretched across the front of the house. We pulled to a stop. I sat, with my car running, and stared for a moment, just taking it in.

Mr. Craig had obviously been a wealthy man. The home was rustic like a cabin, yet with a modern feel of function and elegance. The gigantic front porch was eye-catching. It was arranged with furniture for sitting, and a fantastic bed hanging from four fat ropes. Did he really intend to give this away? What was the scam? A home of this size in Las Vegas would be unimaginable on my salary. What was Mr. Craig thinking?

I turned off my car, grabbed my coat, and stepped out onto the gravel. The cool, clean air filled my lungs. Closing my eyes, I breathed slowly.

Camille was on a phone call in her car, so I strode up the gravel walkway alone. I stepped onto the porch. Running my hand lightly over the coarse rope of the hanging bed, I allowed my thoughts to drift. I pictured myself with a book in hand nestled sweetly in the dozen pillows carefully arranged on the bed. Camille spoke up from behind. I started at the sound of her voice.

"Go ahead." She extended her hand toward the bed.

I lowered myself and enjoyed the sensation as the bed and the pillows supported me. Then sitting up with my feet touching the porch, I rocked the bed back and forth with my heels. "This is what life is all about." I smiled at Camille.

She sat down beside me. "I am glad you agree." A look of nostalgia washed over her. Sighing, she said, "I have always loved this place."

I hated to change the mood, but I had some burning questions. I sat up straighter. "Why would your dad think this place should go to me? There is no way that I can accept this. This is your family's home. I . . ."

Camille lowered her eyelids thoughtfully then raised them, looking at me as if she were figuring out what to say. Then she quietly stood, extended her hand, and said, "Come on. I want you to see the rest of the house."

Biting the inside of my lower lip, I followed Camille through the wide oak door. My breath was swept away as I soaked up the sight before me. How do I describe it? The entry was open all the way to the second floor. A wide staircase flowed down from the second story. Thick wooden beams and pillars brought the feel and sensations of the outdoors into the home. It was beautiful.

I noted a modern kitchen, with multiple ovens and a huge stainless-steel range for cooking. The fridge and freezer were each big enough to hold food for the whole valley.

Up the stairs, the master bedroom was no disappointment. It was surprisingly warm and cozy, and a perfect fit for the home, boasting a separate sitting room with an enormous TV, a gigantic bathtub, and enough space for two of my apartments. My favorite detail was the elegant draping of white netting over the top of the king-sized, canopy bed.

In total, I think I counted four bedrooms and five bathrooms.

After the house, Camille took me to the garage. A shiny, navy blue pickup truck, one side-by-side, one golf cart, and two snowmobiles barely took up any of the space. It was a massive garage. Who needs that much space?

Above the garage sat an apartment, complete with a kitchen, bathrooms, and two bedrooms. I wondered if the apartment was for the butler or for the housekeeper. I asked, "Who lives here?"

Camille laughed. "No one."

After completing the tour, Camille walked me outside and pointed out the perimeters of the property. Fields of alfalfa stretched to the horizon. The lower fields, to the south, were dotted with horses. A few cows grazed in a field adjoining the horses' pasture. This scene, backdropped with the lowering sun, momentarily transported me to a different time and place. It was as though I had just stepped out of the pages of western novel. All that was missing were a few cowboys and the state of Wyoming. (Do they have cowboys in Wyoming?) It doesn't matter. This is all part of a dream.

As I stood, drinking up the view, Camille pointed down the lane to a quaint, yellow home nestled pleasantly against the fields of alfalfa. We passed it as we drove in. I was too absorbed with the view of the big house to notice. "That is where Rick lives. He and his wife Lori take care of the ranch."

"The ranch?" I questioned.

Camille smiled understandingly. "It is a lot to process, isn't it?"

I nodded dumbly. I wanted to say: *A lot to process? This is absurd! What am I doing here? You people are crazy. Keep your big house and leave me alone. I am happy the way that I am.*

"Let's go sit on the porch," Camille interrupted my mental rant. "I will explain all the details."

"Okay." Ugh, why was I so tight lipped?

Following her back to the house, my focus kept drifting out across the scenery. It was mind-blowingly beautiful. It was also very quiet. Too quiet.

A tiny chill bit the air.

We sat on a couple of mission style chairs as she delved into the details of the property. I sat like a blank manuscript, taking in her words.

"The ranch is completely self-sufficient. You see, the alfalfa . . . well hay . . . is primarily sold to ranchers in California. We do store some here to feed the cattle that you saw."

"What about the horses?" The horses were neat looking out there in the field.

"The horses are Rick's. The sale of hay also pays his salary." Camille shifted and stretched against the square pillow at her back. "The acreage east of town is leased to farmers for grazing their animals. The biggest parcel is up the canyon. Some is leased to ranchers. At one time, Dad thought about putting in a resort." She caught my raised eyebrows. With a light laugh, she said, "I think he just got tired."

My thoughts trailed off. My biological father filled my head. I wonder how he would have felt about my experience here today. I wonder, if he had lived, how his life could have been different if Mr. Craig had been able to return his borrowed car? I wonder if he would have looked for me?

"The land, the home, and any amenities were willed to you", Camille explained. All I had to do was agree, and all of it was mine.

It just felt wrong. I don't know why. The uneasiness that stirred was so much greater than anything I had felt with Isaac. There was no question in my mind. I wanted nothing to do with any of it. "Camille, I appreciate you taking the time to fly out and meet with me and . . ." I extended my arm toward the road. ". . . and show me all of this. But this is your family home. There is no way that any of this is for me."

Camille nodded her head and seemed to ponder my words. When she spoke, her voice was as calm as the light breeze. "Lindsey, this is bigger than you or me." She searched my face. "My dad wrote you into his will even before he knew your name. I sat with him one night before he passed. He spoke for forty minutes about his plan to do this for you. It brought him so much joy."

"I really, and truly, appreciate the gesture, but I can't . . . what about your mom? Where will she live? This is her home . . ."

Camille leaned forward. "Lindsey," she put a hand on my knee, "this is the ranch. It's not our mother's home. Dad built this as a family getaway, nothing more. The only person who has ever lived here full time is Rick, and his wife Lori, who take care of the place. It is fully self-sufficient. Money comes in to pay the taxes and the maintenance. It's not enough to live on, but it is enough that you will not have to expend your own finances to take care of the property. That is, if you want to keep those contracts."

My head buzzed with what she was saying. I shooed it out of my mind. "Where does your mother live?"

"Let it put your mind at ease to know that she has a very elegant home in Pennsylvania." Camille smiled. "She had really hoped to meet you but travelling is difficult for her now."

I nodded, understandingly, but still holding a swarm of turbulent emotions inside. "What about your kids, or Spencer's family. Don't they want to keep this house?"

"Again, Lindsey, I wish you would put your mind at ease. Our lives are primarily in Pennsylvania. We rarely get out here, especially with Mom getting older. The Salt Lake office, and this ranch, were Dad's way of getting away, slowing down, and taking a break. You're not taking anything that we aren't happy to give."

Against my better judgment, I agreed to spend the night. Camille put me up in the master bedroom. She insisted. Then she surprised me by not staying. I had assumed that she would also spend the night. She apologized and explained that her husband and baby were staying in Cedar City. She was driving out to meet them. Before she left, she showed me a well-supplied pantry and a well-stocked refrigerator and told me to make myself at home.

Impossible.

Finding a couple of microwave pastries, I sat on a stool at the kitchen island and felt like a marble in a shoebox.

I called my parents to let them know I had decided to stay the night in Cedar City. Mom pressed for more details. I told her a friend wanted me to stay over. It seemed to satisfy her concerns.

It is too sensational for anyone to believe it. But really, this is a true account. Now that I am here alone, I wish that I had brought my sisters . . . or my parents. What was I thinking? How am I supposed to sleep in a strange house all by myself? I would drive back to Cedar City if I wasn't afraid of driving in the dark. I looked outside, and it was really dark. Dark dark. I think I will go and see if there is anything to watch on the TV.

Reluctantly staying here . . . Me

april 8th, Thursday

Miraculously, I did get some sleep. I woke up still on the couch in the sitting room off the master bedroom. The TV was still on. Grabbing the remote, I turned it off. Stretching the kink out of my neck, I stood at the wide window and looked out across the fields. The sun had barely cleared the tops of the eastern hills. A white mist hovered peacefully against the hills.

Bundling up the best that I could, I decided to take a walk before heading for home.

Walking the gravel road, my thoughts spun like a merry-go-round. I paused at a fence to better see the horses in the field. Three came running. I stooped down and picked as many blades of grass that I could gather from the cold ground and extended it to the horses. They each tried to nose in on the tiny feast, causing it to fall out of my hand and onto the ground. I decided to try again.

I bent over, tugging for all I was worth at a stubborn patch of grass, when a mustard yellow pickup truck pulled up alongside me. At that same moment, the grass broke free sending me flat onto my rear. The damp ground went right to my skin. My face flushed red.

An older man with gray hair and brown leather cowboy boots stepped out of the truck chuckling.

"Let me guess. I can bet your parents call you Grace." He laughed some more.

I fired off my best teacher glare. It lasted less than half of a second. The burly cowboy stretched out an enormous, calloused hand. I took it. His hand completely engulfed mine. Then, like a bale of hay, he yanked me to my feet.

"I'm Rick," the cowboy introduced himself. With a wry grin he asked, "What are you trying to do? Poison my horses?"

I looked worriedly down at the wet clump of grass that dangled in my hand muddy roots and all. I stumbled out an apology. "I'm sorry," I said as I quickly tossed the grass to the ground. "It's poisonous to them?" I peered up into the man's etched face. It was rugged and leathery from years of working in the sun. As I watched, his features dissolved into a big cowboy grin. His eyes twinkled like a western Santa Claus.

"Nah, it won't hurt them. I was just messing with you." He pointed at the tossed clump. "They don't really care for the mud, though. You could pull the roots off."

I nodded, staring at the clump as if it were a lab experiment in school, and I was a failed student. Which, I guess I was.

Rick leaned on the side of his truck. He cut to the chase. "So, whadda ya think? You gonna keep the place?" He spit something onto the dirt. I was preparing an answer when he added, "You'd be an idiot not to."

His abruptness caught me a little by surprise. It was unexpected to hear someone else have an opinion on my unique, crazy, awesome, puzzling, and slightly overwhelming decisions to be made. I replied, "I want to think this through." For *my* future. I flicked a few clinging gobs of mud off my hand. I avoided Rick's eyes. One of the horses grunted and nodded, as if putting in his, or her, two cents.

Rick didn't miss a beat. "Well, there ya go." He pointed a thumb toward the horse. "Even ol' Chester agrees with me."

Feeling a cold wetness on my rear, I twisted to investigate the nice wet spot on the back of my pants.

Rick rubbed a thumb against his nose and chuckled.

Honestly, the old man had a way of putting me at ease, even with a wet seat.

Digging the mud out from under my thumbnail, I said, "It seems really odd that complete strangers would want to plop a mansion and a ranch into my lap." I stopped digging and met his eyes. "Don't you think?"

Rick appeared completely undisturbed. He reached into the cab of the truck and retrieved a bag of roasted sunflower seeds. (That's what he'd been spitting.) He extended the bag to me. With a shake of my head, I declined. Rick tossed a few into his mouth. After spitting out some shells he suggested, "Maybe you're looking at it backward."

"How do you mean?" I squinted into the morning sun as I looked up into his face.

"Have you considered that you might be giving them something . . . by taking the place?" He shook a small fist full of seeds back and forth before throwing them into his mouth. A gesture I could imagine he had repeated many times in his life. I waited for him to explain. He grabbed another handful of seeds out of the sack.

I was still confused. "How do you mean?"

Shells flew from his mouth like black birds flying south. He spoke, "Closure."

"Closure?" Puzzling. "I don't really know what you mean."

"Look, kid. This family has been living and working because of the shadow of a man they barely met. You are that shadow incarnate." More sunflower seeds vanished into his mouth.

"But *I* didn't do anything. I'm just a boring schoolteacher that rarely looks beyond my own agenda." So, I did it. I admitted my self-centered nature to a stranger. Not just any stranger, mind you, a cowboy. A rough and tough, work-the-land, type of guy. I must really be losing it.

To console my feelings, I reached for the bag of sunflower seeds. Rick passed it willingly. Grabbing a fist full, I tossed the seeds up and down in my hand like Rick had done and I stuffed the fistful into my mouth only to discover that they were cayenne-pepper flavored. My throat burned like I had swallowed a branding iron. Rick thumped me on the back a couple times as I choked and coughed, spitting the seeds all over my shoes.

Perfect. Maybe this day was indicative of what my life would be like if I were to take this ranch.

Rick squinted, gazing across the field. "Did you know your dad?"

"No. I didn't know him at all," I cackled, swallowing hard to soothe my throat. I kicked the mess off my newest tennis shoes.

"Life's funny, ain't it?" Rick said as more shells flew out of his mouth. He extended the bag to me again. I held up my hands in refusal. He bobbed his head in response and continued his dialogue. "I didn't know my daddy either. He died before I was old enough to walk. He was a soldier in the Army. It was some routine military drill that took him. Some kind of flying accident. My mom broke down after he passed. She kind of let herself get swallowed up with grief, I guess. My uncle took me in. He was the rancher in the family. Raised me to it. I've never looked back, or regretted any of it." He looked at me. "I'm just saying things don't always play out the way you think they should. Sometimes you just have to hang on for the ride."

I nodded stupidly, puzzled by his telling me all of this. I shook blood into my frozen fingers. "I am really not an outdoorsy, hike in the wilderness, rope a calf, kind of girl."

"Come on." Rick motioned with his head for me to climb into the cab of his truck.

I shook my head. "I've got to go put my things in my car. I need to go back to the house."

"Well, hop in, and I'll drive you there."

Exhaling, I turned and studied the dirt road. It was a good distance back to the house. I was cold. My stubby toes were chilled to the bone. I climbed in.

Once I was buckled in, he said, "And . . . I'll give you a tour." He grinned. Off we went.

Riding shotgun in the mustard-colored truck, we bounced over dirt lanes separating the fields. Laying aside my big decision to be made for a moment, I admired the budding green fields. The hills held the periphery as though they were placed just for guarding this land. With a sigh, I had to admit that Mr. Craig had picked a lovely piece of land for his ranch.

The thrill of owning my own land tickled at my senses. My sisters would love it. It would undoubtedly blow my mother's mind. She would have plenty of opinions about it all. Honestly, the thought of what I could get from the sale of the place also stirred my interest. That is what Camille and her brother told me. I *could* sell the place. I imagine such a nice place could see me through my financial worries for quite a while.

Rick returned me to the house. "Think about what I said," he instructed just before he drove back down the road.

Cowboys . . . Me

april 9th, Friday

The cowboy, with a bag of sunflower seeds, fostered my courage to stay another day. Spring break is passing way too fast.

I lay in the large master bedroom this morning staring up at the ceiling fan, toying with the idea of living at this ranch. I played some scenarios that were dramatic and fun, ones that included a very fit, tan cowboy riding in to save the day. Silly stuff.

Rick's barking dog in the distance steered me back to reality. No point in wistful daydreaming.

Today, I decided to follow some of the back roads that Rick showed me and take a morning jog. Good thing I had packed my running shoes when I left home for my "vacation."

I greeted the barking dog fenced in on Rick's property, a beautiful golden lab. I jogged on. The dog chased after me inside his fenced yard, tail wagging.

With the morning mist still hugging the air, I explored. The cool bite to the morning air had me breathing deeper than I ever thought I could. Except for the incredible quiet, this could be a beautiful life. There is just so much silence. It is a strange sensation to be completely alone with my thoughts. I should have snatched my headphones from out of my car.

After the jog, a shower, and a toaster pastry, I took the liberty of calling Camille. The call went straight to her voicemail. I told her that she did not need to take the time to travel out to the ranch. I let her know that I'd reached my decision. (I guess being alone with my thoughts helped confirm what I had felt all along. There was no way that I could take someone's house, or ranch. It was too much. Spending the two nights was enough of a gift.) "I want to sell." I told her I didn't want any of the money. I recommended that she donate it or put it into their business or something.

After the call, I hit the road.

I did as I said, and I stopped by to see my parents. Mom was in the middle of hanging new curtains in the dining room. "Lindsey, what do you think of these new drapes?"

"They look good. I like them," I said with my thoughts elsewhere.

Mom smoothed the cream-colored fabric and said, "I have decided what to do with your *Isaac* wedding dress."

I looked at Mom quizzically. "Are you going to make curtains out of it?"

Dad walked in, "That's not a bad idea."

"Oh, no. I've decided to save the flowers and donate the dress. There is a girl in our ward that needs a dress, and I think she is about your same build."

"She can have it."

Mom smiled.

"How was your trip?" Dad pulled out a chair and sat down.

"Um, it was good."

"Did you get to see any of your old friends?" Mom asked.

"No. Not this time."

"But you made a new friend? What is her name?"

"Well, it's Camille." I hesitated and decided to come clean. "Remember the letters from that attorney? Camille is one of the attorneys. I went to Salt Lake to meet Camille and her brother. They wanted to tell me a story about my dad."

"What story?" Mom quipped.

"He saved a baby's life."

"Well, isn't that fantastic." Dad smiled a genuine smile. "I think that is a great thing. How did they know about it?"

"Camille, the attorney, she was the baby. They just wanted to say thanks."

Mom stood silent. Her expression was unfamiliar. I wondered what she was thinking, but I let her keep her thoughts. It was none of my business. "Well, I need to get back."

After quick hugs, I left my parents pondering on the information I had just shared. I made certain that I said nothing about my dad's death or the ranch they had offered me. That was a conversation I really didn't want to have. At least, not today.

I am nestled safely in my comfortable apartment now, breathing the smog filled air that I call home.

Good night . . . Me

April 10th, Saturday

I spent today working on an article for an education magazine. Nothing fancy. Just another piece on childhood literacy and parent involvement. This one is a paying opportunity. A girl can always use some extra spending cash.

I wish that I could say that nothing from my conversations with Camille, or my days at the ranch, pestered or stole my thoughts. But honestly, I think that for every minute I spent writing, I spent three minutes thinking about Camille, her words, and the ranch. What an experience. I'll never forget it. Complete strangers wanting to give such a huge gift for a five-minute act of kindness from a man they didn't know. It's incredible.

Now, I am going for a swim. I will touch base when I get back.

Swimming . . . Me

Later

Okay, so the pool was fantastic. Just what my tired brain needed to reboot and refresh. Then I got out.

Following an impression, I peered out the windows of the pool house before walking out alone, in the dark. (I know, Mom, don't scold me.) I had a feeling to check on my car. Cozy in my towel, swimsuit, and a pair of sensible shoes, I walked with my dripping hair out to my parking space.

You will not believe what I have to tell you. I don't believe it! Words fail me! I can't piece together the right ones to untangle my spaghetti bowl of emotions. Horrified doesn't even scratch the surface. Furious? I'll go with that. Well that . . . and a heaping spoonful of just plain angry.

My windshield was smashed. A rock the size of my head was still resting on the dash. Someone had obviously grabbed one of the many landscape rocks and heaved it into *my* windshield. Aaaarrrgggghhh! I wanted to punch someone. I rang my hands through my wet hair again and again as I stared at the wreckage and bit back the desire to lash out in a fit of fury.

Steaming, I took a closer look at the damage. It appears that the little vandals were in it just for the thrill factor. I opened the doors and the trunk. I checked everything. I even looked under the seats. Nothing was taken. That was something. There really wasn't much in there that would be of interest to anyone.

Surveying the parking lot, I wondered if any other vehicles had been targeted. I didn't see any other victims. Only mine. My head screamed.

I punched a quick phone call to Dad. He gave some needed counsel. Next, I called my insurance. What a mess.

After working through the details with my insurance, I made a quick call to the police and then one to security. Hopefully they can nab whoever it was on the parking lot cameras. Grrrr!

Dad sent me a message. He and Mom are bringing me their extra car tomorrow. What a blessing.

This just in: Camille texted:

> *Hello Lindsey, I hope you are well. There has been an offer on the ranch. Are you still interested in selling? I will look forward to hearing from you. Camille*

Yes, I am interested. I needed to text her.

Then, I got a message from Ted. Okay, this one I do need to explain. Ted is the cousin of a friend at work, Alicia Sills. Alicia teaches third grade. The message:

> *Hey, my cousin Alicia gave me your number. I hope this isn't too stalker-like. Texting wasn't my first choice, but I chickened out on giving you a call. I wanted you to have the chance to laugh at me without me knowing. I was hoping you could meet me for dinner this coming Thurs. I will be eager to hear from you. Ted*

Hmm. Dinner. With a stranger? I like food. Maybe he was the one who smashed my windshield? Well, that remains for my posterity to discover.

Flabbergasted, and still needing to text Camille . . . Me

April 1th, Sunday

Church was great. I got to help teach the four-year-olds. What a blast. They are hilarious!

I saw Mom and Dad. They brought me the Toyota.

I just got off the phone with Camille. I decided to call her. She said the offer that came in was well below the asking price. She wanted to know if I was willing to accept such a low amount. I don't have an opinion on the price. It still feels like I am being dishonest, even stealing, when I think of that beautiful home and property. I told her to do what she feels is best. I think she is going to shoot down the offer.

I still think about the two nights I spent. I think about Rick, the iconic cowboy. It's easy to see why Camille loves the place so much. I can see why her dad chose that spot as his escape. After having my windshield smashed, I could enjoy a getaway, too.

On a whim, I texted Ted:

> *Ted, It was gracious of you to give me the option of laughing behind your back. I will meet you Thursday for dinner. Does 6 work for you? I was thinking Chinese.*

Dinner with a stranger for my getaway . . . Me

april 12ᵗʰ, Monday

Today on our field trip, my darling fourth graders staged the first ever blow-fish, flash mob! They orchestrated the whole thing on the bus behind my back.

It went something like this: We visited the aquarium. I said in my teacherly tone, "Now if you like sharks, boys and girls, this is the tank for you."

A voice from the lineup of students shouted, "Now!" No less than sixteen faces pressed up against the glimmering glass and puffed out their cheeks with a blast of air. All I saw were backs of heads (except for the six kids that refused to be a part of the flash mob). Well, I'm sure the sharks got a good view from their side of the glass. It was stinkin' funny. I wish I had a picture. Now, I just hope that the blowfish mob doesn't all break out with impetigo all over their faces.

I need a field trip detox.

I do have some good news. My insurance has taken care of things. I will have my car all fixed by Thursday. Yeah! It has taken longer than I thought. Gotta love all the paper trails that make life happen.

Camille called. "Lindsey, I'm so glad I caught you. I have some news about the offer."

A twinge of regret stabbed in my gut. I brushed it aside. I had to do what I felt was best. "Did they buy?"

"The offer was very low. With the water rights and the mountain land considered, this offer came in at less than fifty percent of the value. I know you have the right to sell, but I couldn't see letting it go for pennies."

"No. That wouldn't be right." I agreed on that.

"Oh, I'm so glad you're okay that I didn't accept. I was worried you would be disappointed."

"No. I'm not disappointed at all. I still feel like it's your house. It feels so strange to be any part of it." I paused to think, then asked. "What about Rick? Can I ask what will happen to him with another owner taking the place?"

"That will depend on the buyer. They may hire him to stay."

"But there is a chance that he could lose his work at the ranch?"

"Yes, that is a possibility."

Camille left me with a lot to think about. She said the ranch is still mine until it sells. I thought about Rick. I would hate for him to lose his job.

Ted texted back:

> I like Chinese. Since you were not very specific . . . ha ha ha . . . I assume you are not planning on microwaved, frozen entrees. How about Asia House at the Bay Fair downtown?

I have never been inside the Bay Fair. It seems nice enough, but I *hate* driving downtown. Besides, he sounds awfully smug, but I do like a nice meal.

Ugh, I will deal with it all tomorrow . . . Me

april 15th, Friday

A ream of paper wouldn't cover the last twenty-four hours. So, grab a spoon, a tub of ice cream, and settle in. You have got to hear this.

Yesterday morning dawned bright and warm. I jogged to the park and did six flights of stairs before getting ready for work. A tall blueberry smoothie, straight from the blender set me up for the day.

I arrived at school just in time to see smoke spewing from the roof. The fire alarm was blaring. Adults congregated and worried together. I joined the crowd. Our diligent principal and custodial staff were busy on phones. We were not allowed to go inside the building. Too many potential liabilities.

The fire crew arrived shortly after. They took over as we all waited. All I could think about was my half-completed language arts lesson plan that still rested on my desk. I needed it for today. I was counting on the few minutes before the students arrived to finish it up.

I watched the smoke and pondered my lesson until the buses started to pull into the student loading lane. Students were not allowed to get off. This created problems for the ones who needed a restroom, breakfast, or were causing problems for the bus driver. The other challenge was that the drivers all have more than one route.

I sprang into action and helped as best as I could. We divided up the buses among the teachers and took turns walking small groups of students to the nearby Seven Eleven to use the restroom. (Nearby being roughly four blocks . . . big blocks.)

Funny thing, while I was on my third trip to the convenience store, I couldn't help but notice a very nicely dressed couple. They were both very designer, I mean . . . fancy. I also noticed, I caught it in glances, that they were very much into one another. They looked happy . . . and kind of sparkly, if that makes any sense. (But more on this later.)

With the third group of students safely back on the bus, we received the official word that all of the students were to be bussed back home. All were accounted for. Parents were notified.

After it was deemed safe, faculty and staff were allowed to enter the school, but we were given the day off. I grabbed a few things from my classroom. On my way out, I slipped around the barricade and stole a peek at the cafeteria. I couldn't see much from my vantage point, but I could see some of the beautiful morning daylight streaming into the cooking area through the ceiling.

The principal gathered us for a quick debriefing on the lawn. One of the exhaust fans had sparked and caused the fire. From the amount of damage, it appears that the fire had already been burning in the crawlspace before the fire alarm went off. The principal expressed grave concern over the faultiness of the system. She also said that the big issue was not being up to code. She worried that we would not be able to reopen very soon.

What a deal. I am grateful the students had not been able to step inside.

Well, that was Thursday morning. Let me fast forward to Thursday evening, right around six o'clock.

I bought a new top with my unanticipated free time. It is cute. A nice cream color with black accents. Super cute. With my favorite pants and my best black flats to cover my feet, I was ready for Ted . . . so I thought.

I strutted into the Bay Fair. (I opted to meet him there. I didn't want to depend on a stranger to get me home. Street smarts and all.) The burnt-up school ceiling was not even on my mind. I was ready for a great evening. It just had to be great. I had all the right vibes about it.

Asia House was easy to find. An impressive line was forming. Apparently, it takes a reservation to get in. With my very best poise, I approached the hostesses. They asked, and I gave them my name. Surprise, there was a table ready. Wow. I was beginning to like this. I strutted again past all the people waiting in line.

I was led to a seat beneath a red and gold fringed lantern. A candle was lit for me. I perused the continent sized menu. I had no worries. A guy who had the thoughtfulness to make reservations was nothing to worry about, and given the prices on the menu, he was not too poor.

Hindsight, I should have slurped down the free glass of water and walked out.

Pausing my perusal of the menu, my heart stuck in my chest. I mean stuck. Not a pitter patter of fluttery feelings. No, this was like a 1970's four-wheel drive bucket of rust stuck in the deepest mud hole. Stuck. And a little bit sick.

A man slid into the seat across from me. Moving aside the continent-sized menu, I locked eyes on Ted. Tall and handsome, perfectly dressed, Ted. He was none other than the man I spied at the Seven Eleven earlier in the day. Yes, the same well-dressed guy that I saw very smitten with a lovely female . . . very smitten.

With my heart in the mud hole, can you guess what I did? You will never guess because any sensible human would have either found an excuse and left . . . or simply left.

Staring at Ted, I unstuck my heart and suddenly thought the whole thing was wildly hilarious. With a stupid grin, and biting back a laugh, I donned professionalism and stuck out my hand. "Hi, I'm Lindsey. Thank you for making the reservation. This place looks great." He took my hand, first in one of his, then he wrapped his other hand around our clasped hands. Quaint. I grinned cheesily. I was determined to have a good meal anyway, whatever his ethics might be. Besides, I was, thankfully. driving myself home. It is funny how the menu took on a new life. Suddenly my tastes became very pricy. And yes, I was going to have dessert.

Ted was a great talker. As I stuffed my face, he daintily fed himself. He was even coy enough to reach across the table and feed me appetizers from his hand. (I hope he washed.) He spun tales of his family, work, and future ambitions. I listened stupidly. I say stupidly because I maintained a look of real interest, but I honestly missed a good third of what he said. It is hard to really put effort into a man who is a stinker.

I was a little bit of a brat. I wanted to try a couple of the desserts, so I acted as though I could not decide . . . which is partly true. I was egging him with the hope he would order both. It worked. I managed to snarff it all down. He didn't seem to notice, or if he did, he gave no indication.

After he graciously took care of the bill—honestly, I think I could eat for weeks on the price of that one meal—he circled around behind me and helped me stand. Very chivalrous. He offered his arm, yes, his arm, like we were grade school kids about to dance the Virginia Reel. I hammed it up. I took his arm with relish. Even if he wanted it back, I did not give it. I thought it was funny. I did not care what he thought about me. It was a very relaxed evening for me.

He guided me on a tour of the Bay Fair. We window shopped. He talked. He was brazen enough to make allusions about seeing me again. I held my breath to hold back a snort as he poked around the topic. Nope. This was the only time I would ever spend with Ted.

The night ended very idealistically. He escorted me to my car. Once again I felt the urge to snort. I scrunched up my cheeks in a cheesy grin, and I slid into my car. He closed the door for me, and I was off.

And good riddance of Ted.

Though my stomach was impossibly full from my performance, I ducked into the grocery store on my way home. Awkward situations have a way of making me crave cookie dough. I picked up a tube of chocolate chip cookie dough and tore it open with my teeth. I drove one handed and savored the sugary delight. Eight tiny bites in, I was finished. The cookie dough hit the trash as soon as I was home. Sometimes just a little sweet is soothing to the soul.

This morning, I received a message about the school. School is canceled through Tuesday of next week while damages are assessed. Starting Wednesday of next week, students will be bussed to Elkside Elementary where we will have a split schedule until the school year ends in May. I will share a classroom with another fourth grade teacher. The other teacher will teach from eight until noon. I will teach from one o'clock until five o'clock.

We were allowed one more opportunity to go to our classrooms to get supplies. I spent the better part of the day gathering, transporting, and adjusting to the new arrangement. I visited my "roommate" teacher at Elkside Elementary, and she helped me to settle, a little, into her classroom. We have worked out the logistics, but I spent the rest of the afternoon and into the evening with my plan book trying to fit six hours of curriculum into four hours of school. Without the lunch break and only one recess, I think we will manage.

In case you were wondering, I did get a text from Ted:

> *Hey, Pretty Girl,*
>
> *I can't remember when I have felt so comfortable around someone. I really enjoyed my evening with you. You didn't even laugh in my face. I'll take that as a good sign, although your smiles may have been your polite restraint. No, seriously, I had a good time. I look forward to our next time.*

Game over. I don't want to play anymore. I deleted the text.

Nothing from Camille tonight. I'm actually relieved. I'm finding it more and more difficult to think of someone else owning that property. Yet, how can I be the one to take it?

I'm going to bed.

Good night, journal . . . Me

april 17th, Sunday

I followed a change of course today. I attended the singles ward. It had been a long time. It just seemed like it was time.

I really enjoyed the meetings. Everyone was very nice. I was invited to a potluck on Friday.

Camille called while I was at church. She didn't leave a message.

Mom and Dad stopped by. They picked up their car. I told them about the ranch.

"They just want to give it to you? Two hundred acres." Mom settled onto the couch to sort out what I had shared.

Dad was more practical. "Lindsey, this could be an important opportunity for you. Have you taken the time to weigh it all out? This isn't a decision you should make without considering all aspects of what they are offering you."

"I suppose you're right," I said to Dad as I sat down beside Mom. "I keep thinking about it. But it is in the middle of nowhere. I mean, there are a few houses out there, but not many. You have to drive into Cedar City to go to the store."

"But is it really that far when you think of how long your commute is here, when the traffic is bad? It might be about the same," Dad offered.

"I suppose that's true." I looked into my Mom's face. She was quiet again. I wondered if it was difficult for her to hear things about my dad. Maybe it was a little something like me hearing about Isaac.

Dad counselled me to ask Camille for more time to consider my options. Mom, surprisingly, didn't express an opinion either way for the rest of their visit. I think it was a lot for her to hear.

That's all for now . . . Me

april 21st, Wednesday

First day in a shared classroom. It was actually kind of fun. The short schedule really narrows the focus to the things that matter most. I think I could get used to this. I didn't really get home too much later than I normally would. That is nice, too.

The principal met with us today. The damage to the school was much greater than was originally thought. Anyway, long story short, there isn't any budget for the repairs and updates that are needed. The district is giving all of us a heads up that the school could be shut down.

I'm not worried. There are always so many teaching positions open in the district. I just hope I can land something relatively close to home. I hate a long commute.

Ted texted again. He is persistent. I deleted it without reading it.

Bye bye, Ted . . . Me

april 24th, Saturday

Because this week has tumbled out of control, I am starting with the foolish news for the week. I saw Ted again. Twice, in fact. The first was on a billboard. A digital one. He was advertising investments with his perfectly white teeth and designer hair. The second time was at the potluck yesterday. (Yes, I went, and I even picked up some homemade looking food from the deli for my part of the potluck.) You'll like this, he had another girl on his arm. He didn't see me, so I finally let out that snort I had been holding and followed it with a hearty laugh. Then, I left my potluck on the food table, waved to a few friends, and comfortably walked out. Some things are just better left alone.

Now, I will circle back and write like an adult. I do have to backtrack some. Don't let me lose you, but we have to go back to Thursday now. Early Thursday morning Detective Jade called my phone. I haven't heard from him since Isaac was sentenced. I jumped for my phone and grabbed it just in time. I will skip the onrush of crazy emotions that his call stirred. He asked me to meet with him. Since school didn't start for a few hours, I went right down.

Being back in his office felt like playing a repeat of a detective movie scene. It was all the same as it was in January, the flutter of uncomfortable emotions, the smell of the office . . . I even think I was wearing the same outfit that I was three-and-a-half months ago. I was certain that Detective Jade was wearing the same outfit, but I bet he didn't care. He shook my hand. I can't remember if he did that last time.

Detective Jade dropped into his chair, motioning for me to sit as well. "I appreciate you making the time to come in. I have something that I feel you need to hear."

"About Isaac?" I asked, fidgeting with my purse strap on my lap.

Shifting the holster that hung from his shoulder, he leaned his big forearms on the table. "Guys like Isaac are pawns in a much bigger picture. Most of the time pawns like him don't have a clue of what kind of a hole they are digging for themselves."

His words were cryptic. "What do you mean?"

"Since Isaac has been in custody, he has opened up about some of the layers of his involvement with a much bigger drug-running operation." The detective leaned back into his chair.

"Is he in danger?" I didn't know if I cared. "What does this have to do with me? What about his fiancée . . . Melissa. Is she being called in?" I asked.

"Isaac shared with us that he gave your name to one of . . . what you might call . . . his *higher-ups* in the business."

My gut twisted and lurched. "What . . .? What does that mean? Does that even matter at this point?"

The detective held up a finger and cut me off. "He gave your name because he used you as the excuse, or scapegoat, for flushing the drugs. He told his 'boss,'" Detective Jade made air quotes with his fingers, "your name and that you were the one responsible for him tossing the . . . merchandise. Isaac told them that you had other plans for him. The way he put it to them, Isaac made it sound like he was going to start trafficking for you."

My face turned cold. Again, all the blood drained from my hands and unattractive feet. I do not know where it went. I only know that suddenly I was cold and shivering all over.

Leaning closer, the detective's voice thumped on my ears like two-ton bricks. "We have reason to believe that you could be a target." He paused and seemed to assess my reaction before he went on. "These guys play for keeps. Thousands of dollars won't be just forgiven and forgotten. You're lucky you haven't been victimized already. I've seen their handiwork before. Trust me, they will make sure you know the score when they decide to make contact with you."

From cold to hot. My blood started pumping under my skin. "Are you saying that I am not safe? Am I in danger?"

"Yes." He sat straight, his eyes dark and grave. "We think so."

I twitched slightly under his stare. "Why are you telling me now? Haven't I been at risk all these weeks?"

Detective Jade raised his finger again. "Isaac just dropped this bomb. I thought we had squeezed all he had out of him, but, almost like an afterthought, he mentioned giving you out."

"What am I supposed to do? What do I need to do?" My words came fast.

"You need to take some measures for your own safety. Basic stuff. Do not go anywhere alone. Always be in a crowd. Stay home after dark. Dump all your social media. Get rid of anything that gives any personal information until we have pulled these guys in and shut down their operation."

"I can't." My nerves were sparking and dancing with fear.

"You can. Unless you want to find yourself stuffed in a dumpster . . . you certainly can." He pounded his pointer finger on the tabletop for emphasis.

"No . . . I mean, my job. I have no control over some of these things."

"You're a teacher, right?"

I nodded. "Yes. There are websites that have my information. Where I work. What I teach. Even how much I earn. I am an open book."

"I get it. You're employed by the state. It makes it hard to be invisible," he empathized. He leaned back and pushed out a heavy breath. "Well, take whatever measures are needed to lock all that up. You don't know what you're messing with here. You're lucky you haven't found yourself gagged and beaten. They must have other irons in the fire that take priority over you . . . and Isaac's piled up mess."

My head started to pound.

"Look," Detective Jade advised, "Play it smart. If you feel like you are being watched, get somewhere that you feel safe . . . or call us. Watch out for any 'accidents,'" more air quotes, "that could involve you."

My ears twinged at the word accident. "What do you mean by accidents?"

"It could be anything. Anything to send you a message. Stuff to get at you. To cause fear." He studied me.

My head reeled. My thoughts jumped to the school . . . and my windshield.

"I may have been sent a message." I quickly related all the details to the detective.

He pressed back into his chair again. His spider fingers flexed up and down against each other. Shaking his head, the detective mulled it over. "Tough to say. Could be coincidences. It could also be that they don't see you as a threat. Since you're not trafficking, they may not care, or they could be biding their time waiting to see if you will make a move."

"Make a move?"

"Steal their business . . ." He rocked forward and waved over another officer from the corridor. "This is Detective James. Tell him what you said about that fire."

I just sat like a machine and answered Detective James's questions. Words tumbled around the room. "Further investigation . . . possible arson?" Ugly words tripped through my brain. I tried to squish them out and hide them under a blanket of happy thoughts.

Detective Jade wrapped up our conversation, and I was off to work. I kept all the ugly fearful thoughts tightly wrapped behind my concentration on teaching my students.

After school, Annie called to let me know she and her family are in town. They asked if they could spend the night. "Of course," I said. I needed something joyful in my life.

Once the young ones and the hubby were tucked into bed, Annie and I sat at the kitchen table and talked.

Annie poured us each a glass of milk. "Have you thought anything more about that land?"

I nodded, stacking Oreo cookies onto a plate between us. "I've thought a lot about it. Especially today." I dunked a cookie in my milk.

Her eyebrows arched, and I recognized the big sister tone that accented her words. "Are you still planning to sell?"

"I need to tell you something." Milk dripped from my cookie back into the glass. I set the soggy cookie on the table. Something I would never do. I just did not have an appetite to eat it.

"What? Is it about the land?"

I found myself hesitating. It felt like saying it out loud would make it true . . . that my life truly was in danger.

"What?" Annie repeated, sliding the cookie plate closer to her glass of milk. Meeting my eyes, her eyebrows crashed together as a nudge for me to speak.

"First . . ." I stumbled, "you can't tell Mom, and no, it's not about the ranch." Annie's eyes still held mine. She gave me her *duh* expression. "Okay . . ." It was full disclosure. I told Annie everything: Detective Jade's concerns and advice, my smashed windshield being a possible warning, and the potential threat of the fire at school . . . potential threat.

Her voice raised a notch but maintained its hush because of the sleeping children. "Do you think that fire *was* a warning to you?"

Rubbing my face behind my hands, I let out a long breath. "I don't know what to think."

"And your windshield? This is really frightening." Her cookie broke between her fingers, splashing into her milk in two pieces.

I wanted her words to stop. Her anxieties were not doing anything to comfort mine.

She pushed again. "You shouldn't keep this a secret. I think you should tell Mom and Dad."

"No . . . I don't want them to know. Mom will have a fit." My soggy cookie was making a puddle of milk on the table. I stood and tore a paper towel from the holder. "Don't say anything. I'll figure this out." I fished for validation. I wanted her to back me up, to agree that I had it all under control, but Annie was wiser than that.

"Lindsey, get out of the clouds. You're in real danger. I think you should move in with Mom and Dad until the police get all these guys locked up." Her bossy sister tone softened. "I'm worried now."

I have to admit that seeing Annie so worked up stirred my insides. A fearful knot sank cold in my gut as I wiped up my cookie mess.

Annie came to her own decision. "I am telling Mom and Dad. You can't keep this to yourself." She waved a cookie at me. "I think you need a bodyguard."

I stared at her.

Setting down the cookie, she changed her mind. "Better yet, you need a dog."

Oh, brother. Why did I open my mouth? "No, I can't get a dog."

She pointed her finger. "I know, but it is a good idea."

I felt obligated to put her at ease, but what could I say? "It's probably just a bunch of coincidences. My windshield was probably just a bored kid that needed some excitement in his evening. And, the school is old. They said wiring sparked the fire, so there's probably nothing to it. The detective was just being overly cautious."

"What are you going to do if they find out it was set on purpose . . . for you? I mean, you watch the news. This is scary. If you've got a bunch of criminals thinking you are stealing their business, who knows what could happen to you." She paused to let her words sink in. "Are we safe right now? Here in your house?" Her already big eyes widened with sisterly fear.

I skirted her questions by telling her we could talk more about it later. It was a school night, and it was late.

I went to bed, but I couldn't sleep. I know Annie wasn't sleeping either. She had done a good job at scaring the both of us.

It was hard to watch Annie and her family leave on Friday morning. I realized how comforted I was by having them in my apartment. As I watched them drive away, I was distinctly aware of the crawly feelings on my skin, as though someone were watching me. Was it real? Was it my mind playing tricks on me?

I stayed at home until I absolutely had to get to school, and I came home promptly after. I brought all my planning home.

Another sleepless night passed slowly. At four o'clock in the morning, I made some hot chocolate and watched a Christmas movie. It helped for the moment.

Still struggling under the weight of it all, I called Dad.

Biting back tears, I unloaded all my worries on him. As always, he was calm and even in his guidance. He recommended I come home. I wanted to, but there was no way that I could feel good about walking out on my job before the year is finished. I told him I would think about it.

I hate the way these thoughts take over and paint horrible images in my head. I hate all the unknowns. I almost wish someone would come after me or make a more obvious threat. At least that way I would know they were really trying to eliminate me. If I survived, maybe I could move on with my life. Ugh! I have got to get out of my head. I need to make someone some cookies.

Then this morning, like an answer from heaven, Camille called. And . . . I don't know . . . maybe it was because I hadn't slept. Maybe, in a roundabout way, it was because of Dad's advice. I may have been a little impulsive, but suddenly I told her I would keep the ranch. It just felt like a good idea to get out of this city. Go someplace smaller, quieter. Maybe I can follow the detective's advice a little easier out in the middle of the sticks of Utah? I told her I would move as soon as school is out.

She was ecstatic.

"Oh, Lindsey, I have prayed that you would feel right about taking this special place. I know it would mean so much to my dad. You have to know, as well, that having you there will secure the work that goes on there. It takes the pressure off of Rick and Lori worrying about things changing hands."

"That's good. I don't want to change anything, but I don't have the smallest clue of how to run a ranch."

"I will help you in whatever way I can. You can't imagine what this means to me."

I appreciated Camille's words.

My next move is to let the detective know that I am getting out of the city. I hope he approves. After that, I need to find a job in Southern Utah. Camille said the ranch pays for itself, but I'll need a job to pay for my life.

I hope I haven't just made my biggest mistake yet.

Good night. I hope . . . Me

April 25th, Sunday

Sitting in church today, I was completely at peace. Fresh starts. New beginnings. These were my thoughts. None of it was laced with fear or trepidation.

Excited for my new adventure . . . Me

April 27th, Tuesday

I applied for a teaching position in Cedar City. They have a few openings. I also broke the news to my parents. Mom is still processing it all. She voiced some strong opinions in all directions. Here is a sampling:

"What is wrong with moving back home? You can't go out to some ranch and live all by yourself. How is that going to make you any safer?"

"Mom, I won't be completely alone. There is a couple that lives close by. There are other homes out there."

"I still think you need to come home." Mom shook her pointed finger. "You need to be where you can be checked in on. Not off in the toolies."

"Mom, it's a beautiful place."

"It sounds like it's out in the desert. Why do you want to live there? I thought you were going to sell it."

"I was, but, Mom, I feel really good about this. It'll be easier for me to hide away."

"Well, you may have a point there." She lowered her hand to her hip.

"You and Dad can come and visit any time you want. And, I'll be closer."

That won her over, for the moment anyway.

Susy and Annie gave their support when I called them. They both asked if they could come and stay with me at the ranch. That could be fun.

Now, the more I think about this, the happier I get. I hope I can just quietly fade away and hide in the country.

I hope I can get a job.

Crazy? Maybe . . . Me

april 29th, Thursday

I feel my destiny is unfolding. I got the call today. I have an interview next week in Cedar City!

Now, I simply need to complete the school year without any catastrophes that relate to my life. Right?

Wish me luck!

Moving soon . . . Me

May 4th, Tuesday

I am impossibly exhausted. I took a personal leave day and drove to Cedar City this morning for my interview. I had to be there by nine. With the time difference, I had to leave here at five a.m. Waking up at three thirty is mind numbing.

I chose my black skirt suit to wear with a white collared shirt. I chose tasteful shoes with low heels.

My stomach flipped a few times, but, other than my nerves, the interview went well. Six principals and the superintendent sat around a long rectangular table. I sat like the guest of honor at the head. Each took turns asking me questions. They were all very nice. When they asked if I had a grade preference, I did mention that I would like to teach upper elementary. I hope I didn't limit my chances of getting hired.

I will know by morning. Calls will go out by then.

Camille and I met up after the interview. I drove out to the ranch. This time was completely different. I was driving to visit my home.

Rick the cowboy was there. I met his wife, Lori. They have been maintaining the house while I have been making my decision. Lori had a hot lunch ready for all of us. My dancing nerves spun up to full blown jitters as I sat down with the others to eat.

It was strange to consider that I would soon be sitting at the table alone, as its owner. Maybe I am not ready for this. Honestly, I don't know that I could ever truly be ready.

Camille must have noted my nervousness. Throughout lunch, she periodically squeezed my hand, or put a hand on my shoulder. It helped . . . I guess.

Papers were placed in front of me after lunch. They were all the technicalities for me to take over the property. I know I should have listened better, but the warm open-faced turkey sandwiches that Lori had fed us, combined with my early morning, had lulled me into a zombified daze. I mechanically signed everything. I did not read a single word of any of it. Camille handed me copies of everything. If I get desperate for something difficult to read, I can pull it all out again. At any rate, it is unchangeable now. I am the owner of a huge home and an enormous amount of property.

After quick hugs, I was back on the road to Las Vegas. I have school to teach in the morning. So, though the ranch belongs to me, I have some loose ends to tie up before I can move in.

I wish my dad, John, was here to see it. I wish he were here to know how his act of kindness has blessed others. Blessed me. Certainly more than I could ever deserve.

Humbled . . . Me

Later

I got it! I got the call. They didn't wait until morning to let me know. I have just accepted a position to teach sixth grade in Cedar City, Utah in the fall. I will be teaching at Hathaway Middle School. I will specialize in teaching language arts. Woot!

Now, I've just got to finish out this school year and move out of my apartment.

Whew!

Too wound up for sleep . . . Me

May 19th, Wednesday

Okay, so now I am completely freaked out! Detective Jade invited me into his office again yesterday. *Strongly invited.* They finally got the full report on the fire at the school. I choked.

Evidence of tampering *was* found. Something with the wiring that did not match what it was supposed to be. In a nutshell, there was more to that fire than just old fans on top of an out-of-date school.

Aaaggh!

That was what was screaming in my head as the detective reviewed the report with me. He did say that there was the possibility that the malintent was meant for someone else or a different purpose.

"What do you mean?" I asked. "What am I supposed to do?"

"Well, this could be the work of a disgruntled student or even a parent that had a problem. You never know." He tapped his pen lightly on the computer monitor.

"What about the cameras? Did they catch anything on them?" I was grasping, and my voice squeaked as my throat constricted with anxiousness.

"Not enough to give us anything to go on. Some black smudges of motion. That's all we got." The detective pushed back into his seat. "The cameras are some of the oldest we've seen in a school. We made sure to let the administrator know that they've got to get some new equipment in that place."

I stared dumbly at the man, willing this all to go away. I worked hard. I was kind to people and animals. Why was this happening to me?

"Are they going to replace the cameras?" My mouth must have been in "teacher mode" to worry about the cameras. Honestly I don't care about the cameras. I will no longer be there once this school year winds up.

Sucking in a slow, deep breath, the detective leaned forward. He drummed a peppy cadence with his forefingers on the edge of the table. He pointed the conversation in another direction.

"Did you know any of Isaac's 'work' associates?" He framed the word *work* with air quotes.

"No." I shook my head vehemently. What was he getting at now? Did he think I was mixed up in all of this? Was that what the detective was fishing for? "Not at all. I never went with him to his job." My ugly left foot twitched and jumped under my chair. I pressed it flat against the floor hoping no one had noticed. Nerves. I did not want my jumping foot to make me look guilty. I chewed my lip.

The detective launched a few more questions at me. "Did you know any of his friends? Did you meet anyone who might have been in any way connected to pedaling the drugs?"

"No." I *was* being interrogated. Agggh! I scrolled through the Isaac file in my head. Was there anyone I knew that was a friend of Isaac? Did he have friends? What did we do when we were together? It was like trying to pull images off of a white sheet of paper. It didn't work. It was blank. My head was blank. "I don't think so."

Slowly an image percolated through. I held up my hand, raising my index finger. "There was a party, after a basketball game . . . kind of a party. We went. That was unusual. Isaac is not much of a sports fan."

"Go on." The detective motioned with his tanned arm. "Tell me what you remember."

I zeroed in on the conversation at hand. "It was nothing much . . . just a bunch of college students going crazy over a game." I surveyed my memory of the faces in that group. Was there anyone in that group that had the look of an arsonist? Is arsonist a word?

"What else do you remember?"

The detective typed rapidly as I pieced together as much of the gathering as I could remember. There wasn't much. "Honestly, what I remember most was that I was wearing new shoes that night, and my feet hurt. A bad online purchase. I'm sorry." I looked mournfully toward the floor. I left out the fact that I had purposefully purchased the shoes a half a size too small in the hopes of making my feet less noticeable.

The detective, unaffected by my shoe story, probed for more details. "Describe the people you remember. Was there anything about that gathering that stood out? Anything that seemed out of place?"

Little details began to pull together. "Actually, I do remember stooping down to loosen my shoelaces, and I thought I saw one of the guys put something into Isaac's hand. Whatever it was, Isaac dropped it into his pocket. I assumed it was gum. I just remember that I thought it was weird that Isaac would take gum from someone and not chew it. I thought it was rude, and Isaac always seemed to be so conscious of how he came across in public. Anyway, I just thought it was weird."

"Did you see anything else? Could you see what it was, if it wasn't gum?" His eyes were steady on mine as the detective waited for me to answer.

"No. I only saw Isaac take *something*." I lowered my gaze again and pressed my palm against my bouncing leg.

"What did the guy look like? The one who gave Isaac *something*."

Looking up at the far wall, I let out a breath. "He was a lot like Isaac. He was tall. Dark hair. Nice looking clothes."

"Any distinguishing features?" The detective's fingers hovered above his keyboard.

I chewed lightly on my lower lip as forgotten details tumbled from my memory. "I do remember he wore a button-up shirt, and the sleeves were rolled up just below his elbows, like yours." I pointed at the detective.

The detective stared and motioned with his head for me to get on with it.

I stammered, "He was wearing a nice watch. I don't know the brand, but if I saw it again, I would recognize it." Ugh, I was yammering like an idiot. I needed to get to the point.

The detective typed something and paused again, eyes steady on me.

"I remember he had a tattoo. It was on his forearm. I had forgotten, but I remember staring at it while he and Isaac talked." Wow, that took me a long time to sputter out those details. I am not usually so sloppy with words. Maybe I would do better if I could write these things down. I wonder if the detective could give me a sticky note and a pen.

As if on cue, Detective Jade suddenly pushed a notepad across the desk and handed me a pencil. "Will you draw it?" Did he read my thoughts? Doggone it . . . I knew there would come a day that I would regret all those times I skipped out on that required art class my freshman year. I took the notepad and pencil. I did my best to draw a cartoon seal. It seemed to satisfy the detective.

Once that was addressed, I steered the conversation to my decision to leave Las Vegas. "I have decided to move."

The detective's eyebrows bunched. I went ahead and explained the whole story. The detective sat back in his chair, his eyes fixed on me, as I told my unbelievable story. When I finished, he leaned forward. Rubbing a hand across his chin, he seemed to chew on my words. "Where is this property? Do you have an address?"

"I do." He pushed the notebook my way again. I quickly wrote the address.

"It won't stop them, you understand?"

I nodded, casting my eyes to the floor. The detective didn't seem overly thrilled with my choice.

He spun the notebook to face him and typed into the laptop. Spinning the computer, he pointed at a map. "This is the place?" He clicked on an image of the house. It was a real estate listing. It must have been from when Camille was trying to sell it. The house was labeled as "Sold."

The detective scratched his head. He blew out a noisy breath. "This could go two ways. You move out there, and you never hear from these thugs. Or, you move to the boonies and they dispose of you without any witnesses."

I started. "I like the first option."

He nodded, his face sober. "You'll need to watch yourself out there, the same as here. What I told you before still holds. Don't go anywhere without your phone. You call for help even if you only suspect something is going on."

"I will."

After our visit, I rushed right to school. My mouth taught the curriculum, but my head danced around all kinds of evil scenarios. I was scaring myself with all of the possibilities.

I am still scaring myself . . . Me

May 27ᵗʰ, Thursday

Okay, I am super excited to move, but I have to say I am drowning! Getting ready for the end of the school year, packing my stuff, and being ready to move are killing me! My dining room is buried with school items. Everything else I own is boxed up in the living room. My mattress is the only thing left in my bedroom. It is leaning against the wall. Mom and Dad were generous and rented a trailer for me. They have offered to come and help me haul everything to the ranch. I am super grateful. However, Mom is requesting that I spend the weekend with them in St. George.

Got a call from Cedar City. A teacher has dropped out of teaching in the summer program, and they offered me the position. I said, "YES!"

See you in Cedar City . . . Me

June 5ᵗʰ, Saturday

Sorry that I haven't written sooner. I need to get you up to date. Here goes:

I stayed a couple of days with my parents. Mom was thrilled. I was nervous about the trailer being parked in their driveway, but Dad assured me my things would be fine. It was kind of nice to relax and unwind with them. Maybe I was just a little bit afraid of my future. I mean, I really like being independent. It's just that I can't say that I have ever been independent in a huge house with acres of land between me and my next-door neighbor, not to mention miles of land between myself and any *real* civilization.

It's exciting though, and I've been so busy that my thoughts haven't had time to drift to the reason I have moved here. Isaac's cohorts have stayed out of my brain. I think this move is a good thing.

Mom, Dad, Annie, Susy, and their kids all made the trek with me to my new home. We were a funny caravan. I led the way alone in my car, blaring the only country music station that I could stand in honor of my new country life. Dad and Mom followed in their truck, with the trailer in tow. Behind them were my sisters in their cute, trendy, crossover vehicles.

With small people getting under foot, we unloaded all of my things. It's amazing how much I appeared to own when it was all stacked in my apartment. Here, it looks like a little collection of trinkets, nothing of significance.

Ah, the power of square footage.

All my family was planning to stay the night, but one thing led to another. Kids were fussy. Mom was fretting. Dad settled things by recommending that I needed to get my feet under me in my new place. He put everyone up in a hotel in town.

I am here alone.

Let me describe for you what I see right now. I am seated at the kitchen bar. West-facing windows frame a perfect sunset. Furnishing that are elegant, tasteful, and a little bit rustic, top-of-the-line appliances, stone counters, and a sweeping staircase to the balcony above are all in front of me. At the bar, I can look to the south and to the west. All of it is picturesque.

Is this really mine?

Rick and Lori also came to help with the unloading. Lori was a gem and brought homemade tamales for all of us . . . Yum!

My sisters all oohed and fawned over everything as I walked them through the house. Mom was surprisingly quiet. Maybe it stirred up thoughts of my dad? I don't know. I didn't ask her. Dad was very practical about all of it. He kept saying things like: "Wise investment," "Property value," and "This land will only appreciate over time." I have to confess I kind of tuned it out.

Don't worry, though. They will all be back for breakfast. Mom and Dad are bringing the ingredients for some homemade buttermilk pancakes. Tomorrow we are going to christen the kitchen . . . or something like that.

Some of the realities of this responsibility are facing me now that I am here. I'll tell you what I mean.

How am I going to keep up with the yard work?

What about the utility bills? The power and gas bill on a home this size must be ridiculous.

What about property taxes? I know nothing about property taxes. I rent apartments.

Am I responsible to feed any of the animals?

What about snow? There are snowmobiles in the garage. I've never shoveled snow in my life.

Camille undoubtedly covered some of this the last time we talked but I was so overwhelmed with it all at the time, I remember nothing. Groan!

I'll talk with Dad.

I am actually glad to have this time alone to get to know my house. It's like a scared animal. We just need some time to warm up to one another, the house and I. After I finish today's *missive*, I have scheduled a date with the gigantor-sized tub in my new master bathroom.

I guess there are some perks to this situation.

Finally home? . . . Me

June 6th, Sunday

My new home hummed like a party this morning. All my family gathered in my kitchen for breakfast. I invited Rick and Lori. There was so much noise and laughter. It rolled up the stairs, from out of the kitchen, and filled all the quiet corners of the house. I loved every minute of it. I busied myself with the dishes and wiped down the counters as all the conversations swirled around.

Once the dishes were done, and all of my guests had left, I still had time to go to church, so I attended my new ward today. It was nice. I met the bishop and a sweet lady that sat next to me, Sister Vandamm.

After church I took some time and called Camille. She patiently answered my questions. I felt a little stupid to be asking so many questions after I've already moved in, but it needed to be done.

I took just a moment tonight and stepped outside to look up at the stars. It's true what they say. Seeing the night sky without light pollution is breathtaking. Yet, standing there for that brief minute, in the dark, stirred up a frenzy of nervousness. I pray no one finds me here, no one who wants me dead.

Well, I am off to bed.

I teach summer school tomorrow.

Hopeful . . . Me

June 7ᵗʰ, Monday

I may have officially found my calling. What a great day! I have eight students. They are all students that are struggling with their grades. They have all been assigned to summer school. I thought it was going to be awful. I was anticipating lots of sass and back talk, but it was a really great first day.

Rick let me ride one of the horses with him this evening. It was a little scary. I honestly thought that I was doomed to fall off. You will be happy to know that, not only did I stay mounted on the furry creature, but we became friends. At least, I think so.

Back to school tomorrow.

I can't believe how quiet it is. All the time.

Finding my peaceful . . . Me

June 8th, Tuesday

What a DAY! I am so frazzled that I do not have a clue where to begin. I am steaming. Bah! I'll spell it out for you. Here goes.

After teaching my last rotation of classes, I was cleaning up some of the supplies that we used when I saw what appeared to be a curl of smoke float past the window. Well, given my recent past, my senses fired. I went into full-blown ninja mode. Racing out the door, I rounded the corner. Three of my pupils sat on the sloping grass with their backs to me. All three held cigarettes. *You little stinkers,* I thought. I was certain that my students were better than this. I quickly decided to let them know they were caught. I cleared my throat obnoxiously.

All three of the girls jumped. Two bolted down the hill, tossing their lit cigarettes onto the grass. The third just sat there, her eyes the size of soccer balls. The burning cigarette still smoldered between her fingers. I piped up, "Are you going to run too?"

Her huge eyes welled up and spilled over. She shook her head dejectedly. The cigarette tumbled from her fingers. I took two steps and smashed it into the grass with my shoe. I snuffed out the other two.

Elizabeth, my student, just sat, her head hanging low.

"Come on," I motioned for her to stand.

She silently obeyed, all the while avoiding my eyes.

"You realize I am going to let your parents know about this." I studied her face for understanding.

Shaking her long blonde hair, she whispered, "It wasn't me."

I asked her, with just a glint of fire to my tone, "That lit cigarette in your hand? It belonged to someone else?" I waited for her reply.

Tears streamed over her cheeks. Her hair fell forward, hiding her face.

"Do your parents pick you up?"

A shrug.

I dialed the number that I had on file for her home. I got the *This number is no longer in service* message.

Lowering my face to look into her eyes, I asked, "Is there a number that I can call to get ahold of your parents?"

She swallowed, glanced at me, and quietly shook her head.

Perfect. "Do you have a phone?"

Another headshake.

Great. This just keeps getting better.

I really didn't want to stay and wait for her parents. I looked around the parking lot. Most of the kids had already been picked up. Letting a breath of frustration steam out slowly, I said, "Well, I had better wait then."

Elizabeth moved slowly toward the low retaining wall that separated the parent pick up from the bus loading. She sat down heavily. Something was muttered.

Standing, I leaned toward her. "What did you say?"

Sniffling, she repeated softly, "I didn't smoke."

Yeah. You just magically had a lit cigarette in your fingers. My sarcasm was thick in my brain. I thought it best to keep it there. I shook my head, but I said, "That's good that you didn't smoke. We can talk more about it with your parents."

While Elizabeth sat, I moved a few paces away from her. I called the homes of the other girls, hoping to catch them as soon as possible. I managed to speak with both sets of parents. They were both very supportive of me and very worried about their daughters. Melinda's mom did own that a package of cigarettes came up missing after Melinda had visited her grandpa who smokes. Both sets of parents said they would follow up with the girls. Phew.

I would touch base with my administrator in the morning.

I put my phone away. Time seemed to march by as though riding on the back of a snail. Was her family *ever* going to pick up this child? I sat on the wall a few feet from Elizabeth. Neither of us spoke. She wiped her sleeve across her eyes a few times.

The parking lot completely emptied of vehicles with the exception of my car and the evening custodian's truck. All of the kids were long gone. All but one.

I glanced at my watch for the fifteenth time. I couldn't believe I had waited this long for a parent. I do prefer face to face conversations over phone calls, when it is something difficult that needs to be addressed, but this was getting ridiculous. I turned to Elizabeth, who still maintained her silence. Just then a red pickup truck sped into the bus loading zone. Before I could ask, Elizabeth jumped up, rushing toward it.

The driver's side door flew open and a tall muscular man dashed around the front of the truck to open the door for Elizabeth. He kept repeating, "I'm sorry. I'm so sorry. I got tied up. I'm so sorry."

I marched up and cleared my throat a little louder than was necessary. The man stopped in his tracks. He looked straight at me.

I cut off any chance he may have had to speak. "Excuse me, sir. Can I speak with you for a moment?"

He closed Elizabeth's door and approached. He was huge. I mean in a pit bull kind of way, ripped muscles, shaved, flat-top hair, and penetrating blue eyes. I stood firm. I refused to be intimidated. This was too important to ignore.

His blue eyes darkened. His eyebrows notched upward.

"Sir, I need to speak to you about Elizabeth. There was a situation this afternoon that has me very concerned." I unconsciously placed both my hands on my hips.

Tipping his head suspiciously, he asked, "What situation?"

"I caught Elizabeth and some friends smoking after classes today. I couldn't get you on the phone, so I waited here with her so that I could talk to you. This is a very serious matter. Not only is it illegal, it is opening the door for all kinds of health problems, not to mention setting a pattern of poor decision making for her life." I sucked in a breath to continue when he flashed a raised hand to cut me off. It was such an authoritative hand that it stopped me mid-inhale.

Opening Elizabeth's door, he spoke briefly with her in quiet tones. This was a good sign. I straightened and mentally prepared the second wind of my speech.

Boy, was I wrong.

After gently closing the passenger door, Mr. Pitbull stepped closer. My first reaction was to step back, but my feet were glued to my spot with teacherly obligation and concern for the child. Speaking low, his words were clipped and emphatic. "Look, I don't know who you are, or who you think you are, but you have some serious personal reflection to do if you think Lizzie had any part of what you just described to me." His volume mounted. "Did you even ask Lizzie her side of the story?" His volume rose in seemingly calculated increments. Finding my feet, I forced myself to take a step back to keep a spit-free distance from the man. "You sat here waiting just so you could throw her under some teacher-made label that defines any kid with a cigarette in their hand as a future menace to society. If you knew anything, you would see this for what it really is."

I was not going to stand there, especially after waiting so long, and let him criticize me.

"Look, I saw the cigarette in her hand." I pointed my hand emphatically.

Fire ignited his features. The muscles in his jaw jumped in and out.

"So what." He growled. I think steam escaped from his ears. "What difference does that make? You said there were others. Where are they? Did you wait around to pounce on them? No! I don't think so. You waited around, to pounce on the victim."

"I . . ." I began again. He gave me no chance to jump down *his* throat and voice how I waited patiently with his daughter for an incredible amount of time and how he should be thanking me for not leaving her here alone. Humph!

"No. You know what? I'm done with you. I'm done with this . . ." He waved his hand as if officially signing me off. Then shaking his head he circled around the truck, climbed in the cab, and sped off through the bus loading zone.

I was not going to just stand there, after such an encounter. I hurried back to my class, grabbed my things, and headed for home.

Still reeling from the encounter, I put on a Hallmark movie to distract myself from my emotions, and now I am writing to you. My head keeps replaying the conversation with that awful man . . . over and over. I have so many *would have, should have, could haves*. I wish I could have a do-over. I would not have let him spout off and insult my character like he did.

Huffy . . . Me

June 9th, Wednesday

I passed yesterday's events on to our administrator, and things will be handled according to procedure. What a way to kick off a day.

I waited, and watched, for Elizabeth to come to class today. I actually started class two minutes late, expecting her to arrive. I did want an opportunity to visit with her. I kick myself for not taking the chance yesterday as we waited for her dad. The sharpness of his words still burns.

After some serious reflection, and putting my pride on the back burner, I can admit that my actions were dreadful. I think that is a fitting word. Dreadful. I should have asked Elizabeth more questions. I should have asked her to tell her side of the story, somehow. I should have made some effort to get to know her, yet there I was in my high-and-mighty-ness. I thought that it was somehow more effective for me to keep silent so that her story would not change or shift. I figured that if we didn't talk, I would have full control of the account of the events. My perceptions have changed. Brother!

All day long I watched the clock, but Elizabeth never arrived. The day began, I taught, and the day ended, all without her arrival. My heart sickened at the thought that my actions yesterday were possibly impeding her education. I hope her dad is not so nearsighted to let his anger at me keep her from learning the things she needs to be successful in school.

Every student in these classes are enrolled based on a referral. All of these students need the leg up that summer school will give them. After reviewing the work that was turned in yesterday, these kids are *really* behind in their command of the English language.

I gave the students the writing prompt of: *If you could visit any place in the world, where would that be, and why?* With choppy grammar and creative spelling, most of them wrote of big cities, New York and the like. A couple of them wrote of locations in Europe, but Elizabeth wrote about home. She described a setting of laughter at the dinner table, washing the dishes with her mom, and listening to wonderful stories told by her dad. Her sincerity tugged my heart strings. (I did have a difficult time imagining her dad telling any wonderful stories. All I could see was the image of him giving me an ear full.)

I hope she attends class tomorrow. She really has the potential to go very far.

Concerned . . . Me

June 10th, Thursday

No Elizabeth today.

After work, I weeded the front planter. I kind of like having dirt on my hands.

One thing is for sure, I am grateful the dad I have does not behave like Mr. Pitbull. Goodness, can you imagine?

Still concerned . . . Me

June 11th, Friday

No class today. There is no summer school on Fridays.

I called Mom.

"You're coming over on Sunday," she declared, with water running in the background.

It wasn't a question, but I answered anyway. "I wouldn't miss it." It's her birthday. I can't wait. Not only will I get to see my family, but it will give me a chance to focus on happy things. I need that. I need a break from worrying about Elizabeth and the encounter with her father.

"Good. Now, don't go and spend anything on a gift. I have all I need. You just concentrate on staying safe up there."

"I do. Thanks, Mom."

Happy Friday . . . Me

June 12th, Saturday

Hooray! I found my mailbox. Well, really it was Lori who knocked on the door this morning to let me know that my mailbox looked very full.

"Mailbox?" I asked. "I have a mailbox? Where is it?" (No snarky comments, please, posterity. I mean, really, it's just a small oversight . . . not realizing that I have a mailbox. Right?)

Lori smiled in a loving grandmotherly kind of way. "Yes, you have a mailbox, come with me and I'll show you where it is."

"You must think I'm a complete idiot for not even knowing how to find my mailbox." I pulled on my sneakers.

Again, Lori smiled. "Not at all, sweetie. You have taken on a lot this month. You probably haven't had any reason to get the mail."

I stood, ready to go.

Lori motioned toward the kitchen. "You may want to bring a sack."

Nodding, I poked a plastic grocery bag into my pocket.

We walked together to where the private road meets the county road. I'd driven by them dozens of times, but I had never made the correlation that one of the quaint mailboxes was mine.

Sure enough, I knew in an instant which box was mine. The one jammed completely full, store ads poking out and rustling in the early breeze. Hurray for the sack!

I tossed it all on the kitchen counter when I got back home. As I did, a long white envelope shot out of the bag and onto the counter. I wondered if it was something for Camille's family. I picked up the envelope. It was addressed to me. Unexpected.

Sliding my finger under the flap. I tore it open. Inside was a single sheet of white paper. I pulled it out and unfolded it. Another smaller paper was inside the folded page. It twirled to the floor. The large, folded page appeared to be a spread sheet of some sort. Stooping over, I picked up the little paper that fell. Turning it over in my hand, my eyebrows flew up and my mouth dropped open with surprise. It was a check. It had my name on it. It was for sixteen thousand dollars!

I carefully positioned the check on the counter. Then I flattened the spreadsheet out in front of me. The header was a cattle company—Juniper Run Cattle Co. Columns with dates and dollar amounts were accounted chronologically. What was this?

I immediately texted Camille.

The wait was excruciating. I left the check and the spreadsheet on the counter and busied my brain with learning how to use my new washer and dryer. (Thank you Youtube.) I also tackled the all-important task of cleaning the floors and the bathroom. Owning a home is a lot of work.

Camille finally texted back.

> Good morning, Lindsey. Thank you for your message. Yes, that check is meant to be for you. I am happy to review the details with you. I am at a conference this weekend. I would love to talk with you tomorrow if you are available. Please let me know what time is best for you.

With a couple more texts back and forth, we agreed to talk tomorrow at two o'clock.

I bought mom a new purse for her birthday. Yellow, trendy, and cute. I hope she enjoys it.

Finishing laundry and sorting the mail . . . Me

June 13th, Sunday

Mom's birthday was full of all the expected routines and good times. As usual, she spent her day preparing food and looking after everyone else. She is quite a gourmet. The purse was a big hit with her. Even if she didn't love it, she would never tell me.

I am eager for sleep, but I will prop my eyelids up with match sticks if I have to. I have got to tell you about my conversation with Camille. (Thankfully, I was able to talk to her while Mom took a nap.)

"Lindsey, it is great to hear from you," Camille's voice was light and comforting as I sneaked onto my parents' patio to visit with her.

"Hey, thank you for calling me back. I am sorry to bother you, but I just didn't know what to even think of that check that was sent in the mail."

"No problem," Camille assured me. I had a hunch that she would have used those words even if she were trapped in an ice block that was slowly being lowered into a steaming pool of man-eating sharks. "Have you had a chance to look over those accounts that I emailed?"

A light bulb dawned in my brain. I had three separate emails from Camille that I had not even opened. I kept pushing them to the bottom of my to do list. "No," I replied honestly.

"That's okay. You can go over them any time. They are more detailed and will give you accounts and information that I will attempt to skim through."

She was the model of politeness. My thoughts went to my students. How many times do I get on their case for not paying attention? "Thank you. I really appreciate you doing this. I'm sorry for all of the trouble and hassle. I feel a little awkward about everything. I feel like I am the child that's been given the best Christmas gift in the world, and I am helpless to know what to do with it."

"You are just fine. By accepting our father's gift, you received all assets of the estate." She was all business.

I quickly said, "I remember you saying that. What does that mean?"

"Well, to sum it up, the estate is primarily a home, or structure, and the additional properties. There are three small businesses attached to the land."

I listened like a fourth-grade student as Camille summed up the workings of these small businesses. This is what I understood:

Ranchers lease land to keep and graze their animals. A small percentage of the money for the lease comes to me to maintain the roads and the well.

A cattle ranch also runs cattle during the summer months on a large portion of the mountain land. Again, a small percentage of the money comes to me as per a written agreement. This is also to be applied toward additional maintenance, as needed.

Two independent farmers lease acreage to grow alfalfa and sell it as hay to ranchers in California. Here, again, a small percentage is paid to me.

Okay, I think that tells it all.

Basically, the two hundred acres that go with this place are moneymakers. I guess that makes me a proprietor. Do I even know what that means?

Camille went on to explain, "If you review the emails I sent, you will see how the funds have been used over the past ten years, or so."

"This is what you meant when you said the house pays for itself . . ."

"Yes, exactly. And as you can see from the amount of the check, it's not enough to live on."

". . . and these are the contracts that you didn't want to have to change hands . . ." I shifted in my chair wondering how I was supposed to keep up with any of this.

"Yes. I was a little selfish. I'm sorry I shouldn't have said any of that to you. It is all yours to do with as you please. I really shouldn't try to influence you."

"I'm still baffled by that. I mean, I'm grateful, but wouldn't this all be worth a ton of money to your family?"

"You remember how I told you that my dad bought the land and built the house just to have a place to get away?"

"I remember."

"The reason he chose that spot was at the time the land was selling for pennies. He could have bought the whole town for less than ten thousand dollars."

"But what about now? This has to be worth so much."

"Well, like Spencer said, I'm a little sentimental about the ranch. So, it never was about the money for me . . . or for any of us, really."

"So, that sixteen thousand. Is there something specific I should do? You mentioned the roads . . ."

"It is yours to use, but if you want to deposit it into the sinking fund, that is something you could do."

Of course. I knew she had mentioned this fund before. "Can you tell me more about that?" I wished I had brought a notebook to write everything down. I was still reeling a little from the fact that I had businesses to think about.

"Absolutely. Dad wanted the home to be one hundred percent self-sufficient. This was his way of preparing against future catastrophes. Even before the home was fully finished, the land was parceled out and put into use. All of the profits from the use of the land have been deposited into the sinking fund for several years. Through the years, a few minor things have come up. About five years ago, the pump on the well had to be replaced. Every year, because of the snow, the road needs to be graded and a new layer of road base is brought in. Just maintenance needs. These are all things that add up, as you can imagine. The sinking fund takes care of all of this necessary work."

I was grateful for Camille to explain it all so patiently. "Thank you for teaching me all of this. I never would have thought anything about a well or about the roads. I guess I am pretty uneducated in some things." That was a clear understatement.

"You are wonderful, and don't worry about any of it. When you get a chance to look things over, let me know. I will be happy to answer any of your questions."

"Thank you." It sounded so lame. Two little pitiful words to express appreciation for a massive gift that I could never, in a thousand lifetimes, repay.

Camille had taught me a lot during our brief phone call. She taught me patience. She taught me perseverance. She taught me that I really should study out the details before signing my agreement on any inherited estates. She taught me that saving for a rainy day is not only a good idea, but on a ranch, it is a necessity. Goodness. I have got a lot more to learn.

Once I arrived back home, I read page by page through the files that Camille and Spencer gave me. I also perused the online accounts. It was evident that I had been tremendously graced by the unselfish generosity of two fathers that I would never meet. Theirs and mine. I cried for two hours.

This is why I am exhausted.

On a materialistic note . . . the sinking fund has a balance of $67,031.54. That's a lot of sinking fundage. I am overwhelmed. I certainly do not think of that big chunk of money as being mine. It can just sit there, and I will deposit the sixteen thousand to go with it.

I'm tired. I don't want to think anymore tonight.

School tomorrow . . . Me

June 14th, Monday

Have you ever met someone who was bent on ruining your life?

Elizabeth was not in class again today. I couldn't let another day go by without finding something out about her and whether or not she was going to return to school. I pulled her file and found another number listed. I thought I might get to talk with her mother. Unfortunately, I was blessed to have another *lovely* tête-à-tête with Mr. Pitbull.

Before I could even ask about Elizabeth, he commenced with a full blast verbal assault.

"I've said all I care to say to you, Mrs.—"

"It's Miss . . ."

"Fine. Miss . . . Whatever, you have no reason to call this number ever again. Elizabeth will not be returning to your program. End of story. I don't have time for this."

He ended the call.

My heart hammered like a freight train. Tears threatened, but willful stubbornness forbade them from spilling.

Needless to say. That one conversation cast a heavy tone on the rest of my day. It was now a black t-shirt kind of day . . . blah . . . Mondays.

Right now I would sure like to take a chunk of that sinking fund and do some shopping. Maybe I could invest it and live off the interest. I'll retire from teaching right now.

I want a hot dog.

Grrr . . . Me

June 21st, Monday

Okay, the disastrous struggles of my Mondays are getting old. And this one isn't even over yet. So, I will venture in another direction for a few moments of happy distraction. Here is the happy part. My students are making fantastic progress. Yippee!

Well, that was short lived. Enough happiness. Back to the woes of a Monday.

This evening I was all prepared to climb into a steamy hot shower. No, I can't just begin there. I need to paint the full picture. Let me back up.

After my students left for the day, I combed through all of their writing. I then spent roughly two hours building lessons based on the indicators that I gleaned from their work. (These kids are still struggling with basic grammar, but I am determined to have them writing essays like champions.)

I got home about six o' clock. I was tired, but I wanted to get in a quick jog and some yoga before I had dinner. I ran until I was worn out and soaked in sweat. I slurped down my water bottle and then completed twenty minutes of power yoga. I was dead.

I turned some music on the TV and headed for the shower.

Now, the doozy. The water did NOT turn on. I tried seventeen times. Throwing on the fluffy, white bathrobe that came with the house, I rushed to the kitchen and tugged on the lever of the faucet. Nothing. No water.

Snatching my phone off the counter, I parked myself on a bar stool and texted Lori:

Lori, I don't have any water.

I paced.

This sort of thing never happened in my apartment.

It was with these thoughts twirling around in my skull that my phone vibrated. Hooray, it was Lori!

"Hello, Lori," I gasped. I was desperate for help.

"Hey, Lindsey. This is Rick." He sounded *way* too calm.

"Oh, Rick. Hi. I don't have any water."

"Lindsey, none of us have any water. It might be the pump, but I would be surprised. We just had it fixed. Could be the well has finally dried up."

My stomach churned up new sensations, a garbled tornado of confusion, ignorance, and panic. *Well? Dried up? What?!* "Can we get it fixed tonight?"

Deep chuckles from the other end of the phone. "That would be something, but no, I don't think we're going to get anything fixed tonight. I'll head out to the pump and take a look at it. I will have Lori text you if I find anything."

How was I supposed to survive? I guessed I was going to have to go back to town and buy some gallons of water. I mean, I had to have water to flush the toilet, didn't I?

"Okay . . .?" I felt, once again, the keen, and familiar, sense of being overwhelmed.

"Hey, Lindsey?" Rick added before he hung up.

"Yes."

Rick's tone deepened. "Do you have friends that drive a black Escalade?"

My heart flipped. Suddenly I was frightened. "No, not that I'm aware." I didn't want to, but I asked, "Why do you ask?"

Rick grunted then went on. "I've seen one twice now. The first time I passed him out on the paved road. Today I passed him . . . well, I think it's a him . . . there was someone in the passenger's seat, but the glare of the sun made it hard to see much. Anyway, today I passed the Escalade as I pulled into my drive. They were heading down the road at a good clip, coming from your place."

Hairs stood up on the back of my neck. "When?" A shiver zipped up my spine.

"Oh, about two thirty."

"Maybe they live nearby." I desperately hoped.

"Nope. I would know if anyone had bought a shiny new Escalade. This one had Nevada plates."

A ragged sigh rushed from my lips. Neither Camille, nor Rick knew anything about my reason for leaving Las Vegas. I paused to consider what to tell him.

Rick cut me off. "I don't get the feeling that they were just off the beaten path. Anyhow, I'll keep an eye on your house."

My insides pitched and tossed, causing me to momentarily forget our complete lack of water.

Rick brought it back. "I'm gonna head up to the pump. I suppose you will have to use some of that that they've got stored in the basement."

"Basement?" There's a basement?

Rick chuckled. "What did you do, Lindsey? Put yourself in a place and hide under the rug?" More chuckles. Rick thinks he's so funny.

"I guess I did." My face flushed a little.

"Look, girl. There is a basement that is under that garage. I would recommend that you scout it out. You know, go exploring. You might ought to get to know your property. Oh, and . . ." another *let's laugh at Lindsey* chuckle, "while you are scouting out the basement, maybe toss a few glances around in the garage and see if you can discover your lawn mower. No water won't be much of a problem if you can't get out your front door because your lawn has you locked in."

Snarky old cowboy. "Ha ha . . ." I smirked into the phone. I can do this. I can be a responsible homeowner. I did notice that the grass was tall, but I wasn't about to tell Rick that I thought that there was a service to take care of it. "Thanks, Rick."

Once I got off the phone with Rick, I locked all the doors and closed all the curtains. A crawly feeling about the black Escalade clung to me like a hovering mist. I tried to shake it off. Putting on my pajamas, I braved the garage.

Since living here, I have only been inside the garage a couple of times. I think it's easier to park out front. The fancy pickup and the snowmobiles are still there. Camille said they are mine. I really have no idea what I will ever do with them. Then I saw it. I had never noticed the door sitting there in plain sight. I opened it. Eureka! I had found the basement. Light from the garage streamed in. A set of wooden stairs descended into the dark.

Flipping on the light switch, I stepped carefully down the stairs. Rounding the corner at the bottom of the stairs, a long room opened up in front of me. It was roughly half the size of the garage. The center of the room was occupied by neatly organized shelves, from floor to ceiling. Wandering between the shelves, I was floored by the amount of food and other supplies that were hidden down here. There were sleeping bags, tents, fishing poles, and other gear. True to Rick's word, there were several five-gallon jugs of water in blue-colored plastic bottles.

It proved a real test of my strength to lug the awkward jugs up the stairs and into the house. Determined to fill the tub and get a bath, I first planned on bringing in six jugs. I resigned myself to three after bringing up the first one.

Like a true pioneer, I cleaned myself and even washed my hair, using up only one of the blue jugs. They are not user friendly in the least. It was a pain in the neck to get the job done, but I did it.

Hopefully the water will be back tomorrow. Hopefully the black Escalade was a fluke.

I'm beat . . . Me

June 23rd, Wednesday

I am officially sick of not having running water. I contemplated using the custodians mop faucet to take a shower at school. I hate lugging water from the basement. I hate taking a bath from a bowl.

Today I wrangled the lawn mower. It won. I had it running for just a few minutes before it died. I don't know what's wrong with it. I bit back the impulse to run to Rick for help. He strikes me as someone who would be very lawn mower savvy. I mean, he and Lori had this place looking like a fancy resort. (I'm not saying that I have turned the place into a dump, but it is looking slightly shabby with me at the helm.)

Later

Rick stopped by with an update on the well. It is the worst news that it could be. Our well is dry. They have to drill in a new location. I didn't really catch everything he was saying, something about surveyors and a drilling company. I don't really know. I did zero in when he mentioned the price of it all, roughly forty-five thousand dollars.

That's a lot of money. I am extremely grateful for that sinking fund.

Oh, and he kindly fixed the mower. Silly thing, why did it choose to run out of gas while *I* was using it? Goodness.

The good news is I have not seen the Escalade.

Working to figure things out and grow some grit. (Can grit be grown?) Until next time . . . Me

June 25th, Friday

Well, I caved. I'm at Mom and Dad's house and staying in my old bedroom. I got hungry for a hot shower and being able to get a drink of water without a lot of effort.

Ah, comfort.

There are still some hurdles with the well. Rick explained it all to me, and I caught the gist of it all. I have a new appreciation for the early settlers.

I cannot imagine toting water from a stream on a daily basis just to meet the barest human need.

Ted texted again.

Hey, Pretty Girl, Just wondering how your day is going.

I wonder if he has a program that sends out blanket messages to all the females in his contacts.

A storm has rolled in. Nothing like rainstorms in the desert to soothe the weary.

Sleep tight . . . Me

June 27ᵗʰ, Sunday

When it rains, it pours . . .

Detective Jade called me bright and early this morning. He has some video feed and some pictures that he wants me to see. He wants to see if I can identify a person of interest.

More later . . . Me

Later

I had to beat feet out of St. George to meet up with the detective. The storm still raged, but I missed driving through the worst of it. That's a positive. The wind must have been blowing over sixty miles an hour. Lucky for me, the wind was raging northward as I was heading southwest across the desert. The roads were wet but safe.

Detective Jade took me into a small conference room. Two other detectives joined us in the room, a man and a woman. The man sat at a table with a laptop. A large TV hung on the wall. The man brought up the video feed for all of us. At first, there was nothing but a pixelated gray screen with black shadows. The shadows emerged, and the man slowed the video.

On the TV, a dingy yellow light barely illuminated three men in what appeared to be a parking garage. It all looked pretty normal to me. There was an envelope that changed hands among the three.

The man at the table spoke up, "There." He paused the video.

I looked from Detective Jade to the man for some explanation. Both had their eyes steadied on the screen.

Detective Jade said, "Zoom it in. She needs to get a clear picture."

Laptop man nodded, I watched the image on the TV scroll and expand as he zoomed in on the extended forearm of one of the men on the screen.

After a few keystrokes, the laptop man pronounced, "That is as good as I can get it."

The woman replied, "It will have to do."

Turning her attention on me, I noticed her sharp features. Piercing black eyes with a head of glossy black hair, all neatly tucked into a bun at the base of her neck. Her appearance was striking, and a little intimidating. I bet she was a tough cop.

She spoke to me. "Step up to the TV."

Of course I obeyed. I even managed a little smile.

Detective Jade and the woman, maneuvered forward, flanking me on either side. The Detective asked, "Do you recognize it?"

"The tattoo?" I asked.

"Mmm hmmm." The detective bobbed his head and folded his macho hairy arms over his chest.

Tilting my head from one side to the other, I walked even closer to the TV. My face was less than a foot from the screen. It was dark. It was blurry. (And I am sure I was standing way too close to the TV.) But it was familiar, a blue seal with a ball balanced on its nose.

"That's the same tattoo." I nodded and met eyes first with the detective and then with the woman. "That's Isaac's friend, the one from the party," I confirmed.

Quick glances and a couple of nods went around the room. The detective unfolded his arms and pulled a chair out from the table. "Lindsey, I think you had better sit down."

The pointed-faced woman inhaled and exhaled loudly, taking the seat directly across the table from me.

"Isaac's friend there, he's a loose wire, but we can never pin anything on him. All we ever get is circumstantial evidence. Nothing ever hard and fast. He leaves a place, and drugs appear. Or, he leaves a place, and someone gets their teeth knocked in. He's been a suspect in two counts of arson. He's got some big money backing him, high dollar lawyers, and such." He pointed a thumb toward the TV. "Let me make it clear that you need to be careful."

The room suddenly felt tight. A lump heaved up in my throat. What now?

I made it as far as Mesquite, then I stopped for the night at a quiet hotel. My brain was too rattled to keep driving, and I was a little spooked by it all.

I skipped dinner. My nerves were in a mess, plus shopping on the Sabbath was a no go for me. I texted Mom and Dad. I left out significant details. There were a couple of missed calls from Rick. I'll touch base with him tomorrow. It's going to be a long commute to work in the morning.

I'm nestled in with the Food Network, and I hope that sleep will conquer all.

Frightened . . . Me

June 28th, Monday

Sleep did not conquer. It's three minutes past midnight.

I can't take being in this hotel any longer.

My head refuses to shut off.

I'm packing my little bag and heading for Cedar City. I've got a class to teach.

See you in Cedar City . . . Me

In Cedar City

Can I cry?

I made good time driving home, thinking I would have plenty of time for a shower. (Because they have to have that well fixed by now, don't they?) I walked in my door at a quarter to two in the morning. Flipping on the kitchen light, I made a beeline for the kitchen sink. Turning the knob, I slumped. Still no water.

Whatever . . .

The house was surprisingly cold. All the hairs on my arms stood tall. A rustling, like a sail unfurling echoed through the house.

Silently placing my purse on the counter, I left the kitchen and switched on the living room light.

I gasped at the sight that assaulted my eyes. High above the staircase, a section of my ceiling was missing. Gone! Chunks of wet sheetrock dangled like chewed off fingernails. A heavy tarp flapped and rattled over the hole. A dark, wet trail stained the carpet.

Through the haze of my shock, a voice called. "Lindsey?" Again, it shouted, "Lindsey? Are you in here?"

Turning my head, Rick strolled around to the bottom of the stairs.

He perched a foot on the bottom stair and leaned against the railing. "You probably wouldn't believe it, but it was a lot worse yesterday." I think he expected those words to console me. With a lift and a bob of his head like he was greeting someone, he added, "I left you a message."

Hunching forward, I wiped my nose on the hem of my shirt. "Worse? Is that even possible?"

Rick half grunted, half laughed, and nodded. "Come on upstairs."

Panic scratched and digged at my insides. "I don't have time for this. I have a class to teach in a few hours." My legs remained motionless under me.

Motioning me up with his head, Rick repeated his invitation. "Come on up." He waved for me one more time and climbed the stairs toward my room.

With glazed eyes and robotic movements, I obeyed.

My jaw involuntarily dropped at the sight of my room. It looked like a scene from a Star Wars movie, after the Death Star had fired on a planet and sent a million bits of debris flying. Clothes, shoes, personal belongings were heaped and strewn and stacked. Where was my bed? The carpeting was rolled up from the edges with fans positioned and blowing under it.

"It's a little loud in here," Rick shouted as he dodged around the fans and led me to the closet. The beautiful walk-in closet. He stopped at the doorway, allowing me to go first. A mess of wet sheetrock dangled. The carpet was completely removed. The floor was splintery wood. The shelves and closet rods were mostly bare. A few precious items remained. I lifted a jewelry box that I have had since my tenth birthday. Tipping the ceramic box, water streamed to the floor. I set it back on the shelf, defeated.

"What happened, Rick?"

Pointing to his ears, he yelled. "I can't hear a word you're saying. I can barely hear Lori on my good days." He smiled at that. "Come on. We'll go back downstairs, and I will catch you up."

Once again, I followed.

In the kitchen, Rick helped himself to two mugs from a cupboard. I sat and stared. Like an old pro, he poured water from a jug into the stainless-steel tea kettle that came with the house. Turning on the burner, he next fished out a tub of hot cocoa. He measured two scoops into each mug.

Rubbing my face and checking the time, I kicked myself for assuming the water would be back on. I could have showered in Mesquite.

Rick dropped spoons into the mugs. I decided to face the music, so to speak. I had no clue what to do. "What happened, Rick?"

"Well, that storm that blew through here brought a mess of wind with it. I bet we had seventy-five mile an hour gusts. A wind like that isn't very choosy about what it destroys. Did you take a look at the trees?"

"No," I shook my head slowly, "I didn't notice anything on my way in. I was just worried about work." My chin sat lamely in my hand.

The kettle whistled, and like he had heard my thoughts, Rick offered, "If you don't mind things being soggy, your house will wait patiently until you are ready to work on it." He poured steaming water into the cups.

I shook my head again. "I don't even know what to do."

Handing me one of the cups, Rick said, "Well, here's what I'd do. First, contact your insurance. You want them to pay for as much as they will. Next, I'd find you a contractor. When those gusts started hammering, it lifted the metal right off the roof, taking the ridge cap with it. That's why you have a pond in your room. A lot of water routed itself right in there."

"I noticed," I mumbled with my fingers curled around the steaming cup. "What about the gaping hole in the roof."

"Well, now that's the fun part."

I raised my eyebrows. Fun?

"This is where you have got to get on your insurance. As near as I can figure, whoever put the roof on shortchanged Mr. Craig. It seems to me they were maybe a little shy on the number of screws they used to anchor down the sheeting. It makes no sense that the wind could pull it off, but it did. You had a full four-foot-by-eight-foot board of roof sheeting play follow the leader with the metal you lost. I wonder if it was even screwed in at all." Rick took a sip. Wiping his lip, he muttered, "Messy business."

My head was pounding. Priority one: get to work. I don't want any personal crisis to taint the good impression I'm trying to build with my employer. Priority two: Call Camille and find out about the insurance. Priority three, and three-and-a-half: Get the house and the well all in working order.

Rick went on talking, "I know a guy that could get you patched up again. He would do the job right."

Music to my ears. Lifting my face to meet Rick's, I asked, "How do I get a hold of him? I need to get this taken care of before another storm hits . . . or before it starts to grow mold. Right?"

Finishing another sip, he lowered his mug. "I can take care of getting him out here. He'll probably need half down."

"Half down? Don't people usually pay for things when the job is complete? What if I give him the money and he skips town?" I lifted my mug and took a sip.

With a chuckle, Rick smiled, "I can tell you *are* a city girl. He's not gonna skip town on anybody. He's gonna need money to pay for the supplies."

Swallowing, I replied, "How do you know you can trust him?"

Rick's eyes got a faraway look. "I knew his dad."

I appreciated what Rick was saying, but I was beat. Everything was crashing and crumbling around me. "And, why does that mean I should trust his son? Maybe his son is a flake? It is tough to tell, these days." I took another sip. The hot cocoa was soothing and good.

Shaking his head, Rick's focus turned back to me. "I would stake my reputation on this guy."

"How did you know his dad?"

"We served in Vietnam together."

My opinions took a full turn. If there is one group of people that stir my deep, heartfelt gratitude, it is the veterans. Courageous souls, all of them.

"Really?" I spoke the word in awe, not so much as a question.

Rick ventured on. "Yep. Mack was his name. After the military, Mack went into construction. He set up a pretty good business. Now his son is here and picking up where his dad left off."

I was resigned. "Okay."

Rick thumped down his empty mug. "I'll give him a call right now."

"Rick?"

"Yep."

"How did the tarp get on the roof?"

Rick's warm chuckle brightened the space between us. "Well, that was my handy work."

"Rick?"

"Yep."

"Thank you."

Weary . . . Me

Later

Now, where do I begin . . . again!!!

(Taking deep breaths . . .) I managed to contact my insurance, with Camille's help. They are sending a claims adjuster out to take pictures and assess damages. I also managed to get myself put together and go to work. It was a fine day at school. I was even feeling a little optimistic. How foolish of me because when I arrived home, you cannot guess who was standing on my lawn! Mr. Pitbull! (I know there are limits to the amount of exclamation marks a person should use because it makes the writing look/sound like shouting. Well, I AM SHOUTING!!!!) Mr. Pitbull was on my lawn! AAAAAGGGGGHHHHHH!

I stepped tentatively from my car, like I was on eggshells. Then I remembered that he was on my turf. This is my house, and my furtive steps transformed into heavy stomps. I stomped right up to where he and Rick were visiting.

"Hello," I stated boldly. I was stirred, churning, livid, and ready to dropkick him off of MY property!!!

With speed that could crack a neck, he turned his wide, surprise-riddled eyes and plastered them on me.

"You?" He bounced his gaze off of Rick as though searching for an explanation.

A wave of sassiness washed over me. "Yes. Me." I then took the opportunity to cock one of my hips and rest a hand on it. "I live here."

Mr. Pitbull then did something unexpected. He actually appeared to back down. He even took half a step backward. Maybe I was just that intimidating.

Ah Hah! I wanted to blurt it in his face. *You're not so intimidating when I have the home court advantage, are you?* But I didn't say anything. Instead, I smiled . . . with a little eyebrow raise.

Rick spit a shell from his mouth. "Looks like you two know each other."

Mr. Pitbull, once again, reacted in a way that I did not think was in his capacity as a human being. Rubbing at some invisible dirt on his face, he actually looked bashful, ashamed even. Licking his lips, he shifted his weight, glancing first to the sky then down at the ground. He folded his arms. I turned off my cheeky smile and folded my arms to match his, while keeping my eyebrows raised. He blew out a weighty breath, dropped his hands to his sides, and squared his gaze on me. His eyes matched his cobalt blue shirt. Then, he spoke. "I owe you an apology."

The world stood still.

I waited, surprise clearly evident on my face.

Mr. Pitbull pulled in another deep, and heavy, breath. He said, "I had no right to treat you the way that I did. I was completely out of line. I apologize."

Stunned that these words were coming out of the same mouth that had fired off so many insults, my eyebrows crashed together, and I turned to Rick for an explanation. Rick shrugged and spit another shell in reply.

What was I supposed to say? How was I supposed to react? What did he, Mr. Pitbull, expect? I couldn't find it within myself to say that everything was okay, to say that I forgive him. I didn't feel it.

"Well," Rick closed the silence. He thumped Mr. Pitbull on the back, cutting off any need for me to reply. "Thanks for fitting this mess into your schedule. I know your plate is full. I appreciate your help. Get us a bid, as quick as you can, so we can get you some money. I know you've put some other projects on hold to take care of this." Rick looked at me. "We appreciate it." With his hand resting on Pitbull's shoulder, Rick grinned. Then addressing his words to me, he said, "Don't we, Lindsey."

"I'm sure." The words spit out of my mouth like a rotten piece of cabbage.

"Now . . ." Rick steered Pitbull down the sidewalk by his shoulder. "I had just a couple more questions for you before you have to get back to your other work."

I watched as Rick and Mr. Pitbull left the front yard. I had zero interest in what they were saying. With only an irritated glance over my shoulder, I marched into the house.

Blast! Still no water.

What a day . . . Me

June 29th, Tuesday

I left for work as early as reasonably possible. I wanted to leave before Mr. Pitbull started for the day. Pulling onto the road I resigned myself to the fact that he'd be repairing the house, and I should be grateful.

And, as much as it pains me, I'm glad someone will be at the house during the day.

When I arrived home after work, I was relieved to see that the tarp on the roof is gone. The missing piece of sheeting has been repaired.

Needing to run off some nerves, I took a jog out past Rick's house and onto the paved road. I didn't go too far. I didn't dare. Maybe one day I will get to feel completely safe.

I don't regret my decision to move here. I know that sounds crazy after all I've been through, but it's true. This place is remarkable. Even if the sinking fund will be empty by the time the well and the house are fixed, I plan to see this through.

This just in . . . a text from Rick:

> My guy won't be back until Friday. He's got to finish another job.
>
> Also, the drilling rig broke down. Should be back Friday as well. Have a good night. Oh, Lori says to look in the fridge :)

I dashed to the fridge. Ah, what sweet bliss. She left me a plate of her homemade lasagna. Heaven. At least the microwave still works, and thank goodness for all those jugs of water in the basement.

I just might make it after all . . . Me

June 30th, Wednesday

Today was the last day of summer school. It felt good to get my room set up for the start of school in August. I stayed longer than I probably should have. That's an understatement. I hit my stride with my planning for the year, and I didn't want to leave until I was finished. I broke every bit of advice Detective Jade had given me. It was well past Cinderella time when I left the school, but it was so comforting to have everything ready to go. So, I braved being alone and driving in the dark.

On my way home, I stopped at Mr. B's Fast Food for dinner. It's the only place that is open all night. Feeling like celebrating, I ate inside the restaurant. There were a few other late-night diners, so I wasn't totally alone.

It was a quarter after one by the time I drove home. Once I hit the gravel road, I was surprised to see headlights coming the opposite direction, and fast. I swerved to the edge of the gravel as they flew by. A trail of dust hovered in the air. Through the rearview mirror, I could barely make out the vehicle. It was some kind of SUV. Steering back onto the road, my senses prickled.

I pulled to the front of my house. A shiver trilled up my spine. Quickly scanning my surroundings, I considered that I might be overreacting. I hustled into the house. Dropping my purse down onto the counter, I paused. I felt distinctly like I was being watched. Hairs stood. The shiver returned. It was certainly an eerie sensation.

Thoughts of Detective Jade and the pointed-faced woman drummed. Was I being watched?

Fighting the paralysis that cemented my feet to the kitchen floor, I slipped my phone out from my purse.

Chiding my reactions, I moved from the kitchen to the living room. Flipping on all the switches, the big room was fully illuminated.

Something moved outside across the window. My heart hammered, and I jumped instinctively. It was probably just my imagination. *Wasn't it?*

I was fully exposed behind the wide windows. Acting as though everything were fine, I stepped back into the kitchen. You never realize how many windows are around you until you are trying to be invisible. No matter where I went, the massive windows had me exposed. Inside my head, warnings from Detective Jade argued with my wish that I was merely overreacting to nothing.

Call Rick, my thoughts pulsed.

I punched a call to him as I wondered if it were even possible for police officers to patrol this remote area.

Rick didn't answer.

Given that it was after midnight, he had probably been in bed for hours.

Thinking carefully, I hastily made a new plan. Snatching my purse from the counter, I resolved to drive down the lane and stay with Rick and Lori. Yes, I was going to act like a two-year-old that refused to sleep alone. It was time for me to couch surf at their house.

I'd never parked in the garage. I guess I felt a little claustrophobic, even though the garage has plenty of room for my car next to that inherited truck. Now, I wished I would have gotten over my phobia and parked my car in there. It would have been a lot easier to slip into the garage than retrace my steps out to the driveway.

I had to do it. I had to go back outside.

Slinging my purse onto my shoulder, I fisted my keys in my right hand. Stuffing my phone into my back pocket, I gave a quick shake of my head, inhaled deeply, and opened the door. My insides fluttered and chugged. Tremors took an involuntary hold of all my muscles. I tried for all I was worth, but I could not keep from shaking. I couldn't step out the door.

A sound like a thousand firecrackers going off in unison exploded through the night. A bright flash burst in the not so very far distance. Stucco and wood splinters sliced into my skin. I threw both my hands hard against the kitchen door, slamming it with bitter force. Fumbling for the lock, I cranked the dead bolt into place. Tremors took over my body. I dropped to the floor. Looking up, I screamed as a man's pale face passed the window. Flipping over onto hands and knees, I crawled around the island and pressed my back firmly against the dishwasher. Momentary safety. Gasping for breath, cold sweat formed on my skin.

Help! I needed help.

Grappling for my phone, I was horror struck to find my pocket empty. Craning my head to see, but not be seen, my heart thudded. From my vantage point, I spotted my phone just below the kitchen door. If I moved, I would be fully exposed. My breathing surged in rapid waves. Who was firing at me, and where were they now? My head spun. I felt like I was going to pass out.

I needed to pray.

Resisting the scream that threatened, I looked desperately around. What were my options? The open floor plan of the house was not my friend. I considered making a run for the garage. I could take the truck and drive all the way to town. The keys were hanging right inside the garage door. I think I could make it.

Something banged against the door. Wood cracked. Whoever was out there was coming in.

I had to move. It was now or never. Where was Detective Jade when I needed him?

I jumped to my feet just as the door flew open with an ear-splitting crack. Not pausing to look, I bolted for the garage door. I could make it. A hand shot out of nowhere. In a grip like metal chains, my intruder clutched my arm. I twisted and yanked to break free. Hard steel pressed deeply against my neck. I halted my straining.

Yanking my arm, my attacker spun me around to face him. A frosty pale complexion with eyes that burned like coal stared me down.

An involuntary gasp burst from my mouth. Inside my chest, my heart labored like it would beat itself into shreds.

My attacker pinned my arm hard behind me. With a pistol still at my neck, he shoved me forward toward the living room.

I stumbled twice over my clumsy feet before he pushed me down onto the couch, his pistol still aimed at my face.

"What do you want from me?" I shrieked. The words spilled out uncontrollably.

My attacker spoke. A slight accent thickened his words.

"There are accounts that need to be reconciled, miss." He paced back and forth in front of me, never dropping his eyes or his aim. He had to be well over six feet. His shoulders and arms bulged under a wrinkled, pin-striped, black button-up shirt. His hair, brown and long, was tucked behind both ears. His black eyes were the most unnerving. It was as if he had no soul.

He stopped pacing. Facing me head on, the lunatic roared, "Isaac dumped a hundred-fifty thousand dollars' worth of profit!"

Red hot adrenaline surged. I shouted at the man, "What does any of this have to do with me? Isaac is in prison."

His face sparked with rage. "You think I don't know that Isaac is in prison?" He shook the pistol at me. "Ha! Do you think if he wasn't, I would be here with you? Now, close your mouth, and listen to me . . . pay close attention to what I have to tell you."

With his disgusting face just inches from mine, he seethed. "I know you have money. A lot of money. All you need to do, to go on with your happy little day, is give me what I came here to get . . . the money Isaac lost."

His voice crawled across my skin like a thousand black widow spiders.

Detective Jade's advice reverberated in my skull. A list of don'ts. I had broken all of them. Alone . . . After dark . . . I blew it. I blew them all. Meeting the cold eyes of my intruder, I wondered how I could turn back time, leave work earlier, and get a very large dog so that I am never alone at the ranch. The intruder's eyes twitched. His face muscles contracted and flinched, contorting his already disturbing features into an expression that could draw a chill from a fireplace.

I needed to answer. I needed to say something to buy time.

I had broken so many other rules. I decided to use honesty. Afterall, it is the best policy. I don't have any money at the house other than my emergency hundred-dollar bill in my purse. Thankfully I had replaced what was stolen by Isaac. I hoped it would be enough to buy me some time. *I hoped.* Responding honestly, I began, "I don't . . ."

I never finished my statement. Outside the open kitchen door an engine roared, tires skidded on gravel, and a door slammed. All in rapid succession. Fast feet pounded up the gravel walkway.

My assailant briefly lifted his attention from where I sat. He looked over me to the open kitchen door. Instinctively, I turned my head.

A familiar face filled the doorway. It was the man from the party. The one with the tattoo. My heart rate ratcheted up to full tilt. *How do I get out?* my thoughts screamed.

Sprinting, the second intruder, the one with the tattoo, closed the distance between himself and my captor. I jumped as Tattoo Man punched the huge man squarely on the jaw, without slowing a step. The pistol flew as the big man stumbled sideways, knocking over one of my chairs.

Before I could even consider grabbing for the gun, (not that I would know how to use it) Isaac's friend snatched it from the floor. His movements indicated that this was not his first time in this kind of altercation.

Like he had elastic bands attached to his limbs, the large, black-eyed man righted himself, but he was too late. The gun was in the hands of the tattooed man.

Instead of directing the pistol at me, Tattoo Man, sighted the pistol on the bigger man shouting, "This is what you do?"

The big man lunged forward. Tattoo Man twisted out of the way and fired off a shot. A window exploded. I screamed. The big man dodged out of the line of fire by dropping to the floor, breaking off one of the coffee table legs on his way down. I flinched and covered my ears. I needed to get out.

I tried to inch away while the two men grappled with one another.

"Sit down!" Tattoo Man roared at me. He must have rearview vision. The pistol was steady in his hand, though not presently aimed directly at me . . . but it *was* in *his* hand with *his* finger over the trigger. I sat. Quickly.

The big man reared up and lunged for Tattoo Man. Blood seeped from a wound on his cheek where his face had caught a corner of the table.

Tattoo Man was too quick. With a stone expression, he maintained his position, pistol aimed, facing the big man. Tattoo Man spoke, the coldness of his voice dropped the temperature in the room a few degrees. "Did you think you could just sneak off and take the money?" He paused, stepping closer to the big man.

The big man didn't respond.

"Did you?" Tattoo Man shouted.

The two men stared at one another, both unflinching, both unyielding.

I began my slow inching again, hoping my movements were imperceptible. Once I arrived at the end of the sofa, I would run.

The big man lifted a palm to his bloody cheek and shook his head. "No. You've got me all wrong." His voice was almost pleading as he spoke. "I told you. You're in on this. I told you." Removing his hand from his face, he wiped the blood from his palm onto the leg of his jeans. The big man then pointed a big finger up at Tattoo Man, which I thought was a brazen act, considering Tattoo Man still had a loaded weapon. Shaking his pointed finger, he argued, "I was gonna cut you in."

Tattoo Man's arm stretched forward, the veins around his tattoo stood out like tree roots. The muscles in his neck twitched and danced. With unconcealed loathing, Tattoo Man pronounced, "We do this *my* way." He glared at the big man for four full seconds before adding, "Ever the loyal friend . . ." The sarcasm in his words could have danced a jig on the tension that filled the room.

The big man tried. "I wasn't gonna skate . . ."

A shot loud enough to rattle the rafters blasted from somewhere and peppered the ceiling. I screamed, covered my ears, and closed my eyes.

Blinking, I moved my eyes slowly across the rug, expecting to see a body there. What I saw instead was another man, a third man, come flying across the room. He must have come in through the kitchen door like the others. In a heartbeat, the new man tackled Isaac's friend to the ground. The pistol flew from Tattoo Man's grip. It landed at the edge of the rug out of the reach of any of the men. Fists flew. The big man yelled, caught my eyes, and took a lunge for me. Rick appeared from out of nowhere. I barreled over the back of the couch. The big man groped at my back trying to get a hold.

The big man was stopped in his tracks by the barrel of Rick's shotgun as it met him squarely in the face. I screamed again. Rick stood like iron. "Now, consider your actions wisely," he said to the big man.

I scrambled across the floor for my phone. Gasping for breath, my fingers shook. On my knees, I fumbled uselessly with the cracked screen. Before I could do anything, sirens blared right outside the kitchen door. Red and blue lights sliced through the night. I collapsed in a heavy heap by the kitchen door.

Two deputies, a man and a woman, stormed through the kitchen door. They spoke to me quickly. I don't remember what all I said. I kept pointing to the living room.

Finding my feet, I trailed the deputies into the living room. The scene was surreal. Rick had the big man on his knees, hands on his head, facing the shattered window. Rick's shotgun was in his back. My other rescuer, whose back was to me, had Tattoo Man in some kind of arm lock.

The deputies handed out the handcuffs. I sat on the couch and tried to remember how to breathe. Rick and the male deputy escorted Tattoo Man and the big guy out to the deputies' vehicles. More deputies arrived.

My house swarmed like a beehive with men and women in tan colored uniforms.

The female deputy borrowed a chair from the kitchen and waited for me to come to my wits before she initiated the questioning. Someone handed me a glass of water. I accepted it absently.

Taking a few sips, I surveyed the room. There was some damage. One table. One window. One shotgun blast in the ceiling. My eyes continued across the scene. One Mr. Pitbull. What? My eyes locked on his. Realization dawned. He was the one who handed me the glass of water. There he was standing in the middle of this scene, dressed in his blue work shirt.

Swallowing, I questioned him, "How did you get here?"

Rick charged back into the house at this moment, cutting off all conversations, he asked, "Are you okay, Lindsey?"

"Yes . . ." I closed my eyes for half a second, exhaling slowly. "Yes, I'm fine."

Rick nodded. His mouth twisted just so. I couldn't help but smile. He had gotten an early start on his sunflower seeds. Maybe they gave him superpowers. Afterall, he was a superhero tonight.

The deputy took detailed notes as I told her what happened from the time I walked into the house. Another male deputy took pictures of everything. Rick filled in the details that I didn't know. Mr. Pitbull spoke to the deputies as he was questioned. The room seemed to spin in circles around me.

I just wanted to have a normal life, a life where I could come home from work, do some yard work, and take a bath. A normal life. Not this!

Rick pulled me from my pity party as I listened to him tell the male deputy his accounting of tonight.

"I am an early riser, so I typically hit the sheets pretty early," he explained. "Tonight, it just so happened that I couldn't sleep. While I was laying there in my bed, I heard a vehicle race up here, and I had seen a strange one pulling out of here once before. So, I grabbed my clothes and my phone and started this way. I saw that Lindsey had tried to call." He looked my way. I nodded and took another sip of water, impressed with Rick's intuition. "She's never called in the middle of the night . . ."

The deputy interrupted. "Was there a reason for the phone call?" He looked at me.

Setting my glass on the counter, I explained, "I felt like I was being watched. It freaked me out a little."

He nodded and motioned for Rick to continue.

Rick spit a few shells into the garbage can before he continued. "So then, while I was checking my phone, a second vehicle shot up the road, and I mean *shot* up the road. He must have been doing sixty. So, the next thing I did was I called the Sheriff's Department. Next, I called Greyson."

"Greyson?" I asked. "Who's Greyson?"

Mr. Pitbull bobbed his head and gave a little salute.

Oh, so that's his name. I probably should have known. Now he will think I am even more of a lame brain. Oh well. As if I care.

The deputies went on with some speech to Rick and Greyson about waiting for law enforcement and not taking matters in their own hands. I tuned it out. Rubbing my temples, I thought about Detective Jade. I thought about his warnings. I gave the deputies his direct number so they could have all the information. I just wanted it all to end.

As my thoughts ran, Rick was on the ball. He shook hands with the deputies and thanked them. I stood, shook their hands, and expressed my sincere appreciation.

Three of us stood and watched them drive down the gravel road. Rick spit sunflower shells out the open kitchen door.

Ragged, tired to the bone, but too full of questions to actually rest, I turned from the doorway and stepped into the kitchen. Shivers danced up my spine with all that had just transpired. I leaned on the island.

Mr. Pitbull, *Greyson*, spoke.

"Rick, if you don't need anything else," he glanced in my direction before continuing, "I'm gonna head back home. I don't want Elizabeth to be there alone."

"No, I think that'll be it for tonight." Rick clasped him on the shoulder, "I owe you one, Greyson. You go on home. Thanks again. I gotta tell ya, though," Rick smacked his hands together, "I could watch you tackle that guy over and over and never get tired of watching it. That was something."

Snapping to my senses, I stood upright and smiled. "Yes, thank you." I extended my hand. I don't know what I thought would happen. It seemed like the right gesture in the moment. The deputies had helped, and I shook their hands. I guess I thought it would somehow convey everything that needed to be conveyed, like "Thank you for barging into my house and taking down a very bad guy" or "Thank you for the glass of water" or "Thank you for covering the hole in my roof."

Pitbull nodded his head but didn't take my hand. He caught eyes with Rick, bobbed his head again, and disappeared into the early morning darkness.

I lowered my silly extended hand.

Rick attempted to close the door behind Mr. Pitbull, but the damage made it impossible. "Guess we'll add that to the list of repairs." He laughed.

"Might as well . . ." My thoughts suddenly tumbled to my parents. "Rick?"

"Yep."

"Don't tell my mom."

"Nope. I'll leave that to you." He laughed. Then he pulled up a bar stool and parked himself at the island. I poured him a glass of water. Taking a slow drink, he set the glass on the counter and asked, "What are your plans for," he checked his watch, "what's left of the night?"

"I know it's weird, but I'm actually kind of tired now. I was thinking I would try to get some sleep, in my own bed."

He nodded understandingly then said, "I'll get some plastic put over that window first thing."

"Thanks." I had forgotten that I had a shattered window. I rubbed my temples with both of my hands. My heart rate had settled down.

"Greyson will be able to replace it soon enough, I think."

I nodded, wrapping my fingers against the smooth sides of my glass. "Okay."

"The drilling rig should be back tomorrow, well . . . in a few hours. We might have water by the end of the day."

Shaking my head, I sighed, "I'm not falling for that one again. I'll believe it when I see it running from the tap."

Rick took another long drink. "Smart." He tapped the side of his head. Changing gears, he asked, "Oh, but before I go, I do have one question that's been naggin' me. How do you know Greyson?"

Setting my own glass down, I replied. "I don't."

"No, you can't tell me that. I saw whatever that was that sizzled between you two when you saw him on the lawn. And he apologized? A man doesn't go around apologizing to strangers just to make his conscience feel better. So, what's the real scoop?"

"I think I should ask you something first."

"Okay. Shoot."

"Why did you call him—Greyson—after calling the sheriff's department? And why the sheriff's department? Don't they have police out here? I didn't even know a person could call a sheriff."

Rick held up two fingers. "That's two questions. Two for one? Is that some of the new math they teach nowadays?" He chuckled. Stepping down from the barstool, he opened the door and spit a few shells.

I couldn't help but laugh. "What is with you and the sunflower seeds?"

"Hey." He pointed a finger at me. "That's three questions."

"And where is Lori? She must be worried." I emptied my glass and set it in the sink.

"That's four. And to put your mind at ease, I already called her while you were giving your report to the deputies. Now, to answer your other questions. We live in Iron County."

"That's not an answer, and I knew that." I leaned against the counter.

"You misunderstand. We are not within any city limits out here, so the county sheriff's department is the law enforcement out here."

"Oh. I didn't know that. I just assumed that police officers were everywhere." I plopped onto a barstool.

Rick held up a finger. "That's one. Next question. Why did I call Greyson? Since you claim to have no intel on Greyson, let me fill you in. Greyson is roughly," Rick held out his hand and wobbled it back and forth for emphasis, "one of our nearest neighbors."

"Does everyone just call a neighbor when there is an armed man breaking into the house?"

"You've gotta hear me out." Rick adjusted his feet on the rungs of the stool. "I knew it would take the deputies some time to get here, and I knew what I heard. Just so you know, gunshots are not a common sound on our street."

"Thank goodness."

"So, I grabbed old Bess there." He motioned to where his shotgun sat propped against the wall. "And I called Greyson. You see, Greyson has more training than those two deputies combined, and he has good instincts. You saw what he can do." He waved an arm toward the living room.

Shaking my head, I mumbled, "I really don't know what I saw." I replayed the pieces of what I remembered in my mind. The whole thing was horrible and scary. The hair on my arms rose again. Shaking it off, I looked into Rick's weathered, but kind features.

"Well, I guarantee that fellow will remember Greyson for the rest of his life." I waited. "Anyways, back to what I was saying, I knew I could count on Greyson to get right over, without asking a lot of unnecessary questions. I know he gets up early. I know he sleeps with his phone."

I was tired of Rick's list of Pitbull's attributes. It didn't fit with what I knew about Mr. Pitbull. "Let me tell you what I know about him," I interrupted. "I know he is rude, self-centered, and narrow-minded."

"What's got your knickers in a twist to make you think that?" Rick studied me over the top of his glass of water.

"The first time I saw *Greyson,* he criticized my methods and my teaching. He spared no insults. As you would say, he gave me both barrels." I crossed my arms over my chest.

Rick seemed to weigh it all out. "Well, I suppose if he felt threatened, he might act like that. I think we all would, but Greyson's taken on a lot these last two months. He might be a little more on edge . . . but considering what he has been through, I can't say that I blame him."

Rick piqued my interest. "What do you mean? What has he been through?"

"Remember how I told you that I served with his dad in Vietnam?" Rick stretched back, keeping his hands steady on the counter.

"Yes."

"Greyson really looked up to his dad. They had a real special bond. After his mission, Greyson enlisted . . . not in the Army like his dad, but as a marine. He did well. The fact that he learned to speak German on his mission was a real blessing to him, I'm sure. Greyson did quite a few assignments abroad. Different stuff. Top secret most of it. Greyson volunteered to deploy more than once. I can't say that I know a whole lot of what all he's done. His parents didn't even know where he was or what he was doing." Rick looked thoughtful. Then, his face brightened, and he seemed to think in a new direction. "Have you ever heard of a MARSOC Raider?" Rick stretched and stifled a little yawn that caught him off guard.

Caught in the contagion of his yawn, I yawned back. "No. What does that mean?"

"A MARSOC Raider is the guy you want on your team and not on the other guy's team. Greyson was part of a special operations team. He is the real deal." Rick gazed beyond me as if reliving a special memory.

"That's nice and all . . ." I do have a great appreciation for veterans, but this meant nothing to me. The guy was a jerk and then out of some weird pang of conscience, he decides to randomly apologize. I think it was more because he wants to get paid. What's the saying? Don't bite the hand that feeds you. Maybe Mr. *Greyson* Pitbull should have had a little more training on social graces and less on close combat . . . but he really did come to my rescue. Blah, that makes it hard to hate the guy . . .

Rick was still talking. ". . . so he left it all behind."

"Wait. What?"

"What happened, Lindsey? Did I lose you?"

"A little. What did he leave behind?"

"His position in the military. His contract was up, so he didn't re-up."

"He left the Marines? Didn't he like it?"

"You really weren't listening." Rick scolded me with his stare. I shrugged, painting on a sheepish smile.

"He lost his parents."

That snapped me back. Even though I don't like the guy, I don't wish that sorrow on anyone.

Rick continued, "He picked up where his dad left off. Greyson finished all the contracts and got the jobs done. I helped him a time or two when he was shorthanded."

"How did they die?" I really hated to ask, but something stirred in me and wanted to know.

"Plane crash. Greyson dropped everything, his work, his life. I think he was engaged at the time, but his fiancée couldn't see herself in the life he needed to live, out here." Rick stood, reached his arms over his head and asked, "What have you got to eat in this place?"

I furnished a package of Hot Pockets from the freezer. Tearing open the box, I put two of them into the microwave. I was fully invested in hearing the rest of what Rick could tell me about Pitbull, I mean, I had hired the guy. I've got to know that he's trustworthy, right? "So, she broke it off? But was he married before? What about his daughter?"

Rick dropped his arms. "Daughter? He doesn't have any kids. He never got married."

"What about Elizabeth?" The aroma of ham and cheese Hot Pockets wafted through the air.

"Elizabeth is his sister. She is quite a bit younger than him . . . kind of the caboose."

His sister? No. That can't be. Can it? Instantly my memories of that day flashed through my thoughts. Elizabeth. The truck.

The microwave beeped. I slid Rick's Hot Pocket to him. Neither one of us dared touch the molten breakfast until it cooled a little.

Rick kept the biography of Greyson going. "Yep. Greyson literally dropped everything so he could get out here and raise his little sister." Sliding the pastry from the baking tray, Rick tossed it between his hands like a hot potato. He blew on it then explained, "It was only two months ago that all this came to pass."

Mimicking Rick, and tossing the pastry back and forth, I digested what he told me about Greyson.

Rick's phone rang. "Hey, that's my pretty bride. I am going to take this . . ." He wagged the pastry at me. ". . . and make tracks for home." He answered his call. "Hello, Beautiful . . ."

Nibbling at my breakfast, something stirred within me. I had just passed through a horrible experience. I came out of it unscathed. I was rescued by a cowboy and a marine. Funny, though, after hearing about Greyson and his loss, what I had experienced was nothing more than a little inconvenience. I wondered if I would still feel that way in the morning . . . well, the actual morning when the sun is bright. I wondered if I would still feel that way after I talked to Detective Jade. I don't know, but I do know that it felt nice to think about someone else for a change. Maybe that is what compassion is?

Rick had stepped out the broken door then stepped back in. "You can't stay in this place. The door doesn't even close. Come on down to our place. You can have the guest room."

I smiled in sincere appreciation. A couple of hours ago, I wanted nothing more than to be snuggled in the security of their home. Now, however, I felt like the storm had passed. I felt like the dragons were slayed and the castle was mine. I felt safe in my own home. "Tell Lori thanks, but I want to stay here tonight. I'll put a chair in front of the door."

"Suit yourself." Rick smiled. "I'm glad you're okay."

I smiled back. "Me too. And thanks, Rick. You saved my life."

"All in a day's work." He grinned, nodded, and was on his way back down the road to his cute house and adorable wife. I hope that I can be like that, one day.

Still alive . . . Me

July 1st, Thursday

Phone calls, phone calls, and more phone calls.

Thanks to the local news, last night's adventures made it to Mom's ears. I could strangle the newscaster right now.

Because of Mom's hysterics, and because summer school is finished, I agreed to stay the night with them. Dad said that Mom just needed the proof that I was really okay. I packed my little bag and headed south. I am more nervous about leaving than staying. The last time I left, my roof blew away.

Off again . . . Me

July 2nd, Friday

Mom's hysteria is eased for the present. She had living proof that I am alive. Susy and Annie brought their families over as well. They would not stop pestering me about it until I shared all the details, so I did. Everything. My family sat transfixed as I spilled it all.

Detective Jade called three times this morning to verify facts. Busy day.

Now I am grateful to be back home, even without water, even with buckshot in the ceiling, even with a broken door frame, even with a broken window, even with a broken table, and even with a closet that still looks like a tornado swept through. This is home to me now. I have defended it. (Okay . . . me, Mr. Pitbull, and Rick have defended it.) Yes, it is home.

Lori sent over a gorgeous loaf of bread. Oddly . . . she sent it with Greyson. He arrived, true to his word, to get the job done. Seeing him standing there in his eye-matching blue work shirt, holding a fresh loaf of bread, I viewed him as a completely different person. His looks transformed in front of me. Mr. Pitbull . . . a man who carries the weight of the world. A man who has a teenage sister to provide for. A man who could fight off the bad guys. He looked like someone I could call Greyson.

"Thank you," I said sheepishly as I took the bread from his hands. I felt like I should say something more, something to ease the awkwardness. I gave it my best attempt, "Lori is a good baker."

"Yes, she is," he politely agreed. "I'd better get started." He bobbed his head and quickly turned before I could formulate any more words to speak.

He, and one of his employees, spent the day here. I made it a point to stay out of the way.

Until next time . . . Me

✿✿✿✿✿

July 3ʳᵈ, Saturday

Today we get to celebrate the fourth of July.

Greyson and his guy have made great strides on the repairs. And GUESS WHAT? I HAVE WATER! I ran through the house turning on all of the faucets. They all worked!

Ah, what a comfort . . .

Funny thing. After the water was up and running, a puddle started to form on the kitchen floor. I asked Greyson's employee to take a look. He looked, and then went and brought Greyson down from the work in my closet. After a little investigation, they discovered that the bullet that was fired at the door hit a water line in the opposite wall where it lodged. What are the odds?

Once again, the water had to be shut off while they attended to the repairs.

I am just glad they were all willing to work on a Saturday. Tonight the city will do the fireworks for the fourth of July. Annie, Susy, and Mom want me to join them in St. George. Because I have Greyson and his helper finishing up, I told them I couldn't come down. I am actually perfectly happy to be here. All of Mom's attention, as of late, has left me feeling a little suffocated.

Greyson's helper left shortly after lunch and did not return. I was curious how things were coming along in the closet. I went upstairs to peek.

Greyson stood in the bedroom, talking softly on his phone. I didn't mean to, but I couldn't help overhearing his end of the conversation.

"I'm sorry. No, I can't leave right now. We wouldn't make it in time anyway. No, I need to get this job done. I know it is a holiday weekend, but

I have to get this finished. I have another contract next week. Look, I will make it up to you somehow. I don't know. Somehow." Greyson glanced up and saw me in the hall. He spoke quickly to the person on the other end of the call. "Hey, look, I've gotta go. We'll talk at home. Okay? Bye." Snapping his phone into the case on his belt, he gave me the faintest sheepish smile. "I'm sorry about that. I try not to make it a habit to take personal calls on the job."

I entered the room and shrugged. "It's fine." Turning for the closet, I asked over my shoulder, "Is everything okay?"

"Yes." Greyson filled a silver trough with drywall mud from a bucket.

I nodded. I was pleased to see the closet looking almost normal. I was impressed with how much had been completed. There were plenty of details still to complete, but things were really looking up.

Greyson approached. "I'm going to go down and touch up the ceiling in the living room. The mud in the closet needs to dry. We'll sand it and texture it next week. I thought we could have it all finished by the end of today, but I guess I misjudged the time. I'm really sorry."

I smiled. "Not a problem. I'm just so grateful to have water . . . and for all this work to be done. You have no idea."

He nodded. "Look, I don't want to be in your way for the holiday. I'm going to touch up that ceiling. Then I'll clean things up and let you have your day without any interruptions."

It didn't matter to me one bit that he was there working, but I didn't want to let on that I had already adjusted my plans so that he could get the job finished.

His phone rang. Pulling it from his belt, he sighed. "I'm sorry. I have to take this."

"No problem." I went downstairs. Lori was at the partially repaired kitchen door when I got there. I gave her a hug and thanked her again for the bread.

"I'm glad you enjoyed it." She ran her hand over the remaining scars in the door casing. "It just makes me sick to think about what you went through."

"I will be forever grateful for your husband and his quick thinking. He really saved me."

Lori came in and patted my face with her warm hand. "We are all so grateful. Rick said it was Greyson that came up with the plan. He is a quick thinker." She stepped into the living room. Spotting the still broken coffee table, she put a hand to her chest and shook her head. "I came to see how you are doing and also to check on Greyson. His truck is still outside. Is he here somewhere?" She looked around.

"He's upstairs." I pointed in the direction of my bedroom closet. "We can go up. He was on the phone when I came down." I headed to the stairs and stopped. *Wait . . . Check on Greyson . . . Why?* I met Lori's kind eyes. "Is everything okay?"

"Oh, yes. Everything is fine." She smiled lovingly.

The frustration in Greyson's voice was evident as we mounted the stairs. Yet, there was a gentle resolve. "We'll take care of it when I get home. See you at home. Bye."

Lori entered the bedroom first. "How is she?"

Greyson clipped his phone back into his belt. "Impossible," Greyson growled.

"What can I do?" Lori asked. "Do I need to go pick her up and take her to our place? She is welcome anytime you know." Lori turned a full circle in the room. "Whew, this is something."

I stepped up alongside her. "It *was* a lot worse."

Greyson raked a hand through his hair. Lori seemed to make up her mind about something. She took the reins. "Greyson, call Elizabeth. Lindsey and I will go get her. It's a holiday. We'll all go and make some fried chicken and potato salad. You come down when you finish, and we'll all have dinner together."

I opened my mouth to protest. I could see through Lori's scheme to thrust all of us together like one happy family. I bristled. "No . . . I . . ."

Greyson also appeared to be extremely uncomfortable and digging for an excuse. " Well . . . I . . . uh . . . Elizabeth wanted . . ." He looked to the ceiling as if to find the answer written there. "Okay," he caved with a sigh. "I'll let Elizabeth know."

"Perfect. This will be fun." Lori looked like she had just been crowned queen. "Are you ready, Lindsey?"

Failing to hide my lack of enthusiasm, I tossed a glance at Greyson. Our eyes touched for a moment. The dread was clearly evident for both of us in that passing glance.

Oh boy . . .

At Rick's and Lori's house, Elizabeth avoided eye contact or speaking to anyone except Lori, which meant she avoided eye contact and speaking with me. Given our history, I could not have expected anything less awkward. This was the first time that I had seen her since the incident at school. I hoped that she might warm up to me, in a professionally-distant-sort-of-way.

Fortunately, fried chicken and potato salad are multi-step productions. This took some of the pressure off. All three of us were busy preparing the masterpiece that would become dinner.

Rick and Greyson arrived at the same time. Lori sent them to wash up. I felt like I was living a chapter out of a western novel where the men folk all come in after the cattle drive and a wise matron sends them all out to wash up. Well . . . I guess I was living it. It was kind of awesome, in a way.

Dinner was on the patio. The summer sun was heavenly. I sat across from Greyson. Our eyes met a handful of times across the table. Neither one of us spoke directly to each other. Rick and Lori carried the conversation. I was grateful. They reminisced about their childhood Fourth of July celebrations. Elizabeth quietly lamented missing the fireworks. As if on cue, Greyson winked at his sister and went to his truck. He returned with a box of fireworks. (What a waste of money, I thought.) Elizabeth jumped from her seat and hugged her brother. (It no longer seemed like a waste of money.)

I desperately wanted to make amends with Elizabeth before this night was over. It gnawed at me without letup. I had done wrong by this child. I sat beside her on one of the blankets as Rick and Greyson lit the fireworks. She was a good audience, cheering them on.

As Rick and Greyson readied the next round, I unloaded what was on my mind, "Elizabeth, I want to apologize to you for not letting you tell your side of things at school. I reacted harshly, and I am sorry."

Elizabeth smiled sincerely with her wide eyes meeting mine. "It's okay," she said.

Relief washed over me. "Thank you," I smiled at her. "That means a lot."

"This is our final round," Rick announced across the fireworks. He patted his belly and said, "Before we light it, I think we should all have a bowl of ice cream."

Lori slapped a hand to her forehead. "Goodness sake. I forgot dessert." Elizabeth laughed.

"Can I help you with it?" I asked.

"Elizabeth can help me get it. You better keep an eye on these boys." Lori grinned mischievously toward Rick.

Rick shook his finger and said, "She's absolutely right. But you'd better just keep an eye on Greyson. I'm going into the kitchen to make sure I don't get short-changed on my bowl." Rick darted after his wife and Elizabeth.

The three of them disappeared into the house. I shifted uncomfortably. I purposefully did not look toward Greyson as he took a seat on the edge of the porch.

His voice startled me. "Miss Jones, that was kind of you to talk to Lizzie."

His face was barely visible in the light coming from the kitchen window. "I made a mistake, and I'm sorry. I owed her an apology." I felt better for saying that to her brother.

I looked up at him. He nodded. I looked away again. I wasn't sure if he expected me to reply. I met his eyes once more as the other three burst from the kitchen.

I feel a little better . . . Me

July 15th, Thursday

My house is all put back together again. There are just a few touch-up details to be done, and Greyson sent his helper over to finish the last of them. I am so happy.

I need to tell you that I went on a date Tuesday night. His name is Bruce. He is also a schoolteacher. We met while I was getting an oil change and he was getting his brakes repaired. We sat visiting in the lobby of the garage and he asked me to have dinner with him. (No worries. He teaches at one of the high schools, so no post-date-working-together-awkwardness.) After all the craziness, a date sounded delightful.

We met at his apartment right after our cars were finished. I left my car at his apartment and rode with him in his Subaru. Thankfully, I dressed up for my trip to get an oil change. I had on a nice pair of jeans and the pale pink top that brings out the color in my eyes.

Bruce talked all the while as he drove us to the east side of Cedar City and up the canyon.

"Did you ever do something really stupid?" Bruce smiled innocently, turning the wheel.

"Just one something?" I asked. "I can come up with a whole list if you would like."

Bruce laughed. His laugh was meaty and warm. "I mean when you were a kid? Something you knew you never should have done."

"Sure. I guess." I raised my eyebrows in his direction.

"Okay . . ." his face lit up with childlike enthusiasm, "so there was this time that I decided to go catch some fish for the family for dinner. I thought it would make my parents happy that I could be so responsible."

"That sounds very responsible." I agreed.

"So, I was only eight . . . and I was tending my little sister. She was five and a half. My mom and my two older sisters had gone to a neighbor's house to take them a plate of cookies or something. That's why my mom trusted me to babysit, I guess. If she was next door, she probably assumed I wouldn't cause too much trouble."

"Smart mom," I said.

"So, anyway, I didn't have much time to get to the pond and catch dinner. Since Mom and my sisters walked next door, I decided that I had an urgent need for the car. I figured I would be back with twenty pounds of fish before they ever knew I was gone."

My mouth fell open.

Bruce talked and talked. "I gathered up the fishing tackle, told my sister to buckle up, put in the key, dropped the car in gear, slammed on the gas, and drove straight into the closed garage door."

I put my hands over my mouth. "That's terrible. Were you hurt?"

"Ha ha . . . no . . . but my sister sure made a scene." His hands flew from the wheel and waved madly in the air. "Waaaaahhhh!" he screamed.

I reached over nervously to steady the wheel as we approached a curve in the road.

Bruce reclaimed the wheel and added, "So, like I said, stupid."

I smiled hesitantly. I should have offered to drive.

Bruce pulled in at a little restaurant nestled in the trees. The restaurant was a log cabin decorated to resemble a hunting lodge. It was quaint and inviting. The hostess seated us at a quiet corner booth. Bruce managed to get me talking through most of dinner.

"So, why did you decide to teach? Especially in Las Vegas . . . dun, dun, dun." Bruce grinned mischievously.

I raised my eyebrows. He was a character. Setting down the dinner roll I had been buttering, I gave him the starched answer that I always gave for this question. "It was my fourth-grade teacher. She left such an indelible impression on me that I wanted to be just like her." I picked up the roll and took a bite. In all actuality, I couldn't say if it was because of my fourth-grade teacher that I became a teacher. I really became a teacher because I felt like it was what I was supposed to do. I can't explain it any better than that.

Bruce laughed. "Cool. Your fourth-grade teacher, huh?"

I nodded, covering my chewing mouth with one hand.

"I was expecting a deep, philosophical answer."

I shrugged. With my mouth still full of bread, I muttered, "What about you?" What was I doing? I never talk with my mouth full.

Bruce placed his utensils on the table and sat erect. I think he was trying to impress me. "Easy answer. It was music." He gave a little bow, retrieved his utensils, and followed my example, slathering butter on a roll.

"How so?" The fresh bite of bread in my mouth muffled my words.

Bruce didn't miss a beat. "Well . . . so there I was, at sixteen years old, sitting at the piano and attempting to play some complicated piece by Chopin or somebody, and it hit me . . ." He spread his arms wide, with the roll still in his hand, and nearly knocked down a passing server with a table-sized tray on her shoulder.

Bruce leaned in. "If no one taught, the best things of life could not be passed on. That Chopin piece would not have existed beyond Chopin." He leaned back. "You see what I mean? Without teaching, society as we know it would end."

"Wow . . ." I responded, wiping my mouth, "that's deep." He had made a good point.

"Actually," he picked up his fork and tapped it lightly on the edge of his plate. Then he pointed it directly at me. "It's a good thing there are other piano students, and teachers, in the world because if it would have been exclusively dependent on me, that Chopin piece would not have made it to the next generation."

I laughed this time. "You don't play the piano anymore?"

Bruce shook his head and emphatically mouthed the word, "No."

The server arrived with the rest of our dinner. I scooted my salad plate out of the way and I asked Bruce, "Now that you've been teaching for a while, do you regret your decision?" He was a nice guy. A little goofy, but safe.

"Nope. Not at all. I love my job." Bruce handed the server the empty breadbasket.

I smiled genuinely. "Then your students are very fortunate to have you as a teacher."

After the meal, we drove back through the canyon and into town. Bruce played some of his favorite songs as we drove. He gave every detail of every musician in every band of every song that he played. It was a little annoying but not terrible.

All in all, it was an okay evening. He was an open book. Here is what I know about him. Bruce, in a nutshell: teaches math, plays the guitar and ukulele, has three sisters, is the oldest grandson in his family tree, served a mission in California (Spanish speaking), owns a set of bagpipes, hates brussels sprouts, and wants to tour Europe next summer.

No sparks were flying, and I am okay with that. No strings. No promised follow-up dates.

I called Susy after the date. Here is her advice:

"If I were you, I'd run a background check on the guy."

Funny, Susy.

Until next time . . . Me

July 31ˢᵗ, Saturday

Lucky me. (Not really.) I get to appear in court in sixteen days. I have to go and testify. Because the investigation is in Las Vegas, that is where I will be appearing in court. Did I mention that that is also the first day of school?

Feeling sick inside . . . Me

Later

Greyson texted:

> *Hello, Miss Jones. As a courtesy, I wanted to follow up with you and check on the repairs on your home. Let me know if you have any problems. I guarantee my work. Thank you and have a nice evening.*

My finger hovered over the text box. He had done a great job. I typed my reply:

> *Hello. Thank you for asking. Everything seems to be fine. Thank you for your work.*

I felt the message was satisfactory. I hit send.

I am tired . . . Me

august 1st, Sunday

After church today, I was studying in the living room when the doorbell rang. I jumped as the first notes of the bell echoed through the house. Since everyone always comes in through the kitchen, I had almost forgotten I had a doorbell.

Opening one side of the double door, I was surprised. There stood Elizabeth in her Sunday best, holding a plate of cookies.

I smiled. "Hi, Elizabeth. You look pretty."

"Hi." She smiled back and quickly spoke. She rushed through her words as if she were afraid that she might lose her courage to speak to me. "Miss Jones, Lori and I made you some cookies. I hope you like them." She handed me the warm plate. The cookies were, no doubt, fresh from the oven. Holding the plate under my nose, I savored the aroma.

Elizabeth glanced up expectantly then lowered her eyes to the porch. She started to turn.

"Thank you so much." It was my turn to speak quickly. "This was really thoughtful of you and Lori. I will enjoy these."

"Miss Jones?" Elizabeth spoke but didn't budge. Her back was partly to me.

"Yes, Elizabeth?"

She looked first at the ground and then faced me. "I just wanted you to know that I am sorry that I didn't speak up at school." Her thick eyelashes framed her eyes. Those eyes stayed centered on me for just a moment. Then she gave a little nod, like her brother so often does and looked away.

What a sweet kid. I smiled warmly back at her. "It's all okay, Elizabeth." Then, I remembered. "Oh . . . Elizabeth, I have your essay. Just one minute. I want you to have it back. You did a wonderful job on it." I left Elizabeth standing in the door as I rushed to set the cookies on the kitchen counter and fished her essay from my school bag.

She cautiously took the essay from my outstretched hand. I watched her as she read over my comments.

"Well done," I said. "You write from the heart. That's one of the marks of a great writer. Keep it up. Your writing will get better and better."

She lifted her face, beaming.

"I know it will," I assured.

"Thank you." She hugged the essay.

"You're welcome."

She turned and walked confidently toward where her brother was waiting in his truck. I didn't notice him there before. He gave half a smile, I think, and waved. I gave him a hesitant wave in return.

Closing the door slowly, I wondered at the whole experience.

Good night . . . Me

august 5ᵗʰ, Thursday

Date number two with Bruce. He is harmless enough, right? This time I did give in to vanity. I bought a new pair of shoes and earrings for the evening. I figured if I am going to listen to him talk all night, I might as well look good.

He asked if I could meet him in town. I thought that was a win-win. I do have some worries that a man could have more interest in this home and property than he might have in me. Not that I am really concerned about Bruce, but you never know.

Bruce took me to an open-mic night in the basement of a record store. He and an old roommate (Tim) played guitars and sang a song that Bruce wrote about his hometown in Wisconsin. Actually, they were really good. The three of us had dinner at Applebees afterward. Again, Bruce was full of stories.

Over an appetizer of boneless wings (I hate chicken wings), Tim and Bruce droned on and on about music. Don't get me wrong. I LOVE music, but honestly, there ought to be limits on some things. Let me share just a sampling of what I endured, an appetizer for you, if you will.

"So, did you buy that amp?" Bruce enthusiastically wiped his fingers on his napkin.

"Yeah, man," Tim boasted.

"What did you end up paying for it?" Bruce lifted another boneless wing to his lips.

"Mmm, I got a sweet deal." Tim also grabbed for the chicken.

"Nice. How much?"

"So, I got the Crush 35RT for two hundred bucks." Tim licked sauce from his fingers.

That's enough of a sampling. I swear they went on about the amp for forty-five minutes. I was halfway through my lava cake before the subject changed. Combine that with Bruce elbowing Tim and goading him to ask our server out on a date because she was "pretty" (Bruce's description) and you have a pretty clear picture of my night.

There are simply no sparks with Bruce.

Signing off . . . Me

august 6ᵗʰ, Friday

A note was wedged in the kitchen door when I got back home from putting some finishing touches on my classroom:

> Lindsey,
>
> Sorry for the short notice. We were wondering if you would like to have dinner with us at our home tonight.
>
> Please give us a call.
>
> Sincerely, Elizabeth and Greyson

I was more than a little surprised. A note instead of a text? Tonight? Seriously? It was a cute gesture, a note tucked in the door. Unusual, but cute. Unnerving, but cute. With Greyson and Elizabeth? Who was behind this little unexpected bit of cuteness? Rick . . . no Lori. It had to be Lori.

Me alone with Greyson and Elizabeth? No way!

I raced upstairs to my bedroom to drop off my things with the note still in my hand. I read it five or six times, at least. Each time I read it, I considered the outcomes of accepting or declining the invitation. Suddenly, I was intrigued. I was up for an adventure.

Facing the full-length mirror, I decided that I was presentable enough. Nice jeans. Trendy shoes. I exchanged my baseball t-shirt for my cream-colored top. I faced the mirror again. Yes, I would do this. Besides, the Fourth of July meal was okay with all of us together, right? It was better than a night out on the town with Bruce. (He had called me at noon. I ignored the call.) And . . . I was starving, so if someone else was offering me a meal, I considered it to be a blessing.

I quickly texted Greyson's number before I chickened out:

Greyson and Elizabeth . . .

No. Deleted that.

Take two:

Elizabeth and Greyson,

No. Still no good.

Take three:

Hi, I would be happy to have dinner at your home.

Done.

Sent.

A reply came a minute later:

We will pick you up at your home at 6 p.m.
Thank you.

Wow, so formal. It was different, in a pleasant way. Nervous flutters twirled in my belly. Wait. They will be picking me up?! That would prevent me from making any fast get away. Should I text back and take my car? I measured the possible outcomes in my mind. If I needed to get back, to get out of their house, I would find a way. Why not see this adventure through? Right?

I used my wait time to touch up my makeup and do some reading. I should say I attempted to read. It was not much use. My thoughts kept drifting, anticipating, and playing various scenarios of how things might unfold at dinner. I hoped I was actually ready for this. What was I thinking? I have got to stop letting my stomach get me into fixes.

No such luck.

At one minute after six, the doorbell rang. I jumped again at both the loudness of the doorbell and the monstrous jitters in my stomach. Goodness. Maybe I should stick with Bruce? Then I won't have to go through this roller coaster of nerves.

I swung the door open and found Greyson standing there in a pair of nice jeans and a crisp, gray button-up shirt that set off his blue eyes. It doesn't seem to matter what he wears, his eyes are striking even if he is Mr. Pitbull.

Elizabeth stood next to him, a bouquet of wildflowers in her hands tied with a pink ribbon. She extended the flowers to me. "I picked these for you."

Wildflowers? Picked, not purchased? Did I just step back in time? My jitters shrank to a quiet patter. "Wow. They're beautiful. Thank you." I marveled at her thoughtfulness. She was not a typical thirteen-year-old. I wondered what her mother was like. Was this girl a reflection of her mother's kindness? I smiled. I inhaled the sweet fragrance. I don't think I had ever smelled anything so lovely. Store bought flowers always smell like cabbage to me. These were divine. I stepped to the side.

"Come in. I will put them in some water." Greyson stepped out of the way and motioned for his sister to enter ahead of him. Elizabeth stepped inside, eyes wide as she took it all in. Greyson followed his sister into the house, looking almost shy . . . or uncomfortable . . . I'm not sure which, exactly.

Greyson inspected the ceiling as we passed through the living room.

"Chris didn't patch that?" He pointed to the buckshot embedded in the drywall from the shot Rick fired. "I will come tomorrow and fix that. Why didn't you say anything?" He looked at me quizzically.

I laughed and said, "I asked him to leave it."

Greyson puzzled over my logic, and I let him. I walked straight to the kitchen and set the flowers into a tall glass with water. Centering the bouquet on the island, I said, "Very beautiful. Thank you, Elizabeth."

"You're welcome," she smiled, glanced at her brother in a way that appeared to say, *I told you so*, and smiled again. Greyson ignored her and continued to examine the ceiling.

What I didn't tell Greyson was, to me, that buckshot represented hope. Even when things are falling apart, and criminals are fighting in your living room, there is always hope.

I stepped up behind him. I asked, "Are Rick and Lori going to join us?"

"No," Greyson answered, looking toward his sister. She was busy straightening a couple of the wildflowers she brought. "It's just us."

Ah, so this was her idea. Perhaps she was trying her hand at matchmaking? Or am I reading things into this simple gesture of kindness. *Watch yourself, girl. Don't get yourself caught up into something you will regret.*

Greyson turned and asked, "Ready to go?" It was a little awkward.

"Sure," I replied. I locked the house, and we were off. Greyson drove. Elizabeth sat in the middle seat. I was grateful she was there. She did most of the talking, pointing out the flowers on the way. It was already proving to be an interesting night. Awkward. Uncomfortable. But interesting.

Rick was not kidding when he said Greyson was "roughly" our closest neighbor. Nestled in the next little valley lay a quaint little community. The homes were quaint and old looking. Green lawns, a few pastures, and some farm machinery added to the picturesque view of the little neighborhood. Greyson pulled into the driveway of a two-story farm home, white with green painted shutters, very *Anne of Green Gables* looking. The surrounding property was green and beautiful. Two small outbuildings stood like Monopoly pieces on the far end of the land. Cottonwood trees swayed in the breeze on either side of the driveway. The place held a sense of love and peace.

Charming.

"This is beautiful," I remarked.

Before I could navigate the door handle, Greyson had walked around the truck and opened the door for Elizabeth and me.

"Thanks." I was a little thrown off by his polite manners.

"You're welcome," he offered as he held the door and I climbed out. Elizabeth followed.

The interior of the home was as bright and welcoming as the exterior. Simple, clean, elegant, homey. A large family photo hung over the piano. A pain stabbed my heart. I looked away.

"Come on in." Greyson led the way to the kitchen. Elizabeth followed at my side, now chattering about a friend that was coming over later for a movie night. Once in the kitchen, all her previous shyness dissolved into a huge grin. She spread her arms wide. "We are having Cooks' Experiment Night."

Greyson half grinned, half smirked, an expression that I had not seen before. Then, he handed me a red and green, ruffled, plaid apron.

I turned the apron in my hand. The word "experiment" had me a little worried.

Elizabeth explained, excitedly pressing her palms together in front of her in a namaste position, "This is a tradition that Greyson and I started a little while ago. Fridays are our experiment nights." She opened her arms again.

"Sounds dangerous," I replied. "Should I go back and pick up some TUMS or something?" Though my mouth was playful, my heart felt the tug. I wondered if this tradition started just after their parents died. Was it Elizabeth's idea, I wondered, or did Mr. Pitbull put this together?

"Maybe," Greyson interjected with his smirk. Elizabeth shot him a mock fiery stare. Greyson raised his eyebrows and shrugged at his sister.

Who would have thought Greyson could joke?

Elizabeth laughed and tied on an apron that was covered with flying unicorns. "We haven't been poisoned yet," she said.

"There are some rules, though," Greyson explained while slipping a yellow apron that was decorated with a chicken holding a spatula over his head. Then, meeting my eyes with his, he quietly added, "Really . . . you probably should have said no."

What did he mean by that? Did he wish that I would have said no? Was he resentful that I was there, in his house? This was all a bit strange. All of this friendliness. I mean, granted, he did save me from bullets, so technically I should probably be the one making him dinner, not the reverse.

Then, in the midst of my befuddled emotions, Greyson winked at me. What was I supposed to think of that?

I masked my worries behind a thin smile. Greyson caught my gaze just as my smile faded.

Elizabeth burst through the awkward moment. She was truly transformed. Waving her hands in front of her, she outlined the rules. "We have to make the meal together . . . from scratch. No shortcuts."

"And . . ." Greyson coaxed.

Elizabeth's eyes danced. She slid a mason jar across the counter until it rested in front of her. There were strips of paper inside. She laughed. Her eyes twinkled with delight. She looked up at her brother, shook her head, and laughed again. Elizabeth held the jar up for me to see. "So . . . Greyson found this idea on Pinterest."

"Oh . . .?" I responded, a surprised grin on my face. Greyson and Pinterest? Interesting . . .

"Yes." Elizabeth clasped the jar with both hands. "We did a family Pinterest challenge. We each had to find a project, and it was a race to see who could finish first." She tossed her brother the stink eye.

Greyson interrupted before she could expound. "Of course, I won."

Elizabeth blustered. "Only because you chose the easiest project you could find." She shook the jar under his nose.

"Well . . ." he defended, opening his arms and shrugging.

Glancing between the two, I asked Elizabeth, "What was your project?"

Greyson snorted. I was thoroughly surprised by his playfulness.

Elizabeth retorted, "Hey . . . I chose a great project."

Greyson sobered. "Yes. Yes, you did. It is just unfortunate that you haven't finished with it yet."

My curiosity was piqued. "What did you choose?"

Elizabeth mumbled. "A pallet bench."

"A what?" I asked. I wasn't sure I heard her correctly.

"A pallet bench," Elizabeth repeated.

Greyson smiled fully, revealing perfectly straight teeth and a light in his countenance that was striking. I lowered my eyes, not wanting to give my thoughts away.

He took a jab at his sister. "Lizzie, why don't you share your pallet bench with our guest. Maybe she would like to sit on it?"

Elizabeth shook her finger at Greyson then laughed.

"What . . .?" I asked. Were these the same two people that I met in July? They were so different. So fun. I never could have imagined them acting this way, and yet, it wasn't an act.

Elizabeth walked to the kitchen window and lifted the blind. With a sigh of defeat, she pointed. "There it is."

I carefully stepped around Greyson and looked out the window. Across the yard, leaning against the fence, sat a single wooden pallet.

I couldn't help the chuckle that flew out of me. I sounded like Rick. Yikes! This life was rubbing off on me. "Well," I collected myself, "you have the most essential part . . . I'm guessing. So, good job," I praised Elizabeth, avoiding any contact with Greyson as he stood politely close to me and peered out the window.

Greyson punched another jab at Elizabeth. "And who brought that pallet home?"

Elizabeth playfully glared at her brother as she lowered the blind against the setting sun.

Greyson smiled. I smiled. For a fraction of a second, we both just stood there, smiling. I broke away, looking down and pretending to investigate my apron.

"Anyway . . ." Elizabeth sang out. "We have a jar of questions." Scooping up the jar, she pointed at it with emphasis.

Grateful for the distraction, I faced Elizabeth. "What do you do with the jar?"

Greyson wasn't finished teasing his sister. "Yes, tell Miss Jones what a great job *I* did with my Pinterest project."

I laughed, "Please. We're not at school. Call me Lindsey."

Elizabeth tossed her eyes up to her brother.

"You too, Elizabeth," I said. "You can call me Lindsey."

"Okay." She grinned. "Lindsey." She seemed to digest it for a second and then continued. "Anyway . . . we each take turns asking and answering questions from Greyson's jar. You only get one opt out."

"Wow." Why not, I thought. It could be fun. Besides, it might give me some more information about these new neighbors of mine. "Okay, I want to do this right." I tied on my apron.

Greyson placed a collection of ingredients on the counter. I couldn't make heads or tails of what the end product was supposed to be. I picked up a jar of garlic powder, a can of mushrooms, and a package of breadcrumbs. "What are we making?"

Greyson gave me a pained expression. "Chicken casserole, if we're lucky."

"Okay, I'm in." My confidence surged. Casserole was something I could do. I pointed the can opener at Elizabeth and said, "Elizabeth, ask the first question."

Elizabeth spun the lid off the jar. "If you could make up a holiday, what would it be?"

I scrunched up my eyebrows, looking first at Elizabeth and then at Greyson.

Greyson raised his hands, "Oh, don't look at me. This is your question." With a pair of kitchen scissors, he worked at opening a bag of frozen chicken.

I leaped, "My holiday would be Cooks' Experiment Night."

Greyson shook his head. Then, turning to Elizabeth, he said, "I don't think she knows what she's gotten herself into."

Elizabeth laughed.

When the finished product came out of the oven, the breadcrumbs were slightly soggy, but the chicken looked great. It was definitely the first time I had ever been given casserole on a date. (Was this a date?)

We sat at a round table. Greyson said a blessing on the food. Elizabeth asked a million questions while we ate. Greyson did steal the jar a time or two. Each time I pulled a slip of paper from the jar, it was a trivial question about favorites. For example, I learned that Elizabeth's favorite ice cream is Butter Pecan. Greyson's favorite kind of chips are plain potato chips, and I learned that Elizabeth's favorite color is purple. Yet, every time I was asked a question at the table, it was some deep probing question that seemed pointed at examining my soul. Goodness.

"One more question," Elizabeth chirped as Greyson and I dried the last dishes.

"Okay, fire away, Lizzie." Greyson took a bowl from my hands and put it in the cupboard above me. I didn't mean for it to happen, but my heart did this little flutter as he reached above me. My cheeks flushed, and

I stepped backward, nearly tripping over my mortifying feet. I grabbed the edge of the counter to steady myself before Greyson could catch me. His arm brushed gently across my back.

Elizabeth saved the day. "Miss Jones . . . sorry . . . Lindsey, this one is for you." With a mischievous look, she held the question stretched between her two hands.

Embarrassed, I said, "Okay, what's my question?" Greyson moved his arm.

Elizabeth leaned across the counter. In her best menacing voice she asked, "What is your deepest secret?"

Seriously! Why didn't I get to ask this question? Besides, there was no chance that I was going to answer this one. Not really. What would I say? *My deepest secret is that I was engaged to a criminal.* Impossible.

I protested, deflecting my fear strategically onto Greyson. "What was the question you got? How many grades of school did you complete? And I get a whopper? My deepest secret? No. I am going to have to opt out." I raised my hands in surrender.

Greyson walked around the counter peering over his sister's shoulder. Drying his hands on a dishtowel, he studied the question. "Yep. Deepest secret." He tossed the dish towel on the counter, pointed right at me, and said, "And you can't opt out. You opted out on 'What is the worst advice you have ever been given?'"

He was right. Dang. "Okay . . ." I paused, not for effect but to consider my out. I hated this. Anxiety swirled and bit at my insides. I was like a little kid again riddled with fear. I looked at the floor, hoping something would pop into my head. Something that was not a lie. Bugger. I exhaled slowly. I chose.

"My feet."

However, if they asked for a view of my feet, I would have to escape.

"What?" Elizabeth leaned farther to get a view of my feet. "Feet cannot be a secret." Since my ballet flats were nothing remarkable, and my shameful feet were fully covered, she announced, "Do over."

Relief washed over me. My heart rate lessened and my breathing returned. I was safe.

Elizabeth sat back, still seeming disappointed. "All right." She shrugged and shook her head. "Well at least your deepest secret isn't that you've killed someone or run a crime ring out of your basement."

Greyson grinned knowingly at me over Elizabeth's comment. He met my eyes.

I smiled suspiciously. "Well, maybe I do run a crime ring. It just happens to be out of my living room and not the basement."

Greyson had to add, "It's just that we already knew about that . . ." he winked at me again.

Unnerving. My heart lurched a little. My smile fell a hair. I didn't mean for it to. Maybe it was the wink, but I did not want to share the Isaac craziness with Elizabeth. I was okay with Greyson knowing about Isaac . . . I guess. I assumed that Rick had already told him everything, anyway.

Greyson raised his eyebrows at me.

I was committed to my silence.

Elizabeth broke the tension. "Lindsey, can you stay for a movie?" Her blue eyes pleaded. "Sharon is coming over, and we could all watch together."

"No, I better not." I untied my apron. "It's getting late."

Greyson stepped close to take it from me. Again, the flutterings at his nearness. *Good grief.* I stepped sideways and increased the distance between the two of us.

Elizabeth was not giving up without coaching me on some more of their family traditions. "We always do a movie after Cooks' Experiment Night. That way, if dinner is gross, at least we'll get to watch a show." She was still intent.

The doorbell rang. Elizabeth sprang to answer the door. She returned to the kitchen with a tall, dark-haired girl that I assumed was Sharon.

Brief introductions were made.

Greyson grabbed his keys, then instructed Elizabeth. "Get the ice cream. I'll take Lindsey home. You and Sharon can start without me. I'll be back in a minute."

"No rush." Elizabeth smiled. Sharon giggled. A new sensation, something unexpected washed through me at their silliness. Were they insinuating there was something between Greyson and me?

Hogwash.

Elizabeth reached and gently hugged me. I returned the embrace.

"Thank you for coming over, Miss Jones . . . I mean, Lindsey." She stepped back. "I'm sorry. I can't get used to calling a teacher by name. I mean by first name." She was a sweet kid.

"It's okay. Thank you for inviting me to dinner. It has been a lot of fun. Oh . . . and good luck with your pallet bench." I smiled at her.

With that, Greyson and I walked silently to his truck. He opened the door for me. Chivalry. Wow. I climbed in. What a different world from my first impression.

"Thank you, again, for coming over tonight," Greyson said as he put the truck in gear. "Lizzie has been pestering me for a week."

"She's a great girl."

"I really worry about her. She's so vulnerable. She never wants to hurt anyone. She doesn't want anyone to be left out. She hates seeing other people get in trouble. She isn't the typical American teenager. Sometimes I wonder if I would have less worries if she were a sassy, self-centered thirteen-year-old." He shook his head with his eyes on the road.

I was surprised by Greyson's openness. "You're doing a great job." I studied his profile as he drove. With the tight haircut, pressed shirt, and Herculean build, it still proved difficult for me to lift my first judgments of his character. Yet, his behavior tonight was nothing but that of a perfect gentleman and a thoughtful and loving brother. Confusing.

"I don't know." He cast a soft smile at me.

Whether it was my professional duty, whether it was my conscience, or whether it was the perfectly pleasant evening we had just spent together, I wanted closure on this episode of my life. I needed to make things right with him. Aside from being neighbors, I didn't see this relationship continuing, so I needed to do it tonight.

"Greyson." I realized that I had never spoken his out loud name before.

"Yeah?"

"I need to apologize to you."

"For what?" He turned briefly to face me. The puzzlement wrinkling his forehead.

I exhaled. "Two things. First, for my reactions toward you . . . and especially for my actions toward Elizabeth on that dreadful day at school. I didn't do my job for her, and I was overly defensive with you. I am sorry . . . and if it matters, the other girls did receive consequences for their actions." Okay, it was out. I said that part of what I needed to say. I waited for a reaction.

To my surprise and relief, Greyson shook it off. "It's in the past." He looked my way again. "Forget about it."

Now for part two. I held up two fingers. "And second, I want to apologize for walking away when I first saw you with Rick the other day. You apologized to me, and I behaved like a stinker. I'm sorry."

He tossed me a sideways glance. "A stinker?" The look on his face was comical.

"Yes, I was a stinker. I am sorry." Okay, it was done.

Greyson laughed pleasantly. "I've taken a few turns at being a stinker. You have nothing to worry about. Really."

We rode in silence the rest of the way. Once again, Greyson was out and around the truck holding the door open for me before I had even shouldered my purse. "Thank you." I slid to the ground and walked toward my home. Pausing halfway up the walk, I turned around. Greyson was just about to step into his truck. "Greyson?" It still felt strange to say his name.

He looked across the hood of the truck at me.

"Thank you for saving my life."

He took a step and said, "You're welcome."

I smiled from the inside out for the rest of the night.

Good night . . . Me

august 4th, Saturday

My family visited today. All of them. It was a good time. Rick and Lori helped Dad and I put on a barbeque. And . . . I might add . . . I did a fair share of the prep and the cooking. Not to toot my own horn, but . . . toot toot! I did a hands-down great job.

Mom twisted her hands with worry as she investigated the living room and the buckshot in the ceiling.

"You can't live alone." More hand wringing. "Maybe your dad and I could come and stay with you until your Christmas break."

"Mom, no way. There is no reason for you to come and stay with me. You are welcome to come whenever you want, but you just can't abandon your lives and come and tend me like some animal in a kennel." The last thing I needed was for my mother's constant stewing to be right under my roof.

More wringing. She was not dissuaded, "Maybe after Christmas those awful men will be locked up in a prison somewhere, and you will be safer."

"Mom . . . they are in jail."

She studied me with a scrutinizing stare.

"I will be fine."

She and Dad did, however, bring their things to spend the night. Funny how living in Las Vegas never proved to be as dangerous for me as living out in the country. I suppose I could still sell and move back. Hmmm . . . if Mom decides to stay for the next few months, I may consider it.

Until next time . . . Me

August 15th, Sunday

Mom and Dad stayed and went to church with me. Odd thing, I don't remember seeing Elizabeth and Greyson there before. I wasn't sure they went to church.

Mom caught me mid-glance at Greyson. (I couldn't help it. I still wonder what he really thinks of me.) Mom curved her lips, lifted her eyebrows, and looked sideways up at me in that way that said, *It's about time you found yourself a man.* It's an ongoing struggle.

As we were leaving, Elizabeth waved at me from down the hall. Standing by Elizabeth, Greyson talked with one of the ward members, a man in his fifties that I had not yet met. Elizabeth's wave turned Greyson's attention for just a moment. He gave me a smile and a nod. He went back to his conversation.

The gesture (of course) was not overlooked by Mom, who asked ten thousand questions as Dad drove us back to my house.

True confession: the gesture was also not overlooked by me. I thought it was nice.

Thoughtful . . . Me

Later

Mom and Dad left. The house is silent.

My sub plans are ready for the first day of school tomorrow. A deep sense of dread is churning and clawing my insides. I am missing the first day of school. I am going to testify in a court of law. I can't take it.

Oh, yeah. In case I failed to mention this . . . Rick and Greyson will be there as well, in court I mean. It makes my head spin. I shudder when I think about what might have happened if Rick and Greyson had not shown up.

Rick just texted both Greyson and I:

> *Hey you two. Why don't we all save some fuel and ride down together tomorrow? Whaddo you think? :)*

The churn in my gut flopped and grinded. Now it was real. I was physically prepared. I had even packed an overnight bag in case the trial went long. I had left a week's worth of sub plans with my administrator as well. Just in case.

Emotionally, I was a scrambled egg.

Riding with Rick and Greyson could be a good idea. I lifted my phone to text when the chime sounded. Greyson had replied.

I'm in. I'll drive.

Now it was up to me.

Lifting my phone again, I considered carefully what I wanted to say.

Okay. Good idea. My car gets better gas mileage, let's take mine.

Rick and Greyson both replied:

Okay.

Sounds good.

Rick added:

Meet at Lindsey's at six.

This was really happening.

Now, more than ever I just wanted to live the fantasy of being nothing more than a happy schoolteacher in a country town.

Pray for me . . . Me.

august 16th, Monday

Welcome to fabulous Las Vegas! Oh brother.

We met up at my place and crossed the desert into Las Vegas. Rick sat next to me in the front. Greyson rode in the back. None of us spoke very much except for Rick. He did the talking, lowering his window at regular intervals to spit shells. If any of them caught in the wind and landed on Greyson, he didn't tell. Needless to say, the wind from his spitting didn't do my hair any favors.

Reclaiming my hairdo with a quick fix in the mirror, Rick, Greyson and I climbed the few steps into the courthouse. We passed through metal detectors and signed in. My nerves sizzled and sparked. I thought I might pass out from the sheer stress of it all.

Court was just like it is in the movies, except this time I was there. We sat in a small room around a table while we waited to be called into the courtroom. Three other witnesses and an officer were there. Silence reigned. A large box of donuts sat in the center of the table for us to keep our energy. Time seemed to tick backward. All I could think about was school and the fact that I was missing the first day of class.

I ate a donut.

Rick was called in. We tossed surprised glances at each other. I thought I would be the first one called.

One eternity later, Rick returned. The clock on the wall read five thirty. I was going to go crazy.

I ate another donut.

Greyson paced like a caged animal, texting and talking to Elizabeth. When Rick came back, he settled Greyson down by calling Lori to go and get Elizabeth.

At ten after six, we were informed that court was adjourned until tomorrow. We were dismissed.

With my blood sugar performing the wave, I wanted to scream. I wanted to march into the courtroom and have a word with all the powers that be. This is a perfect example of what is happening to public education . . . the criminal is taking priority over the classroom. Seriously.

Greyson called Elizabeth.

Rick called Lori.

I called my administrator.

Next, we found a hotel.

Nauseous . . . Me

Later

I'm going to throw up.

Sitting on the tile floor of the bathroom in my hotel room, I'm still wearing feet-hiding heels and a skirt, and I don't care. Every inch of my skin is fully cognizant of every germ lurking on this floor. My back is against the tub, and if I weren't in a hotel, I would be fully leaning on the toilet.

Evil donuts!

I want my mom . . . Me

Later, again

Greyson and Rick lightly knocked on the door that connects our rooms. In the midst of prying myself up off the floor to answer their knock, it all came out. It was not pretty.

Greyson and Rick knocked some more. I was powerless to answer. I gagged and wretched as they thumped.

What a mess.

Greyson burst into the room. He is making a habit of that.

Rick was the guilty one with the spare key for my room. He is still bent on protecting me, but he minced no words when he saw me in my mess. "Oh, I'm out." He vanished back into his room.

Strong arms steadied me as I continued to puke in a very unladylike manner. Definitely not glamorous.

The same arms eased me to my feet and handed me a warm washcloth as the waves of sickness beat at me with daggers of fury.

Face in the washcloth, I slid back to the ground. Round two was about to begin. Greyson rinsed another washcloth as I heaved over the toilet. Gasping for air, I leaned back again. A fresh washcloth was put into my hands. No attempts were made to get me to stand. Greyson sat on the edge of the tub next to me. He held a fluffy white towel in his hands.

"Well," he paused, searching for the perfect words, "at least you have good aim."

I shook my head at his lame attempt at a joke.

After ten more minutes of Greyson watching me sit on the floor, I started to feel better. Pulling my knees under me, I prepared to stand. Greyson was ahead of me. He knelt beside me. "Here, wait, let me take your shoes."

Okay, posterity. You know how this is. Yep, it's my feet. I may have been sick and green and puking, but there was no way Greyson was taking my shoes. I would go to bed with my shoes on. I would climb mountains with them on. I would super glue them to my skin before I was going to let him take my shoes and see my toes.

"No!"

Greyson acknowledged my concern. He paused, knowingly and said, "Oh that's right . . . your deep, dark, secret feet. Well, then at least, let me help you to stand."

Catastrophe averted.

I brushed my teeth.

A smell that threatened to send me back to the toilet followed my every move. I had to get out of my nasty clothes. Greyson, by himself, quietly accomplished all the cleanup that was necessary in the bathroom, but I was disgusting.

After I was sufficiently certain that I was not going to throw up again, Greyson left.

For the record, Rick made it clear that he can't handle barf. "If I see it," he declared, "I repeat it."

I'm glad he stayed out. There wasn't enough room for two at the toilet.

Completely drained, and a little shaky after a hot shower, I found a home improvement show to lull me to sleep. With socks on my feet, and pj's on, there was nothing to stop me.

Or so I thought . . .

Greyson knocked, then entered with a tall soda, brimming with crushed ice. He balanced a Styrofoam bowl of chicken broth in his other hand. "One for the stomach. One for your strength." He set the bowl on the nightstand and handed me the lemon-lime soda. "I hope you don't mind, but I borrowed your car."

With the soda soothing me from the inside out, he could have wrecked my car and I would not have cared . . . well, okay, I might have cared a little.

"Thank you," I said, wishing I could offer more than simple words. I was grateful for his kindness and attention to my horrifying needs.

Greyson slipped out the door.

I need to feel better tomorrow . . . Me

august 17th, Tuesday

Today, Greyson, Rick, and I were each called in turn to testify. It was an experience that I will never forget. Though I was the victim, in that scary courtroom, I felt like I was the one on trial. I can't even remember what I said. I felt like I repeated the same words over and over as I was questioned by one attorney and then another. The judge also asked for clarification. I felt like I was on some kind of merry-go-round, living the same moments over and over. Thankfully, my stomach was in check.

We've been released to go home. Yeah! I can get on with my life. I can get back to my classroom.

Greyson offered to drive. I took him up on his offer. Greyson also furnished Rick with a small, white plastic trash bag from the hotel for his seeds. I laughed at that. I guess Greyson did catch a few shells in the back seat on the way down. This time, I took the back seat.

It was so quiet in the car, I slept most of the way home.

Until next time . . . Me

august 21ˢᵗ, Saturday

I feel free.

The struggles of this week are behind me. My stomach has returned to normal. Even with me being absent on the first two days, the first week of school went well. I did spend the better part of today catching up on things. But that's okay.

I am looking forward to reading and resting tomorrow.

Revived . . . Me

august 22ⁿᵈ, Sunday

What a beautiful day. Today has been a peaceful day of church, reading, and relaxing. Just perfect.

I stretched and picked up my book from the couch when the doorbell rang. Not expecting anyone, I tucked a few rogue curls behind my ear. Opening the door, I found Greyson standing beside Elizabeth.

"Hi," I said.

"Have you got a minute?" Greyson asked, always polite. Elizabeth nodded, smiling.

I stepped back from the door. "Sure. Come in."

"Thanks, Lindsey," he said softly as he walked past. The simple words sent a little shiver through me.

"You're welcome," I replied, closing the door and following them into the living room. "Please, make yourselves at home."

Elizabeth walked to the center of the living room then turned and faced me. With a look like she was about to make an important announcement, she put her hands together and said, "We want to invite you for Cooks' Experiment Night this week." She looked at me, eyes pleading. "You have to come."

Greyson sat down on the edge of the couch, and added politely, "If you have time . . ." I turned to look into his face. His eyes met mine, and neither one of us looked away. His eyes softened. His features relaxed. A magnificent little smile lifted only the edges of his mouth. What could I say to a face like that?

"I would love to," I replied, still looking at Greyson.

"See," Elizabeth blurted, breaking the spell between us. "I knew you would say yes. Greyson didn't believe me." Her eyes narrowed playfully at her brother.

Greyson leaned forward as if to stand. With perfect manners, he started, "We had better let you have your evening. Thank you for letting us drop in . . ."

"Actually . . ." I took a chance, cutting him off completely. I don't know what I was thinking, but I knew I didn't want them to leave, not yet. "Would you like to go for a walk with me?"

"Definitely," Elizabeth declared. She was so much more confident than the girl I met in June.

"Are you sure we're not intruding?" Greyson was so formal. Was it because he was at my house? Was it because there was nothing more between us than a series of hapless events that had somehow thrown us together?

I turned on my most assuring expression. "Not at all."

Elizabeth was so excited. As we walked, she let me know that she had downloaded some new questions for the jar. "I chose the most impossible questions I could find, and I don't think we should allow any opt outs."

"You say that now," her brother jabbed.

"I'll take all the opt outs." I grinned, loving the banter between the brother and sister.

The setting sun framed the trees in gold as we continued down the gravel road.

Greyson pointed at the horses. "Has Rick taken you out on a ride?"

"Just once," I smiled.

"Would you go again?"

"It might be against my better judgment, but yes, I would go again. I'm not the most adept horse rider." I remembered the evening riding with Rick. I was white knuckled the entire time, but I loved it.

"Maybe you and I could ride some time." The light in his eyes was unmistakable. Undeniably, a part of me hoped that light was for me. His face cracked a smile. The smile trickled all the way down to the soles of my shoes.

Elizabeth spoke up. "I'm glad it's you two going and not me." Her blonde hair waved as she shook her head. "Horses scare me."

"I can't get her on one." Greyson reached his arm and pulled his sister to his side. She fell into step beside him. Putting her arm around his waist.

"Nope," she affirmed.

"Rick hasn't given up on trying to persuade her to ride, though." He gave her shoulders a squeeze. "If anyone can get you up on a horse, it'll be him."

Elizabeth shook her head. "I don't think so."

Greyson laughed. Elizabeth stepped from his side.

"Hey, I'm going to go see Lori," Elizabeth announced as we approached the driveway of the yellow house. Then, turning to Greyson, she added, "Take your time, and don't worry about me." She waved a hand and strode up the driveway.

Greyson's eyes followed her. "Lori has adopted her. I'm so grateful. They, both of them, have done so much for me . . . for both of us."

I thought of all the times they had helped me, rescued me, fed me. Goodness. "They are incredible people." We took a few steps in silence. The breeze whispered in the trees. I lifted my eyes to Greyson. His profile was framed neatly by the surroundings. Thoughts of Greyson and what he had done for me wrapped around my mind. "Greyson?" I said, filling the silence.

He looked at me pleasingly without saying a word.

"Rick and Lori aren't the only ones who have helped me through all this craziness. You have too." I continued with what I wanted to say. "At the hotel, I was in a pretty awful mess. I appreciate you helping me the way that you did."

"Well, we knew we couldn't count on Rick . . ."

I laughed, remembering Rick's hasty evacuation from my hotel room. "No, I guess you're right . . ."

He laughed and shrugged it off. "Don't worry about it. Everyone gets sick."

"Yes, but I think most people don't puke in front of individuals who have also saved their life."

"They aren't that lucky."

I laughed.

We walked a few more steps in silence, then Greyson spoke. "How are you adjusting to living here, now that things have settled down?" He caught himself. "That is, I'm assuming things have settled down." He looked at me for reassurance that my insanities were over.

Again I laughed, and it felt so good, so easy and natural. There was nothing forced or pretended. "I hope all of *that* is behind me for good." I shuddered at the thought. Then, I answered his first question. "I think I'm settling in pretty well. I love the house."

"I'm glad," he said.

Our footsteps paused. He met my eyes. A wave of warmth crested and broke in my middle. My heart spun as my head tried to make sense of what I was feeling . . . this pull that I felt toward Greyson.

Before I could take my next breath, Elizabeth raced up to us. "Lori wasn't home, but I told Rick that you and Lindsey wanted to take the horses."

My eyes widened. Elizabeth didn't waste time, did she?

Greyson looked over Elizabeth at me. Without skipping a beat, he asked, "Would you have any time this week?"

"To go riding?" My head was still catching up to the fact that Greyson was asking me out.

He nodded. "If you would like to go . . ."

The words, "I could go Wednesday after school," tumbled slowly from my mouth.

Greyson smiled.

I caught Elizabeth doing the last moves of a micro happy dance. She was a little matchmaker. With the setting sun still illuminating Greyson's enchanting eyes and attractive smile, I decided that I could be okay with that.

And just like that, I had a date for Wednesday.

I think my life has flipped over.

I group texted my sisters:

> *I think I'm really starting to like living at the ranch.*

Susy's reply:

> *It's about time.*

Annie's reply:

> *Okay, you've obviously met a guy. Tell us who he is.*

Another time, my sisters.
Good night . . . Me

August 25th, Wednesday

"Are you up for this?" Greyson asked as he cinched the saddle on ol' Chester.

"Bring it on." I smiled with the best confidence that I could muster, wearing jeans and Lori's borrowed cowboy boots. My legs trembled, but I didn't let it show.

Rick, Lori, and Elizabeth had gone into town for dinner. This left only Greyson and me with the horses.

"Well, then." Greyson smiled. "Climb on."

I lifted my leg and stepped down in the stirrup. I landed gracefully in the saddle. I was beginning to feel pretty good. Greyson reached out a gloved hand and lifted one of mine. I guess my death grip on the saddle horn didn't go unnoticed. I resisted the urge to grip his hand and hold on tight.

"Hold the reins like this." He showed me how, just as Rick had done back in June. Then Greyson stepped back and said, "You've got this."

I blew out a breath. "Yes, I do," I assured myself.

Greyson swung into his saddle, and we set out across the pastures. It didn't take too long for my nervousness to settle. The steady rhythm of the horse's steps wound down my anxieties. My hands, and my head, relaxed. Ol' Chester followed alongside Ladybug, Greyson's horse, without any prompting from me.

"Have you been to The Peaks before?" Greyson asked, looking everything like something out of a classic western movie.

"Nope. The only sightseeing I do is driving back and forth to work." I am so boring.

"Well, I hope you like this."

Looking around, I didn't see anything that looked like a peak. "How far is it?" As much as I was enjoying the ride, I didn't want to be out all night. Not on horseback anyway.

"Not too far." Greyson looked at me. "It's only about three miles on horseback."

Watching him, I wondered out loud, "How did you learn to ride a horse?"

"Oh, Rick taught me. When I was a kid. He and my dad and I would ride out to The Peaks or over to the lake."

"Lake?" I looked around again. All I saw was desert. "There is a lake?"

Greyson pointed across the pasture. "It's six miles south. It's not a bad ride. I could take you sometime . . ." He met my eyes, then seemed to evaluate his words, ". . . if you would like to go. It takes a full day to go there and back. Or, you could camp . . ."

"Oh wow, I think I have enough with riding a horse . . . I don't think I could camp." I didn't add that I had only been camping once in my life and I hated it. I ended up covered in mosquito bites and with a viscous stomachache from burnt campfire food. No, I didn't need to go camping.

Greyson laughed. "I had a hunch."

"What?" I narrowed my eyes slightly. "You baited me. Hmmm, you think you know me pretty well, huh?" Then I laughed and said, "You probably do."

We rode out of the pastures with Greyson dismounting and opening and closing gates as we went. The horses followed a trail into the junipers. We rode single file, threading through the trees. I kept my eyes fixed on the trail as the incline steepened. Greyson slowed up ahead of me. Looking up, I could see craggy rock formations through the trees.

"Is that it?" I pointed.

"Yep. Those are The Peaks."

At the edge of a small clearing, Greyson steered to the side. Swinging his leg, Greyson dismounted. "This is the place." He looped his reins around a branch. Then he stood beside me and patted Chester. "Here, let me take your reins."

With his hand on my back to steady me, I dismounted. Greyson tied Chester to a branch, and Chester immediately joined Ladybug in nibbling the plants on the ground.

I limped and wobbled as I tried to walk. It was unfair that Greyson moved around so nimbly. I rubbed my thighs. Greyson laughed, "It'll get better the more you walk around."

I took his advice and took a few steps in every direction to ease the discomfort. He was right. It did help. I pulled my gloves off one by one. Greyson reached out his hand to take them. "Thank you," I said as I watched Greyson put away the gloves and pull a small cooler out of a saddle bag. He then handed me a water bottle. "This is really beautiful," I said, looking up at the bright summer sky above the jutting peaks. "I don't think I've ever truly appreciated the beauty of the desert, but this is really pretty."

"It's better over here."

I followed Greyson past the trees into the clearing. A panorama opened up of distant hills and the houses down below.

"I can see why you come here. It's a great view."

"I think it is." He looked at me. "I'm glad you're not disappointed."

We took our dinner to a large boulder that looked like a heart jutting out of the ground. Greyson said, "I hope you're not a vegetarian." He held a roast beef sandwich in my direction.

"I'm not a vegetarian." I playfully snatched the sandwich from his hand.

Greyson pointed to a brown house below us. "See that house?"

"The brown one with the trees?"

"That one belongs to a nosy guy." He turned to see if I was listening. "He can't be trusted."

My eyebrows arched. "How do you know him?"

"I've known him since we were little kids. So, believe me, I *know* him." He looked at me sternly, then his eyes crinkled and a smile broke across his face. Shaking his head, Greyson laughed. "My best friend Dave lives there with his wife and two kids. He is like a brother to me."

"A nosy, untrustworthy brother?" I quipped.

"Precisely." Greyson laughed, wadding the wrapper from his sandwich.

We didn't stay long at the heart-shaped rock. Greyson had to get Elizabeth home, and I had work to finish. The ride back was easier than the ride there. My nerves had settled considerably, and I trusted Chester to see me safely back to Rick and Lori's house.

Greyson again steadied me with a hand to my back as we dismounted in front of Rick's barn. "Thanks for riding with me tonight. It's been a while, and I don't think I would have gone if you hadn't gone with me."

"Blame it on Elizabeth," I grinned back at him. Then I added, "I had a great time. Thank you for inviting me."

His blue eyes beamed. It's a wonder that I ever saw a Pitbull in those deep eyes.

My insides shivered.

Saddle sore . . . Me

august 27th, Friday

I smiled like a fool through my classes today. The cause of my merriment? Dinner with Greyson and Elizabeth, of course.

I offered to drive myself, but Greyson insisted on picking me up. When I heard Greyson's truck on the gravel, I have to confess that my heart jumped. In a good way. I grabbed my purse, and I bolted out the door to save him the trouble of walking up to the house. He was alone. My nerves zipped and tumbled inside of me.

Greyson saw me walking toward him. He quickly jumped out, circled the truck, and held the passenger door for me. He stood, ruggedly handsome, by the door as I climbed up.

"Thanks," I said as I pulled my seatbelt into place.

He closed the door and was back in his seat in a flash. "You're welcome." Greyson turned a soft glance in my direction that was trimmed with a beautiful smile.

"How was your day?" I asked as he drove.

"It's been good. Yours?" he asked.

"So good." I smiled. Greyson smiled back.

Elizabeth handed out the aprons when we arrived. Greyson arranged the ingredients on the counter. This lineup of ingredients was more challenging than last week's odd array: an assortment of veggies (some canned, some fresh), eggs, instant rice, and brown gravy mix. "Are we making omelets with brown gravy . . . and rice?" I asked with evident confusion.

"Egg Foo Young," Greyson answered as he melted butter into a skillet on the stove. "Elizabeth, get the mixing bowl."

"Okay." She danced around me and retrieved a large green bowl from the cupboard. "You will love this." She was more confident than I felt.

"What is Egg Foo Young?" I thought omelets sounded better.

Elizabeth handed off the bowl to Greyson. He passed it right to me.

He dished out the directives. "You crack the eggs," he instructed me. "Elizabeth, get that onion chopped."

Greyson and I stood elbow to elbow in the narrow kitchen. I cracked an egg into the bowl, tossing the shells into the trash. I paused, giving Greyson the chance to direct me further.

"More," he barked with a teasing smile. He left his pan to stir the gravy.

"I'm worried." I cracked away, one by one, pouring a whole dozen eggs into the bowl. A large metal whisk was thrust into my hand.

"Now you stir," Elizabeth coached, grinning. She readied the rice for the rice cooker.

I cringed when Greyson slid a mountain of vegetables into the eggs. Yuck. "Wait," I held up my finger, "I bet I can guess the next part . . . stir?"

"You've got it," Greyson cheered.

I plunged the big whisk into the slimy mess. This was dinner?

Elizabeth found my evident consternation to be hilarious. I couldn't help laughing as well, even though I found it all to be completely unappetizing. I don't know . . . this might be more than I can gag down.

I stood by as Greyson scooped out small amounts of the goopy, eggy, "batter" and fried them into neat, round patties.

Elizabeth assembled our plates. A bed of rice, topped with two of the patties, and a thick helping of gravy.

We took our plates to the table. Greyson blessed the food. Elizabeth started on the "impossible" questions.

I liked my first question tonight.

"What's the weirdest food you've ever eaten?" Elizabeth grinned over her plate.

"That's easy," I readied myself for the rebuttal. "Egg Foo Young."

Elizabeth shrieked with laughter. Pointing fingers at Greyson she crowed, "I told you! I told you!"

"What?" I laughed out loud.

Greyson tossed Elizabeth a brotherly scowl, cleared his throat, and replied. "Elizabeth thinks that veggies and eggs should never cross paths."

I kept my personal opinions in my head. I didn't want to take sides, but I was certain Elizabeth had a very good point. Once again, I admired the closeness that Greyson and his sister shared.

"Okay." Greyson would not be defeated. "Let's find out. Let's see if you think this is the weirdest food of your life after you take a bite."

The acid test. "Okay . . ." I stabbed into the gravy laden mess on my plate.

Elizabeth laughed. "Here, let me show you."

Elizabeth expertly scooped up a small bite with rice, a bit of egg patty, and a drizzle of gravy. "It's better if you get some of all of it." She smiled.

Greyson watched, arms folded across his chest, and a look of pure merriment illuminating his features.

I slid the bite into my mouth. My face cracked into a smile. "It's actually good." I held my hand in front of my mouth as I spoke. "Really good."

"Hah." Greyson goaded his sister. "Now who's right?" She rolled her eyes playfully.

"Sorry," I apologized to Elizabeth, smiling. Then following her technique, I scooped up another bite of food.

An hour later, Elizabeth and Sharon were deep into a movie as Greyson and I took care of the cleanup. It's funny. Neither one of us spoke much. It was comfortable to be there working together. I can't really put my finger on it, but I liked it, whatever it was.

After wiping it with my towel, I handed Greyson the last dish. Again, like they had a dozen times, our hands brushed. This time, his eyes softly met mine. Those beautiful eyes. My heart did a little pirouette. Quickly checking myself, I dropped my hand and busied myself with taking off the apron. Tonight I wore the unicorns and Greyson wore the plaid with ruffles. I hung the apron on a hook on the wall with the others.

Greyson put the dish away then turned and faced me. "Do you have to get back?"

Difficult question. *Did I have to get back?* Back to what? Back to my big house? Back to finishing my laundry? Back to binge watching TV as I folded the laundry? If I said that I did have to get back, that would be the easiest. The night could just peacefully end. No strings attached. No awkwardness. No . . . no risk of me falling for this guy who makes meals into memorable events. This guy who opens doors. This guy who is a mother, father, and a brother for his sister. Be smart, girl. I took a leap.

"Nah, I don't have to be home." I watched an indefinable emotion wash over Greyson's face. Was he hoping I would stay? I studied his face again. His eyes beamed like lights but with poised dignity and control. Tough to read. A tiny smile on his lips betrayed what I hoped was contentment.

Unexpectedly. I panicked. Suddenly, I was afraid. Very afraid. I could really go for this guy. This guy who was so different from any man I had ever dated. More serious. More focused. More real. More gentlemanly and kind. Fear clutched my chest. Elizabeth could end up getting hurt. My chest constricted. The air got tight. I needed out. Now!

Greyson opened the back door, revealing tiny strung lights glittering over a quaint deck. A table, chairs, and a swing were placed tastefully on the space. Elizabeth's pallet still waited against the fence. He extended his arm to me. "Let's go outside. I would like to show you around the place."

I stepped through the open door into the night air.

Panic clawed from my throat down to my hideous toes. I had done it, hadn't I? I had already fallen. Why? This was too much! I couldn't speak.

Greyson's hand found mine. His fingers lightly wound through mine. He turned, his face close.

Like a miracle, *or not*, Mom called.

Catching my breath, I spun out from under Greyson's spell. Grabbing my phone from my back pocket, I drilled all my focus into the screen. What was I doing? Without thought or consideration, I turned apologetically to Greyson. On impulse I said, "I really need to take this."

He nodded. "No problem. I'll go inside, so you can talk."

No good. I had to make a bigger deal out of this. I couldn't risk another Isaac-type mistake. I had to get out before my emotions got out of control. Before I kissed too soon. Glancing at my phone as forlornly as I could, I said flatly, "I think I had better take this at home." I am an idiot. Somebody give me a dunce hat. What is wrong with me? "I'm sorry."

Greyson closed the door to the backyard. Concern etched his beautiful features and deepened the blue of his eyes. "Is everything okay?"

"Oh, yeah. It's fine." Digging . . . digging for any excuse. "I just know that this call will take a while. I would be more comfortable at home. That's all." Okay. That's out. And I didn't lie. Mom can typically bend my ear for an hour if she has something on her mind.

"I understand." Greyson's disappointment was clearly written on his face. He lifted his keys from a tray on the counter.

"I'm sorry." I really was. I was sorry that I was making lame excuses to probably the best man that I had ever met.

"It's okay," he said. "We'll do this another time."

"Sure." I smiled weakly.

He took me home. It was a silent and depressing drive. He opened the door to the truck for me every time. We quietly exchanged goodbyes. Behind the closed door to my house, I shook my head. What was I doing?

I called Mom. She had a question about a sweater I bought. That was all. Nothing more. A five-minute conversation about a sweater. Brother.

Too stirred, I called Annie. "Hey, do you have a minute?"

"Sure. What's up?" Annie asked. Mindy was singing a song in the background.

"I think I may have blown it."

"With what?" Annie paused.

I blew out a breath.

Annie filled in the blank. "Would it have to do with a guy?"

"Yes."

"What's wrong?"

"Nothing. That's what's wrong. I'm completely freaked out."

Annie smiled behind the phone. "That sounds like you." She laughed. "So, what's he like?"

"He's a contractor . . . and a marine. He takes care of his little sister. He's the one that attacked Isaac's friend the night of the break in."

"Your rescuer? Wait. You need to fill me in."

"I met him first at school. But then Rick hired him to fix the house." I poured out every detail about Greyson, even my using Mom's call as an excuse to leave.

"Lindsey, I know you've been through some nutty things. But I also know you. Just like with that ranch . . . remember you were going to sell it. Don't you think you'd be kicking yourself if you were still in Vegas living in your apartment. And think about it, if Isaac's cohorts would have attacked you there. You wouldn't have had anyone rushing in to save you."

Her words hit me hard. "What should I do?"

"Give it some time. Give yourself some time, too."

She was right. I needed to give it all some time.

Until next time . . . Me

August 28ᵗʰ, Saturday

I barely remembered that I had signed up to help at the ward party. Greyson and Elizabeth were both there. I busied myself in the kitchen with several other volunteers. Elizabeth and Sharon both stopped by the kitchen to say hi. I didn't see Greyson until the party was over and the church house was nearly empty.

I was alone in the kitchen when he stepped in.

"Hi." His voice was calm.

My insides twirled. My cheeks flushed. I met his eyes long enough to echo, "Hi." I grabbed a dish cloth and began earnestly wiping down the counters that I had already cleaned.

"Can I help?" Greyson asked with class and masculinity.

I shook my head vigorously. "Where's Elizabeth?" I asked, steering the conversation and thinking she might come to my rescue.

"She rode home with Sharon." He stepped closer, picked up a towel and dried a wet bowl that I had left on the counter.

"Oh." I was stuck. I prayed he would not come closer and melt my carefully crafted barriers. He had already wadded up my insides into a sticky glob of happiness, romance, and terror.

He stacked the bowl with others of its kind. I avoided looking at him.

With a nod of his head he declared, "Well, I guess I had better go. Good to see you."

"Yeah, you too," I answered like an automaton. I scrubbed the counters with more vigor. I was a fool.

As if reading my last thought, Sister VanDamm walked into the kitchen. "If I were you, I would grab on to that boy with both hands." She was known for speaking her mind.

I smiled, rinsing the dish rag. I changed the subject. "Well, I think it's all finished. I am going to go home." I stifled a yawn.

Sister VanDamm was not finished. "You know, I was really close to Greyson and Elizabeth's parents. Great people. I think all of us, especially in the ward, are still in mourning." She looked at me to make sure I was listening. "I bet that boy could use a shoulder to lean on. Or an ear for his troubles."

I nodded, feeling obligated to respond.

Like she was a messenger on a mission, she pointed a washed serving spoon at me and said, "You might want to offer to hear his story." With her duty completed, she left the room.

I drove home with my thoughts to keep me company.

I sat on my bed for a full forty minutes with my phone in my hand. I stared up at the ceiling. I glanced toward the closet. Memories of Friday's dinner played in and out of my head. I should call him. Maybe it would quiet my worries if I did? I could say that he had said that he wanted to show me the backyard. I could tell Greyson that I was ready for that tour. What was I afraid of? I had it narrowed down to two items: I was afraid of being hurt, and I was afraid of making another mistake. I don't think either of these ideas are earth shattering. Given my past, I am choosing to be cautious . . . I think?

I tossed my phone on the rug.

Maybe tomorrow will be easier . . . Me

September 10th, Friday

I am sorry, posterity, for neglecting you for so long. Things have been out of control. I will sum it all up to get us current.

Last weekend I went to Las Vegas. Deputy Jade had some reports to finish and wanted me there. Sentencing was passed on my two attackers. They will be in prison for some time. Isaac will see the great outdoors again before either of them do.

Last Wednesday, I saw Elizabeth in the hallway at school on her way to class. It was after lunch. She smiled and waved. I waved in return. I turned to go into my classroom when I spied the two girls from summer school tailing her. My teacher sense tingled. Since it was my prep period, I sprang into action. I scrambled through the busy hallway, trying to close the gap between them and me. As Elizabeth stepped into the doorway of her class, the other two girls pounced. Grabbing onto Elizabeth's backpack, they yanked her back into the hall. "Let go," she shouted. Taking her wrists, the girls stood on either side of her. Elizabeth struggled to break free.

"Hey," I shouted, "what are you doing?"

Elizabeth's eyes were as big as the windows in my classroom.

The two girls dropped her wrists and ran.

"Are you okay?" I asked, jogging up to Elizabeth.

"Yes." Her whisper was barely audible as her eyes filled with tears.

"Come on." We walked together back to the main hall. Looking at Elizabeth, so frightened, I asked, "Would you like to call Greyson? You don't have to go back to class."

She nodded with tears escaping from her eyes. I walked with her to the office where she called.

I watched as she used the phone. I felt so responsible for her safely. "Is he coming?" I asked as she hung up the office phone.

She nodded then she threw her arms around me in a ferocious hug. I tentatively touched her back. I motioned her to one of the upholstered chairs in the office. She sat quietly, clutching her backpack.

I visited with the vice principal while Elizabeth waited on the chair. He asked Elizabeth to write a description of the events. As she worked, I busied myself, checking my box for mail. I didn't want to hover, but I wanted to know she was cared for. I grabbed two boxes of pencils from the supply room. I checked my calendar on my phone. I was beginning to understand just a small fraction of what Greyson must feel in regard to looking after Elizabeth.

Elizabeth handed her report to Mr. Kelly. I sat beside her.

Greyson must have been working close by. He arrived sooner than I expected. Rushing through the main doors, he hurried to Elizabeth. Our eyes met for only a tenth of a second. I stepped to the side and let them talk. Mr. Kelly approached and handled things. It was his job.

With Greyson there, and feeling like some kind of broken third wheel, I slipped out and went back to class. I had a lot of work waiting on my desk and prep time is a precious commodity.

I fought to focus on my work. My thoughts kept returning to Elizabeth and Greyson . . . and Greyson again. He had barely even looked at me.

That sums up Wednesday.

Thursday and Friday, the workday seemed to drag. All my students were glassy-eyed and checked out. It had to be the heat. The poor swamp coolers in the school are not doing much to cut through it.

Elizabeth has a new routine. She comes by my class each day at the same time just long enough to say hi.

I have watched her in the hall. She is holding her head high and keeping herself surrounded with kind kids. What a good kid. Why do others have to make life miserable sometimes?

I stayed late on Friday. Not so late that the sun went down. I have learned my lesson on that one. Having survived my week, I stopped at Mrs. B's Fast Food for a Friday night victory dinner.

It's funny how each time I stop, some kind of calamity happens.

Halfway home, my back passenger tire blew. My dash lit up with warnings. I hobbled the car to the side of the road. Parked in the gravel, I looked around. Sage brush, rabbit brush, and a couple of juniper trees were all that surrounded me. No service stations. Not one. Perfect.

I quickly searched for a video on how to change a tire, eating fries from my to-go bag. I was just learning how to remove the lug nuts when a vehicle pulled behind me and stopped.

I don't know what the odds are. I was never very good with statistics, but it was Greyson. I got out of my car and stood beside it. Before he could open his door, two other vehicles pulled over as well. (I love living in a small town.) Greyson, one grizzled cowboy, and one mom with three kids, all converged at my car. Conversations bubbled all around. Greyson got the jack into place. The cowboy took care of the lug nuts. The mom handed out juice boxes to everyone and refereed her children. She was the first to leave.

Greyson hefted the flat tire into my trunk as the cowboy tightened those lug nuts around the, as he called it, donut.

"You jes' watch yerself around those bends. That donut'll do the job if you don't take 'er too fast."

The cowboy was the second to leave. Greyson, having closed the trunk, attempted to brush tire grime from his hands and made no motion to leave.

"Thanks," I said softly. I set my empty juice box in the car.

He shook his head, deflecting any praise. "It was a team effort."

I turned to my car door. I could drive away. Greyson stood facing me, but I was not facing him. Sister VanDamm popped into my head. I spotted my bag of dinner. Bending in, I grabbed the bag. Extending it to Greyson I said, "A small offering, in gratitude for your assistance . . . But I did eat some of the fries."

Greyson laughed. A pleasant sound. "No . . . but thank you. I have a date."

My smile did not falter. I held the bag steady, but something on the inside wilted at his words. *A date?* Why should that bother me?

"Oh." I quickly bounced back. Stretching my arm toward him again, I asserted, "Well, you could share with your date."

Greyson laughed again. "And spoil Elizabeth's Cooks' Experiment?"

Duh . . . It's Friday. Elizabeth is his date. I could kick myself.

"An appetizer then . . ." I tried.

My heart quivered as Greyson took my extended hand, bag and all, in his. Lowering my arm, we stood facing one another. The earth stopped on its axis. The setting sun burned warm on my skin. I was powerless to remove my hand from his.

Another car raced past us. The moment burst. (Good grief. First, nothing but brush and junipers. Now, four cars in less than twenty minutes.)

I dropped the bag into the dirt. Greyson bent and grabbed it. He had it before I even reacted. He stepped closer. Though we were not touching, I swear I could feel him breathe. He lowered his face. With waves crashing and fireworks blasting inside me, I met his eyes. We each seemed to weigh the consequences of our closeness on our own terms.

Then, I did it. I stepped away because I was afraid. I had been through too much. I wasn't ready for this. My insides tore and unraveled.

As casual as ordering french fries, I said, "I wonder how much rain it gets out here."

Greyson searched my face, not taking his eyes off of me.

I looked away. I tried another topic. "It was nice how everyone stopped to help."

That got him.

He looked across the horizon toward the setting sun. "Yeah, there are a lot of good people out here." He didn't take in the sunset for very long. Turning his face, he held my gaze with his.

Those eyes, deep and tumbling. My greatest weakness. I wonder what he thinks of me? I turned, breaking the spell. "Well, I better take my burger and go then."

I reached out my hand to take the burger back, but Greyson did not surrender the bag. Holding it at his side, he spoke, his voice low, almost a whisper. It tickled the hairs on my neck.

"Will you come and eat with us?"

I was quick with a flippant reply. "Thank you, I appreciate the offer, but since you don't need it, I am committed to that burger."

"Lindsey . . ."

"Yes?" I inched imperceptibly away. My walls were crumbling. I could feel it.

A silence, like the setting of the sun, descended over us as he paused. When he spoke, the words were soft like a breeze, ruffling my insecurities. "I appreciate all that you have done for Elizabeth. Those two girls used to be her best friends. Then out of the blue they turned on her. Thank you for going out of your way to protect her."

His praise caused the color in my cheeks to rise. I smiled and gave a little nod. He was winning. My pulse rate quickened. The scenery around us faded to a blur. All I could see was Greyson.

Greyson exhaled, lowered his eyes and then raised them slowly before speaking, "I want to ask you something."

I studied him. I was caught. Trapped. Heart hammering.

"I was wondering . . ." He looked away shyly then back again. "I was wondering if you would go out with me."

My heart exploded. I had absolutely fallen. Every signal in my mind and heart confirmed it.

But I couldn't. I can't go through this. I can't. I turned and pointed my eyes on the western hills. I couldn't get involved any deeper. What if it ended the same as last time?

Greyson stepped toward me. "I would like to take you to dinner." A pause. I didn't respond. Then, he added. "I was planning to call you this evening, but this is better. I mean, seeing you in person." He gave an embarrassed laugh. "Not the flat tire."

I wished it would have been only the juice lady to come to my rescue. Things would have been far less complicated. With my eyes still looking toward the western horizon, Greyson crossed in front of me, catching my gaze before finishing his question. "Will you have dinner with me tomorrow night? No Cooks' Experiment. We will have someone else do the cooking." He searched my face.

I had been asked out by flirtatious boys. I had been asked out by scoundrels. I had been asked out by brotherly types and shy boys. This was the first time I had ever been asked out by someone with so much sincerity. It was beautifully alarming. I wanted so badly to reach up and trace the lines of his mouth. To touch his face. I couldn't trust myself to be rational. I willed myself to firmness. I would *not* succumb to my emotions and give in to his request. Yet, I couldn't breathe. My feelings for him swam the tempestuous currents of my fears and my resolve to not get involved.

I willed it, and fear and resolve won.

Reaching for my burger bag, I dully replied. "I can't."

Greyson didn't surrender the bag. I quickly snatched it from his hands and dropped myself into the driver's seat of my car. Shoving the key into the ignition I hesitated, a love-stricken paralysis momentarily took over. Unable to turn the key and drive away, I was stuck, sorting through my jumbled web of feelings. Pulling my fears and resolute decision back to the surface, I snuffed out any romance. With a deep breath, I started my car.

Greyson leaned down, resting his hand on the edge of the open window. His heavenly eyes were warm and alert. On his hand I saw the black smudges left by my tire. Threads of agony tugged at my heart. He had done so much for me.

Fear spoke: What did it matter? There was no obligation for either of us to pursue this relationship anymore.

"Lindsey . . ." he started.

The hum of the engine cut him off. I met his eyes in an attempt to share some part of what I was going through. I don't know if he could read the struggle in my face. "Greyson, I can't," I whispered painfully.

"Lindsey, wait," He pleaded.

I pulled the car into gear and rolled forward as the tears came. Greyson watched me leave.

Now, as I sit here in my big house with my cold, mangled burger, I'm a mess. Emotionally. Stress-fully. (If that's a word. I can vouch that it *is* a feeling.) What is wrong with me? Why do I do the things I do? He is the kind of man a girl dreams up. He is honorable, noble, a gentleman, and kind. Again, what is wrong with me?

The burger hit the trash. I cried a few tears that refused to stay in my eyes.

Burdened with stupidness . . . Me

September 11th, Saturday

I received a phone call from one of the ranchers that lease the mountain property for their cattle, Gavin Burd. He called to tell me that some of his cattle had wandered onto private property because the fence posts that secure the gate had broken. He also informed me that he was in California . . . and could I please drive up there and replace the posts, so that the cows stay inside the fence.

What?

Cows . . . fence . . .?

This was definitely way beyond my skill level and comfort zone. I called Rick with an S.O.S. before I committed to anything.

"HI, Rick, Gavin Burd just called and told me that there are a couple of broken fence posts on the mountain and his cows are getting out."

"Sounds like there are some fences to mend." He chuckled at the remark. "I kind of have a strong suspicion that you just might want my help with that process? Because, that's what I'm here for."

Humbled, I hastily replied, "Yes. Could we go up there today? I've never seen that part of the property. I would like to see it if you don't mind that I tag along. Would I need a truck, or can my car go up there? Do you have time?"

"Let me take care of some things. We'll get it fixed . . . most likely today." Rick spit a few shells, the sound was so familiar.

"Okay. Thanks, Rick. Just call me when you're ready. I will call Gavin and let him know."

"Yep. Will do."

An hour later, the doorbell rang. I didn't jump this time. It was odd for Rick to ring the bell. He usually came in through the kitchen.

That should have been my first clue that a conspiracy was afoot.

Dressed in jeans, a yellow Pikachu t-shirt that was a white elephant gift from Susy two Christmases ago, and red Converse sneakers, I swung the door wide.

Standing on the porch was Greyson, looking everything like a cover of an *Outdoor Living* magazine. I caught myself before my thoughts entangled any deeper. My insides swirled.

Why was he standing on my porch?

"Hi," Greyson spoke first.

"Hi." I paused, wondering why he was at my door. Greyson said nothing, so I asked, "Can I help you with something?" I scrutinized his expression. He looked delighted about something.

"Are you ready?" Greyson asked with an easy smile. I had no clue what he was talking about.

"Ready? Ready for what?"

Greyson was unruffled. "To fix the fence . . . Rick said you would be ready. Didn't he . . ." The happy expression on Greyson's face fell as new light dawned. It was evident that we both arrived at the same conclusion, at the same time. We had been bamboozled. Rick set us up. Just for that, I am withholding all sunflower seeds from his Christmas present.

"I was expecting Rick," I said lamely.

"Yeah, I can see that . . . now." The air between us cooled significantly. Greyson cast a glance over his shoulder back toward his truck. "Well . . ." He shrugged and pointed toward his truck. "I have cedar posts in my truck." His tone was all business. Any traces of fun evaporated under the realization that he was here on Rick's account and not mine.

"Did you have to go all the way into town and back?" I worried. I hated to be any more indebted to him than I already was.

"No. I had these as leftovers from a job a few weeks back. In fact, I almost burned them, thinking I would never use them." He stood tall, almost as though he were standing at attention but more relaxed.

"Greyson," I recovered, "you don't have to do this. I'm sure you can think of a thousand things you would rather be doing right now. I don't want to put you out." I could think of a million things that I would rather do than get filthy repairing a fence that is technically the property of the cattle rancher.

Greyson surprised me when he answered, "You're not putting me out." His eyes found mine. Those eyes. I turned away.

Rick was going to hear from me about this. He had no right to send Greyson to my house. This is so awkward. "What about Elizabeth?"

"She's with Sharon." He visibly stiffened. "Look. Lindsey." I loved it when he said my name. "I am ready to go and get this job done, if you're okay with it being me here instead of Rick. He said you wanted to take a look at the property . . . and if you don't want to ride with me, that's okay, too. You could follow in your truck." He paused for a breath then added, "If you have changed your mind altogether, I can go alone and take care of it." He hung his arms coolly at his sides then shrugged. "It is up to you. I have the posts in the back of my truck with my tools. Rick said we were taking your truck, but it's obvious he said none of this to you."

My head swam. "My truck?"

Greyson exhaled, turned slightly, and turned back again. "Look, Lindsey, I don't want to force you to spend time with me. You have your reasons, and I respect that. It's your call. Whatever you want to do. Either way . . . I think we had better get that fence back in working order." The muscles in his jaw tightened. He looked away briefly then locked his eyes forcefully on me.

I wanted to stand there and stare at him, to study his expression and ponder his reasons for being so willing to help me.

So, I asked. "Why would you do this for me?"

Greyson raised, then dropped, his arms to his sides. The muscles in his face relaxed. "I want to help you. And . . . if when I'm finished you want me to disappear, I won't bother you anymore." He searched my face for understanding.

I gave a little nod. His message was clear. I weighed it conscientiously. "I will go with you." It had to be the right thing to do, didn't it? I still needed to learn about this property. I waved my arm in the general direction of the garage and muttered, "We can take my truck. I need to learn how to drive it, anyway."

Greyson's eyes sparkled.

"What do I need to do?" I asked. "I am admittedly pathetic when it comes to knowing anything about repairing a fence."

"I will get things transferred into your truck if you could just open the garage for me."

"Sure." I grabbed my keys off the coffee table and punched the garage door button. I followed Greyson into the garage.

"Wow, that really is a nice truck," Greyson commented as the big door rolled open. He walked to the truck and rested his hands on the tailgate. "Let me know if you ever decide to sell it."

I stood there like a helpless child. "I haven't even started it."

"We'll take care of that today. I'll get everything loaded, but we'd better get on the road. It'll take us a while to get there, and depending on what kind of damage there is to the fence, we'll probably need every minute of daylight. Go ahead and grab whatever you want to bring with you. I will get everything loaded." Greyson spun and walked swiftly to his truck.

I nodded and turned to go into the house. Taking the two steps, I stopped at the door leading into the kitchen. Greyson was back in a flash with cedar fencing posts slung over his shoulder.

I dumbly asked, "What should I bring?"

I listened as Greyson rattled off a list of possible mountain supplies. It was a long list. I zeroed in on ". . . water bottle, snacks, and a jacket." Got it. I turned.

I grabbed a jacket and a water bottle. I put them into the truck. I retreated into the house to grab my purse, and I fired off a text to Rick:

Hey, I thought you said you were coming over.

He replied:

You'll thank me someday :)

As I stepped back into the garage, Greyson was tying everything down. He had the tools and a cooler all loaded.

He opened the driver's side door and stepped back for me to get in.

"Are you sure you want me to drive?" I balked.

"It's your truck." Greyson caressed my face with his eyes, at least, I thought so. That's how it felt with his eyes on me. Then he cleared his throat like a schoolboy. My insides hopped. I put them in check. This was not a picnic. This was business.

The black leather interior was nice. The chrome trim gleamed. I checked my shoes. The last thing I wanted to do was to track dirt into the truck. Looking at Greyson, I announced, "I don't know how to get to the property."

Greyson pulled a paper from his back pocket. "I'll guide you." He took his seat on the passenger's side.

A shiver of excitement raced up my spine as I closed my door. "Okay." I turned the ignition. Thankfully, the neglected truck roared to life. Checking my mirrors, I backed slowly out of the garage. I felt like I was driving from the top of a camel. It was so much higher than my car. I steered onto the gravel road. I felt like I was creating my own lane in the middle of the road. I drove us past Rick's house and out onto the main road that leads back to town. An approaching car unsettled me. From this angle, I was certain I was hogging the entire road. I quickly pulled off onto the right shoulder.

"Are you okay?" Greyson asked nervously.

"Yes." I looked at him sheepishly. "Will you drive? I'm afraid I am going to run someone off of the road in this big thing." I unclipped my seatbelt.

"Sure," he calmly replied.

We swapped seats and drove east through Cedar City and on up the canyon. The road was winding and steep. I turned on my favorite playlist, and we drove the distance without talking.

After what felt like an hour, Greyson turned onto a dirt road and we drove south across the mountain. Two more turns, and we were making dust clouds on a road that was only marked by the tire tracks that were worn into the vegetation. Greyson stopped once to consult the directions he had received from Rick. Lastly, we bounced down a rutted path to the obviously broken gate.

A broken fence post jutted out of the ground, looking like some prehistoric animal had chomped off the top half of it. The top half of the post was strewn on the ground beside it. A brown metal gate lay flat on the ground. What a mess.

Greyson turned off the truck. "Looks like the cows must have pushed their way out. Must have been chasing the greener grass on the other side." He gave a short laugh.

"It's a mess," I said. "Stinking cows."

Greyson was optimistic. "This won't be too bad to fix." He pointed at the view before us. "It's only one broken post, and the gate looks like it is in fairly good shape. It shouldn't take more that an hour to fix." Looking at me, he asked, "Do you want to eat first?"

Looking around, I regretted my shoe choice. My red Converse sneakers were going to be covered in mud. There was no way I was going to tell Greyson that I didn't want to spoil my shoes.

Greyson was still looking at me. I only vaguely remembered that he had asked me a question. I was embarrassed to admit it, but I said, "Actually, I could use a restroom." There was some kind of poetic justice to my plight. I bet I had said the words *you should have gone before we left* to students a thousand times. Now it was my turn. Blast.

Greyson smiled. "Well, you've got a lot of options."

Surprised, I asked, "What do you mean?"

Pointing, he explained, "Pick a tree."

"I see." Not quite what I was hoping for. I hesitated. "What about porcupines? Are there any of those around here?"

His eyes teased. "Yes, but I think you'll be fairly safe."

"I don't know. I remember what happened to *Old Yeller*."

"Old Yeller?" His gaze was quizzical.

"Yeah, the dog. He got a face full of porcupine. I don't want that to happen to me."

"Fair enough . . ." Greyson nodded, seeming to digest my confessed concern. Fully turning to face me he said, ". . . I really think you will be okay." His face softened as though he were talking to a child.

"Just the same," I retorted, "I think I'd rather wait. I'll go when we get back. Maybe we should just get the fence fixed."

"Okay by me." Greyson climbed out, unloaded tools, and a cedar post. I followed behind him, praying I wouldn't make a complete fool of myself.

Stepping from plant to plant, I watched at Greyson dug and tugged at the broken post. Finally, the post gave up the fight. Greyson had won. Using a shovel, Greyson prepared the ground for the new post. He grabbed a long metal bar. He looked at me and extended the bar. "Have you ever used one of these? It's a dig bar."

A what? I shook my head vigorously. I wasn't about to tell him that I had never even held a shovel in my hands until I had taken the ranch. "Tools and I are mostly strangers," I admitted.

"Grab those gloves off the back seat, and I'll show you."

I weighed my choices carefully. Help Greyson. Stand potentially very close to him. Cover my shoes with mud. Or . . . Stay put and watch him do all the work. Responsibility kicked in. This was my property. My broken gate. My problem.

I met his eyes. Snatching the gloves from the tailgate, I stepped purposefully into the wet mud. I could do this.

The work was exhausting. My shoulder muscles screamed, but I enjoyed it. The dig bar was impossibly heavy, but it did an outstanding job of busting up hard soil. Once the post was in, we pulled the gate back into place. Mud streaked my jeans, to say nothing of my shoes. Then we set the gate on brand new hinges that Greyson provided.

When it was finished, I patted the gate and spoke authoritatively to the air, "Okay, cows, do your worst."

Greyson looked at me like I was a nut, but he smiled so sweetly that it was all worth it.

I helped Greyson load up the tools. He pulled a cooler between us as we sat on the tailgate. Opening it, he invited, "Take your pick."

"Thank you. Really." I was humbled by his thoughtfulness. He gave up his day, his tools, and he made us sandwiches. I didn't even think about sandwiches, or tools, or how far away this piece of land really is. Even though it technically belongs to me, I can't say that I would have made any effort to find this place if Gavin Burd hadn't called.

Greyson spoke between bites, "So, what is it like inheriting all of this?"

Swallowing, I answered honestly. "It's overwhelming." Scanning the trees, I said, "It feels like I am living someone else's life. That probably doesn't make any sense." I swung my legs and picked up a slice of tomato that fell from my sandwich and landed on the tailgate. I tossed it into a bush.

Greyson nodded. "Actually, that makes a lot of sense."

Nibbling a bite and swallowing, I decided to take a stab at Sister VanDamm's advice. "What about you? What's *your* story?"

A look of surprise registered on Greyson's face. With eyebrows raised, he studied me. "My story?"

"Yes. Rick told me about you and Elizabeth and your parents, but I would like to know about you, from you, if you'd like to share." My heart hammered. The cooler between us gave me courage. Social distancing at its finest.

Swallowing his last bite of sandwich, he nodded. "I get it. Just one condition . . ." his eyes found mine, "you tell me your story, as well."

"Okay . . . I guess?" I took a sip from my water bottle in an effort to hide my nervousness. I'll just share the boring, obvious details of my story. My life. Nothing more.

Greyson wiped at his mouth with a napkin before he began. "I thought I had my life all planned out. I thought I had calculated every last detail of where I was heading and what life would hold for me. Then, I got the news about my parents."

Twisting my water bottle in my hands, I asked. "What were you doing at the time?"

"I had a great job with the military."

"Marines?"

"Yes." He raised his eyebrows.

"Rick told me."

A nod. "I had just finished an assignment overseas. I was on schedule to re-up my contract when I got the news."

"Re-up?" I took another tiny sip of water. "What does that mean?"

"It means it was time for me to sign a new contract." Greyson wadded the plastic wrap from his sandwich and dropped it into the cooler.

I nodded, trying to understand.

"Every plan I had made unraveled right in front of me. I left my job and took over Dad's business. I know if he were here, he would have counseled me to stay in the military and pursue my career. To be fair, I considered it. Long and hard." Greyson gazed off into the distance. "But, I couldn't uproot Elizabeth. She had to come first. She needed stability that a military career couldn't offer. I would have bounced her all over the world."

"That must have been very difficult . . ." I wonder if I could have given up my personal ambitions the way that Greyson did? I don't know.

He tossed me a half smile. "I moved home. It definitely hasn't been easy, and Elizabeth and I have had our share of arguments." Greyson stretched tall and raked his hands through his short hair.

"You took over your dad's work?" I squinted at the sun.

"Yes. I had to. He had worked his whole life to establish a solid reputation. I'd worked with him off and on through most of growing up years. Even when I was a little kid, he would sometimes take me on jobs. He taught me a lot. Most importantly, he taught me honesty. He taught me that people are more important than money. He was a great man. Fortunately, he was also a very organized bookkeeper. I was able to step in and pick things up and work forward. A lot of his contracts were with people who had scraped and saved to get some things done at their homes. I couldn't feel right about abandoning them and leaving them with a half-finished job. So, that was where I started. I completed all his contracts."

"Now you do your own contracts?"

"I'm learning the ropes." He smiled at my interest.

"What about the military? Do you think you'll ever go back, I mean, once Elizabeth is raised?"

"I do think about it." Greyson took a long drink. "Actually, I'm still a marine."

"You are?"

"I signed into the reserves. This keeps me involved but gives me time to be home to take care of Elizabeth. The only downside is that I have to miss church on those weeks."

"Can I just say, you are doing a wonderful job. With her, I mean . . ."

Greyson shook his head, "Oh, yeah . . . like telling off teachers . . ."
I laughed.

His eyes caught mine and sparkled. He laughed.

". . . something like that . . ." I grinned.

He shook his head. "You've been generous, but I promise you that I haven't forgotten. I am full of shame for what I said to you. I'm so sorry . . ."

Shaking my head, I quickly turned the conversation. I had enough shame in my own behavior on that memorable day, and I didn't want to dig it up right now. "What does Elizabeth do when you leave town?"

Greyson took the bait. "Lori is a lifesaver. When I have drill, Elizabeth stays at their place. In fact, that Sunday when she brought you the cookies, I had just gotten home."

"I remember that day. It was sweet of Lori. They are wonderful people." I fully agreed.

Greyson jumped off the tailgate and stretched. He offered me his hand. I took it and slid onto the ground.

"Let's walk a little." He lightly held my fingers in his. Surprisingly, I let him. I stared at our hands for a brief second. I didn't know if it meant anything. Maybe he was just being polite and helping his klutzy neighbor to stand. I don't know, but I do know that butterflies waltzed to an enchanting tune in me, and I liked it. Yikes!

However, in spite of the beautiful moment, the motion of standing up hit me with the harsh reality that I still needed to go. I really needed to go. I hated to break the mood. I confessed my plight. "I think I had better brave the porcupines."

Greyson handed me a ziplock bag with toilet paper, wet wipes, and hand sanitizer. "Pick your tree." He motioned with an outstretched arm.

Red faced, I walked into the trees at the head of the truck. I walked until the truck was no longer visible. Greyson promised that he'd look the other way, and I believed him. I just wanted to be a good distance away. And I didn't want to get lost. That would be just my luck.

I found Greyson still facing the opposite direction as I tramped through the woods back to the truck. With pink cheeks, I returned his supplies, minus what I had used. I was surprised when he reached out his hand again and took mine. I was again surprised how I didn't hesitate to take his.

"Lindsey, I want you to be honest with me. You didn't want to come with me today, did you?"

I squirmed under his bluntness. Biting my bottom lip, I had to respond honestly. "I was expecting Rick."

Greyson adjusted his grip on my hand but held on. "But you didn't want to come . . . with me . . . I mean?"

I lowered my eyes. "I wasn't eager to come."

He bobbed his head with understanding then looked to the tops of the trees. Taking in a long breath, he said, "If I were more courageous, I'd ask why, but I'm not sure I want to know that answer." He teased me with a grin.

I quickly followed up my last statement. I felt I needed to. ". . . but I'm glad I came." I met his eyes.

Greyson visibly relaxed. "Me too." He gently squeezed my hand.

I smiled shyly. Warmth tickled me from head to toe.

We walked a short distance when Greyson let go of my hand momentarily, then laced his fingers with mine. I could have walked on like that through all eternity. We had only gone a few steps, with his hand laced in mine, when he suddenly stopped. He faced me. Greyson asked me to share my story. My story . . . I told him about my family. I told him about my work.

"So, you're the only daughter of your two parents?" Greyson mulled it over.

"Yes. I'm the only child."

"Was that ever awkward?"

"Only at back-to-school night. Teachers would meet my parents, look at me, and try to understand the genetics behind my appearances." I laughed at the memories.

"Well," Greyson paused. Facing me, he softly said, ". . . you're beautiful. Stunning."

I blushed but smiled. The compliment was warm and sincere. I wanted to fall into his eyes. We walked on.

"You never knew you father?"

"No." A bird fluttered across our path. I jumped.

"You okay?" Greyson asked with just the hint of a smirk on his lips.

"Yes," I stammered, embarrassed.

"You haven't spent much time outdoors, have you?"

"Is it that obvious?" I laughed at myself.

We crossed a meadow to a look-off point. The valley stretched out beyond us. A breeze swept up the mountain, causing me to shiver.

Greyson released my hand and instinctively wrapped his arm around me. I felt so safe under his touch. I leaned into him, loving his warmth. Greyson seemed to catch himself and lowered his arm. He said politely, "We had better get back."

"Okay." I said, feeling disappointed.

Hand in hand we made our way back to the truck. Maybe the mountains were casting a spell? Once we got back, the spell would be broken.

Greyson insisted that I drive. "You'll get the hang of it," he assured, holding the door for me.

"What if I run somebody off the road?" I squirmed.

"I won't let you do that. Just take it slow on the downhill turns."

"Okay."

With a death-like grip on the wheel, I followed Greyson's directions all the way down the mountain.

Too soon we were back. The sun was down, and the automatic lights on my home welcomed us.

Greyson convinced me that after driving down the mountain, pulling the truck into the garage would be easy. He was mostly right. I hit the rack of garden tools and knocked them over.

He laughed as we stood things back up, "Maybe we can put some bumpers on this rack. Then you could run into it all you want."

"Hey . . ." I scolded him with my eyes.

He smiled from his chin to his hair.

We lingered in the garage for a moment. He talked about some of his work. I told him about my students. It was so easy to fall into the circle of his warmth. He kept his distance . . . a little aloof. We didn't touch hands, yet lightning crackled between us . . . or was it just crackling for me? Where were my carefully crafted barriers now? The mountain must still be casting its spell in me. I wondered if Greyson felt it?

He must have felt something. He appeared to be wrestling with thoughts on his mind. He looked down. He took a step toward me, then stepped back. He met my eyes.

Drawing in a deep breath, he spoke, "Lindsey, I have really enjoyed our time together." My heart thundered.

"Me too," I quickly chimed, ". . . today, the horse ride, and the Cooks' Experiment Nights."

"Wait? What? Really?" Greyson's astonishment surprised me. I thought it was evident that I had enjoyed those evenings. "I'm glad to hear it. I wasn't sure what you thought, especially about our corny tradition."

"Are you kidding? I think it's brilliant. I do have a question, though."

"Shoot."

"Whose idea was the note?"

"The note?" Light dawned. "The one we stuck in your door . . ." Greyson grinned, lighting up his eyes. "That was Elizabeth."

"Mmm, so you didn't really want me to come that night?"

"Touché," he smiled, opening his hands in a gesture of surrender, "I was a little apprehensive, that's all."

"Uh huh . . ." I smiled back with just a hint of sarcasm then dusted a streak of dried mud off my jeans.

Greyson softly reached and took my dusty hand in his, carefully wrapping my fingers with his. With his free hand he gently touched my cheek. I lowered my eyes. His fingers were warm and strong. Then he took both my hands in his.

With his voice barely above a whisper, he asked, "Then why did you run away?" His question made a little tear in my heart. It was the same question I had asked myself a thousand times.

I inhaled slowly, as if breathing would stack all my anxieties and fears into neatly organized little packages that I could address one at a time. Letting go, our hands dropped. I took a step away and turned. With my eyes to the wall, I did my best to explain.

"You may have noticed that I don't have the best history with relationships."

Greyson listened without comment.

"I've had my priorities all twisted up." I shifted uncomfortably. "I thought I had it all planned out for a perfect life. Then, I get a phone call. One thing unfolds to another, my fiancé goes to prison, and in the process is engaged to someone else . . . I guess I'm just scared—just scared I'll mess up again."

I turned to face Greyson again.

We stood, eyes gently meeting. Suddenly an alarm sounded on Greyson's phone. He glanced at it and said wistfully, "Dang . . . I've gotta run." He lifted his hand and traced my face with his fingertips. I leaned into his touch, disappointed that the night had to end.

We hurried to unload the extra posts and the tools from my truck and put them into Greyson's truck. Standing in the cool night air, I watched as Greyson strapped things down in the bed of his truck.

"Thank you, again, for your help today," I said, feeling like the magic had slipped away. "I can write you a check . . ."

In a flash, Greyson closed the distance between us. Pulling me tightly into his arms, he lowered his face and softly pressed his lips against mine.

Surprise, resistance, and fear all dissipated into the night. Waves crashed. Lightning sparked. Wrapping my arms around his neck, I kissed him back.

Pulling back, he touched my face. I pressed my face against his shoulder, smiling. Greyson scooped me up into a hug, lifting my feet off the ground. "Lindsey, I don't want a check."

Setting my feet back down, he gently took my face into his hands. I held on to his waist. Leaning down, he kissed me once, more soft and sweet.

"Okay . . ." I finally replied, butterflies flipping and skydiving. "I guess I'm safe then to assume that you're not interested only in my money." I smiled warmly.

He playfully shook his head. Another quick hug and he was back in his truck.

With a little wave and a promise to call, he drove down the gravel lane.

Hmmm . . . maybe Rick had been right :)

:) . . . Me.

September 12th, Sunday

Church was fabulous today. Greyson met me in the parking lot. He opened my door. I love chivalry. I stepped out.

Standing beside him, he wrapped one arm tightly around my shoulders, pulled me close, bent, and kissed me sweetly. My butterflies danced on cloud nine. I drank in every drop of the moment and every drop of Greyson.

Elizabeth was already seated when we walked into the chapel. Her face lit up brighter than the overhead lights as I sat between her and her brother . . . with my hand inextricably clasped with his.

Sister VanDamm caught my eye and gave me a smiling nod of approval. I glowed from my head to my funny toes. I could feel it, all tingly and light.

I never knew that love could feel like this.

Smitten . . . Me

September 20ᵗʰ, Monday

Why does the busyness of life have to interfere with the beautiful times?

I have not seen Greyson since Sunday—a week ago.

Between his work and mine, Elizabeth getting the flu, and an impromptu family reunion with my sisters, we have only been able to call. And . . . if anyone was wondering, I kept tight lipped about Greyson with my family. My sisters, and especially my mom, do not need to know anything. Nothing. At least, not until I know where this relationship is going.

But, hey . . . I did get that donut taken care of for my car. And the old cowboy was right about watching my speed. I got in a hurry one day on a curve, and I slid right off the road. Yeah for four tires!

Greyson and I do have a date planned for this coming Thursday. Our first official date. I am *so* happy. We're going to dinner. We chose Thursday so that we didn't interfere with Cooks' Experiment Night.

He has become so much to me. I think about him night and day. I catch myself daydreaming of him right in the middle of lessons. When I lie in bed at night, I just smile and remember every moment with him. I only hope he feels for me, what I feel for him.

Dreaming . . . Me

September 23ʳᵈ, Thursday

For the first time since meeting Greyson, I got dressed up to see him. It's getting cold now, so I bought a new sweater just for tonight and a new pair of shoes. (Closed toe, of course. You know the deal with that.) Besides, I needed to replace my red Converse sneakers. The sticky mountain mud won that battle.

Greyson picked me up at five. He let me know that Elizabeth was thrilled to have the house to herself for the evening, so I didn't need to worry about her.

Holding my hand, he drove us into town. Since I am crazy for Mexican food, he took me to a little place in the center of town. A home all stucco-ed in white, with green and red trim. A kind lady seated us at a corner table.

A man wearing a sombrero played a guitar and sang happy sounding songs in Spanish. Greyson joined in on a couple of verses. I didn't know he could speak Spanish.

"It helps on the job," he explained.

"Did you take Spanish in school?" I asked tracing the edges of a blue cloth napkin with my fingers.

"No." He smiled and sang another line.

"Mission?"

"Not Spanish." He reached across the table, clasped my hand in his and kissed it. My heart soared. "I learned German and a little Czech on my mission."

"Right ... I remember Rick telling me something about that. I'm impressed."

He sang again. His voice was deep and rich. "Then where did you learn Spanish?"

"I picked some up as a kid. My dad was pretty fluent. He would watch TV in Spanish. I also listen to a Spanish radio station. Oh, and I also bought one of those independent study programs online. I practice when I drive back and forth to work. I'm not super fluent, but I can get by with basic conversations and work-related stuff."

"Wow. I am a slouch. I only speak English. Barely ..."

Our food was delivered.

All through dinner I kept wanting to pinch myself. Was this really happening to me?

After we ate, Greyson drove us to an arcade. We battled each other at shooting, racing, and air hockey. I jumped up and down, doing my victory dance when I scored the winning point on the air hockey table. Greyson circled the table, scooped me up, and spun me around. People stared, and we didn't care.

All too soon, it was time to go home, after all, it was a school night. Greyson, ever chivalrous, walked me to my door. "I'm sorry it was just a simple dinner and games ... We'll ..."

"No ..." I cut him off. "It was wonderful. Best night ever."

We both smiled.

Wrapping me tight in his great big arms, he gave me a kiss that left me breathless. Then he bid me good night.

Still smiling ... Me

September 24th, Friday

It is so late, but I am too happy to sleep.

Cooks' Experiment Night included potatoes, hamburger, shredded cheese, green beans, and tomato soup. I was stumped, again. I thought it might be some kind of strange spaghetti, without noodles, and with green beans instead. I was wrong. As usual. Tonight, I was introduced to Shepherd's Pie. It was fabulous.

While the girls watched their movie, Greyson and I walked out into the backyard. I was ready for that tour. The evening air was brisk. Fall is fast approaching. Greyson pulled on a jacket then brought out a denim quilt his mother made. He handed the quilt to me. We sat on a bench and talked.

"What are you thinking about?" he asked, winding one of my curls around his fingers.

"I was thinking about you. I was wondering how you do it, how you manage everything and stay sane." Pulling the blanket up to my chin, I leaned into him.

"You're being kind. It's one day at a time."

"Do you ever miss your full-time job with the military?"

"I can't say that I miss all of it, but there are things that I do miss. I miss the guys I worked with. I miss feeling like I was doing something for the greater good."

"Do you think about going back?"

"I'd be lying if I said no. I do think about it. I thought I might reenlist after Elizabeth finishes school." He let the curl slide out of his hand. Wrapping his arm around my shoulders, he said, "But . . . I struggle with that."

"Can you tell me why?"

"I like what I'm doing here, too. This community is like one big family, and I have been very blessed. From the moment I got the news about my parents, people have bent over backwards. I haven't had one worry about having enough work, or food. We still have meals coming in from our neighbors, and people are always lining me up with work. Just like Rick did with you." He stroked my hair. "I would hate to walk away from all that."

I sat up, "Can I ask you another question?"

"Shoot."

"It's a personal question. And, you can opt out if you want."

Greyson laughed and pulled me close, kissing me on the cheek. "Tonight is a no opt out night."

"Well, I was just wondering about your engagement. Will you tell me about it?"

Greyson sat up to look at me. "You want to hear about my engagement?"

"Well, from you. Rick told me, but I thought it would be better to hear it from you."

Greyson leaned back. "There's not much to say. We met at a dance. Our lives seemed to be moving in the same direction. We thought we knew what we wanted. We jumped into an engagement. Then my parents passed. It was all a little too much for her. We broke things off."

"I'm sorry."

Greyson started, "You're sorry?"

"I know that when you were going through it, it was a lot harder than it sounds. I'm sorry you had to go through that."

Greyson wrapped his arms around my shoulders. "It was worth whatever it took to lead me to you."

As the evening drew on, I found myself hating to have to leave. My heart physically ached. What was this sensation?

With hands clasped, and fingers intertwined, he bid me good night on my front porch.

Was this love? Honestly? Truly? Is it still too soon to tell?

Or am I just being . . . Me?

September 2ᵗʰ, Monday

"Dave wants to meet you," Greyson spoke loudly over the noise of a saw running in the background.

I smiled. A nervous, but exciting, jolt trilled through me. "The nosy, untrustworthy Dave?"

"The very one. He invited us to have dinner at his house tomorrow. I told him that I would ask you."

Being asked to have dinner with Dave felt like a serious step, somehow. Greyson didn't have parents or other siblings I could meet, so meeting Dave felt like meeting family. I wondered if Dave would pass judgment on me for my suitability to be with Greyson? Of course he would. It's what friends do.

"What time?"

"Would six-thirty work for you?"

"You bet."

Okay, world, tomorrow I meet the nosy, untrustworthy, Dave.

Very curious and rather nervous . . . Me

September 28th, Tuesday

I checked my face in the mirror three times before Greyson pulled up the road. I pulled the door open before he had a chance to ring the bell. The sight of him nearly knocked me to my knees. Collared shirt, classy jeans, and eyes that see straight into my soul.

"Hi," I tucked a curl behind my ear, my insides jumping.

"Hi, Lindsey." From where he held it hidden at his side, he produced a vase of white daisies. "I saw these today, and they made me think of you."

"Thank you." My heart swirled and danced to the moon and back again.

Greyson lifted his hands to caress my face. Softly he lowered his face to mine. The kiss that landed was sweet and warm. "Thank you . . . for coming with me tonight."

"My pleasure."

The flowers were left on the kitchen island. Greyson held my hand all the way to Dave's.

The large house was welcoming and warmly decorated. We were rushed through the door with Dave slapping Greyson's back in a noisy bro hug. Greyson turned to me saying, "Dave, this is Lindsey."

"Lindsey," Dave threw his arms wide, "nice to meet you." Dave lunged forward as though he were going to swallow me in a man-eating hug. My eyes flitted nervously to Greyson. Greyson shook his head, rolled his eyes, and smiled. Just before Dave's arms touched me, he halted and said, "Just kidding." He extended his hand. "Hi, Lindsey. It's nice to meet you." He shook my hand stiffly, with a glint in his eye.

From somewhere behind Dave, his wife Jennifer playfully slapped his arm. She reached for me with one arm and pulled me into a hug. "Don't mind him. Welcome, Lindsey."

"What?" Dave threw his hands out in fake consternation.

I melted when Greyson's hand slipped into mine as Jennifer said, "Come on in, the food is hot."

Two blonde-headed children sat at the table. They looked to be about seven. Jennifer introduced Mandy and Matt. "Twins," Jennifer explained.

I caught Dave tossing Greyson a wink. I hoped that was a good thing. Stealing a glance at Greyson, his smile was all the brighter. I took the wink as a good sign.

Jennifer brought plates of food to the table. "Can I help?" I asked quickly.

Her soft brown eyes twinkled. "Come on into the kitchen."

I followed Jennifer. She handed me a basket of hot rolls and a picture of water. Pausing, she touched my arm. "I can't tell you how good it feels having you here."

"Thank you for the invitation. This was really sweet of you to make us dinner."

"Oh, this is nothing. But you, my dear, are something. You have brought a lot of happiness to Greyson." She patted my shoulder, and I took the food to the table with her words warming me more than the hot rolls.

After blessing the food, Dave leaned on his elbows. His eyes made a beeline to mine.

I took a sip of water to divert his gaze, but it didn't work.

Jennifer slapped his arm. "You're embarrassing," she quipped.

Dave leaned back, reaching his arms out, he defended, "I just want to get to know Lindsey."

Greyson nudged my elbow. I turned. He mouthed the word "nosy" dramatically enough for Dave and Jennifer to see.

Jennifer laughed.

Dave donned an expression of mock injury. Then leaning forward again, he met my eyes. "So, Lindsey, tell me everything about yourself that Greyson hasn't shared."

I choked on my water. "What has he told you?" My eyes darted to Greyson who ducked his head with only a hint of pink darkening the tops of his ears.

"Oh, only boring stuff. You're beautiful. You're spunky. You're adventurous. You're patient and kind and blah, blah, blah . . ."

I looked at Greyson, the blush rising in my cheeks, my heart doing a thousand cartwheels.

Dave cleared his throat noisily to draw my attention back to him. With exaggerated movements he nestled his chin into his hands, his eyes burrowing through mine. "Now tell me the dirt. Who is Lindsey Jones? He said you went to court. What's the deal? Do you have a criminal record?" The playfulness was evident in Dave's eyes, but I was struggling to keep up with his questions.

Across the table, Jennifer groaned and rolled her eyes.

I decided to give Dave some *dirt*. With my eyes narrowed and my voice low, I said, "I got a speeding ticket once."

Dave slapped the table. "Hah," he pointed at Greyson, "I bet you didn't know that, did you?"

Greyson laughed and shook his head. "I admit it. I did not know you had a lead foot."

I shrugged and smiled as innocently as I could. "It's only when I'm late to work."

Dave pointed a finger at me. "Now . . ." I braced myself for the next downpour of questions. ". . . tell us all the boring stuff." Dave poked a bite of roll into his mouth.

I shared the "boring stuff" about family, work, and hobbies. All the usual things that are shared when people meet for the first time. I have to say, Dave was an attentive listener.

After sharing enough about myself, I found the words, "Now Dave . . . share some of your dirt," coming out of my mouth. I think Greyson was more than a little surprised.

Dave set his utensils on his plate. He swallowed, took a drink of water, pointed at his wife and said, "It's her fault."

"Oh, here we go again . . ." Jennifer grinned.

Greyson chuckled beside me as though he knew what was coming.

I shook my head. "What?"

Dave spoke up, "She . . ." he said pointing to his wife, ". . . always does better pranks than me."

Jennifer shook her head.

Matt and Mandy ran off to play.

"Better pranks?" I questioned.

"Yeah," Dave continued. "I had to come up with something really good. Something to really surprise her."

"What did you do?" I glanced at Jennifer then back to Dave.

He leaned across the table, and nearly whispering, said, "I had my obituary printed in the paper. Then, I had funeral flowers delivered to her at work."

Jennifer groaned, but the twinkle in her eye was evident across the table.

"I got her good," Dave whispered.

Greyson laughed into the hand over his mouth.

"Yes, he did," Jennifer picked up the story. "I was sitting at my desk when one of those huge funeral displays was brought in by the delivery driver. He set it up on a stand and everything right there by my desk. Well, that caused a stir in the office. But that wasn't enough. He had contacted my cousin, who works with me, and she came running in with a copy of the paper. The whole office went up in commotion."

"Yeah, but you never forgot." Dave winked at me. "Best prank ever."

As the evening wound down, we said our goodbyes to Dave and Jennifer. This time, Dave put his arm around me. He said, "You are welcome here anytime. I'm not sure about that guy you're with, but you're welcome any time."

I loved it.

Greyson walked me to my door. Holding hands, we laughed again over the tales of Dave. Then sobering, Greyson said, "I'll be home Sunday afternoon."

"Stay safe," I wrapped my arms around him. He held me tight.

What a great night . . . Me

October 2ⁿᵈ, Saturday

Susy and Annie have been begging me to do a girl's lunch with them. With Greyson at drill, this was a perfect time. I drove down, and since all the boys had gone fishing, I picked up Mom at her house. Mom started as soon as I stepped through the door. "Lindsey, it's important that you check in. We don't know what you're doing up there in Cedar City."

"I know, Mom. I'm sorry. I've had a lot going on."

"Annie told us all about that boy you're dating. The one who clobbered that bad man. Lindsey, I am all for you dating. I only worry, with you dating someone so aggressive, if you will be happy."

I let Mom say what she needed. Her words tumbled in and out of my ears as I drove to *Italian Noodle*.

We pulled into the parking lot in time to see Susy and Annie arrive with the kids. Taking a big corner booth, all attention was on me.

Our server had to ask twice to get our order. What a distraction my life has become. Fabulous.

"Okay," Susy said, bouncing Michael, "I seem to be the last to know, so tell us about this guy. Come on."

As I talked about Greyson, my heart burned with feelings that are so hard to describe. In my mind's eye all our dates played out. I loved his every movement, his formal manners, his wit, and his humor. And his protective nature. I loved his creativity, his devotion to Elizabeth. I loved how he teases me and seems to know me better than I know myself. There was no way I could put this emotion into words. So, I described how he looks. I told about our dates. It all sounded so two-dimensional compared to the myriad of feelings that swam in my heart.

One thing . . . I did not miss the irony of sitting at my former reception destination and talking about someone so completely different than Isaac. Nor did I overlook how much I had changed. The things I wanted out of life were so different now than from when Isaac and I were dating. All I cared about then were superficial and plastic to what I cared about now.

Greyson had a depth to which I could never find the bottom. Our lives were built on something more than just climbing the ladder of success in our careers. It was disturbingly wonderful.

Mom was very attentive. "We need to meet him." Mom twirled spaghetti on her fork.

"Lindsey," Susy asked, "have you talked about marriage?"

"No."

"That doesn't mean anything," Mom blurted. "You don't have to talk about marriage for it to be right." She raised her fork and I sensed what was coming. "Look at you and Isaac. You certainly talked about marriage." She took a bite of sausage before adding, "And we know how that went."

I think it will be years before Isaac's name fades from the family repertoire.

Annie leaned forward to wipe Alice's face. "Lindsey, if you love him, let him know."

I carried that thought as I drove back home.

The trees in the valley have put on their fall colors. It's a view that never tires me. As I pulled up to the house, I smiled. Tomorrow Greyson will be home, and not only that, I have invited him and Elizabeth over for dinner.

I can't wait.

I checked my phone before I went to bed, though I didn't expect it, Greyson texted:

Lindsey, I wanted to wish you a good night. I'm looking forward to seeing you tomorrow. Greyson

Fallen . . . Me

October 3rd, Sunday

Greyson and Elizabeth arrived punctual, as always. I was ready. I had everything in place. I had watched some good cooking videos to prepare myself for this. I was brave. I was daring.

I made pancakes!

I also made bacon, prepared sliced strawberries, and provided a can of whipped cream. It was to be a meal that legends are made of.

Greyson swept me into his arms when I invited them in. With his hand at the back of my neck, he kissed me, warm and lingering.

"Okay you guys," Elizabeth commanded. "I'm here, remember?" She marched into the kitchen.

Greyson released me slowly. His eyes held mine. My face flushed. Through the rush of emotions, I remembered why I had invited them. Dinner.

We followed Elizabeth to the kitchen.

"These are really good," she gushed as we sat around the table finishing the last bites of the meal.

"And you said you couldn't cook," Greyson chided. "Now we know better."

"No," I corrected, stabbing the last strawberry. "I said I didn't like to cook. I never said I couldn't."

After dinner, we went to work on the dishes. Elizabeth stood beside me and we worked together. It made me happy that she was so at ease in my world.

And then like a plague, my past descended to destroy my happiness. Here's what happened:

Greyson stepped back into the kitchen after kindly taking out the trash. My phone, sitting on the island, chimed. A text message. With my hands up to my wrists in soapy water, and Elizabeth drying and putting things away, I ignored it. Whatever it was, whoever it was, it could wait. The screen illuminated. The chime sounded again.

Greyson picked it up and offered to hand it to me.

I laughed, with my hands dripping, and said, "Go ahead and read it to me. It's probably my mom."

Elizabeth took a plate from my hand and began drying.

Looking over my shoulder, I saw Greyson's expression turn dark. Concerned, I twisted as far as I could without dripping water onto the floor. "What does it say?"

My beautiful happiness shattered.

Greyson read:

> *Hey, Pretty Girl,*
>
> *I've had you on my mind all week. I loved seeing you in Vegas on Saturday. Hope you are coming back soon. Not sure I can make it through the week without your sweet kisses.*

I have never thought of silence as deafening, but there it was. It was as though the room had exhaled all of the air that was in it and replaced it with a heavy dead space. I knew it was Ted. I knew he had obviously mixed up his contacts and sent me a message destined for one of his other girlfriends. I knew all this. And I knew that Greyson, and especially Elizabeth, knew none of this. I was painfully aware of how this message made me look. Not to mention the fact that I had not spent any time with Greyson or Elizabeth on Saturday. They didn't know I was with family all day in St. George . . . but to them, I could just as well have been in Las Vegas "sweetly kissing" Ted.

I turned quickly from the sink, water dripping from my hands. I reached to grab my phone. I wanted to explain, but my words got stuck in my mouth. I felt so stupid.

Elizabeth's eyes were wide and innocently seeking an explanation as I floundered. She, at least I thought, had not yet labeled me as guilty of any unseemly offences.

But Greyson.

Muscles twitched in his neck as his jaw contracted. Lifting his eyes to mine, my heart split for the pain I saw written there. Then, taking the hand towel from off of the island, he placed it in my dripping hands.

"Greyson," I quickly tried to explain, "it's nothing. It's a random text to a wrong number." My words chirped out. Why was I feeling so guilty? I had done nothing wrong . . . well, okay going out with Ted and recklessly flirting with him was wrong, but that was months ago. Why should it haunt me now?

Cool and composed, Greyson turned to me and said, "He is in your contacts. It's not a wrong number."

"I know . . . It is someone I know, but that text isn't for me." It was as though Greyson didn't hear me.

He turned to Elizabeth and said, "We'd better go."

If his words had been daggers, they couldn't have hurt me more. I lowered my eyes. Tears brimmed. Why was it impossible for me to speak? Where were my words? Why couldn't I explain this stupid situation.

Elizabeth threw her arms around me in a quick hug and thanked me for dinner. Greyson left without a word, my heart seizing with each step he took. Elizabeth caught my eyes before she walked out the door and gave me a look that seemed to indicate that she still had faith in me.

Clutching the towel Greyson had handed me. I raced to my room like a child, threw myself on my bed, and cried until I fell asleep.

Stupid . . . Me

October 17ᵗʰ, Sunday

It has been three weeks since I last saw Greyson. I called twice. He didn't answer. I texted once:

> *Greyson, I am so sorry for this misunderstanding. I hope you will forgive me. That message will forever haunt me. I went on one date with Ted. It was a long time ago. Since then I have received several texts from him, all addressed to Pretty Girl. I was with my family on Saturday. My family wants to meet you. I hope they will have that chance. I hope I will have the chance to see you, too. I'm so sorry. Please call me.*

I hoped for days he would reply. He didn't. I wish it didn't hurt so bad.

I tried again today to reach Greyson. I made cookies. I hoped to catch him at home after church. I rang, but nobody answered. I left the cookies with a note:

Greyson,

Please call.

Lindsey

I have buried myself in work during these lonely days. I volunteered for three committees. The work fills the bulk of my thoughts, but Greyson is still there in the edges . . . but . . . if I'm honest, he actually fills the bulk of my thoughts. Work is just a distraction.

I try for all I am worth to carefully place my loads of work in the front and center in my brain. I have even taken up daily jogging and massive amounts of yard work to distract my mind. I guess I am thankful there is plenty to do, I just wish it didn't hurt so much to be brushed off without the chance to explain.

Oh . . . and to cap things off with another one of life's twisted ironies . . . I got another text from Ted. It was sort of a farewell to the troops, or in his case, girlfriends. He is engaged and is to be married next Saturday.

Ugh . . . Me

October 2ⁱˢᵗ, Thursday

With my alarm clock screaming, I woke up early. I've really been enjoying my early morning run lately. I'm getting stronger, and I'm feeling some small fraction better about my current circumstances.

I left the house under low fuzzy clouds. All sounds were muted. Snow threatened. My lungs burned in the cold air, but I felt strong. Out on the main road, I was running toward home when a familiar truck approached in the distance. My insides shook. Pulling my beanie down low, I ducked my head and watched the street. After all this time, I prayed he didn't see me. I could do this. I could close this chapter in my life. It's what he wanted . . . right? If he wanted to know my reasons, my side of the story, so to speak, he would have answered my calls *or* my texts . . . *or* . . . not kept his eyes off me at church. (Elizabeth still smiled and waved, but she's also loyal to her brother. I debated trying to contact Greyson through her, a note or something, but I decided I had better not.) Greyson had made his decision perfectly clear. Yet, seeing his truck approach in the foggy morning light, stabbed me with daggers of grief that I could not have foreseen. Tears that I had bridled prickled and stung in the edges of my eyes. I willed them not to fall.

As the truck drew closer, I sorted through my feelings. As much as I wanted to be invisible. As much as I wanted him to drive on by, I also knew how much that simple act was going to hurt me. I burned to get to talk to him, just one chance. That's all I would ask.

Head down, I raced harder. Tears spilled, burning my eyes and blurring the road ahead of me. Blinking, I wiped at my eyes with my gloved hand. Bad choice. Whatever residue or dirt that was on my gloves was now in my eyes and burning like crazy. New tears spilled recklessly. They kept coming. Blinking hard, it felt like having a jalapeño pepper smeared in your face. I was a running faucet. The burn was so intense I could hardly keep my eyes open. Greyson's truck was almost to me. Blinking and squinting I looked up as I heard his engine closing the distance.

And then . . .

One little rabbit brush at the edge of the road caught my shoe and sent me sprawling. Arms flying to break my fall, I twisted and rolled as Greyson sped by. I landed hard on my left elbow and hip. My face hit the ground, sliding in the gravel. I could hear tires skid . . . or was it my face. I rolled to a stop face up under a sagebrush.

Stunned, I lay motionless for a moment. Footsteps pounded in the gravel. Hands slid under me and helped me to sit.

"Are you okay?" a voice said. A familiar voice.

Hunching over, I steadied myself. With searing pain coming from somewhere, I pushed up my beanie that had slipped over my eyes. I gazed up at my rescuer through my flooding eyes. Greyson had arrived. (Great . . . Was he going to think I pulled this stunt on purpose?)

"Lindsey . . ." His voice saying my name stabbed a jolt of pain right through me that was deeper than anything else I was feeling. "Are you okay?" His concern triggered another jolt. The pain was intense. It seemed to be getting worse. Strangely, it seemed to be coming from my left wrist.

"I'm fine." I managed, folding my legs up under me to stand. Greyson pulled twigs from my beanie.

He took my elbow. I shrugged it off, wincing at the movement and tumbling against him. Holding my left forearm against my torso, I repeated, "I'm fine. I don't need your help."

He touched my cheek with his glove. I jerked away. Bad choice, shooting pain raced down my leg from my hip. I winced. Fresh tears sprang. Not again . . .

Greyson drew his arm across my shoulders. I don't really know how it happened. I don't know if I fell. I don't know if it was because he pulled me in. Maybe it was some instinctual desire to be comforted. Maybe I was in shock. All I know is that the moment his arm stretched across my shoulders, I melted against his chest. My left wrist pounded and throbbed, sending shooting pains in all directions each time I moved it. I tucked it between us as I leaned on him and shook and sobbed.

Tightening his embrace, ever so gently with one arm around my back and the other cradling my neck, he held me in both his arms and let me cry.

The purple clouds above opened and puffy white snowflakes floated down.

Tears flowed in hot rivers down my cheeks. Greyson lifted my face in his gloved hands, wiping the tears with his thumbs. "Lindsey, do you have your phone."

I nodded with an unattractive sniff.

"Okay. Let's get you into the truck. I want you to call your school . . . or whatever you have to do to get a substitute. I'm going to take you to InstaCare. You need an x-ray."

I tried to shake my head in protest. Pain flashed. I winced hard.

In his truck, Greyson flipped the heater on high. Balling his coat, he propped it under my leg. He fashioned a sling for my arm out of a ratchet strap from his toolbox. He watched over me as I made three calls, and he typed and sent two emails for me.

"Are you good?" he asked, placing my phone beside me on the seat.

I nodded and sniffed. "Yes, everything's taken care of."

"Okay. Let's get you looked at." Greyson carefully buckled me in.

"I need my purse." My voice was cracked and hoarse from the sobs and the dirt I had eaten when I fell.

"We'll stop by your house."

He spun a U-turn as the wiper blades pushed the fluffy white snow from side to side.

Still delirious, or still in shock, I blubbered loudly, "I'm sorry, Greyson!"

Fresh tears sprang, as if a dam shattered. What was the matter with me? Why was I falling apart like this? I wanted it to stop. I wanted my blubbering to go away, but still it gushed. Still, my eyes flooded. Agghhhh . . .

Like he was comforting a sobbing child, which I was, he whispered, "Shhhh . . . Shhhh . . ." He patted my knee lightly. "It's okay. You can tell me all about it later. Right now, I think you should rest."

"No . . ." I shouted through the sobs. I was a sniveling mess. "No . . . I want to tell you now."

Greyson must have realized that he had lost to me. He drove silently. Patiently.

"You didn't answer your phone, Greyson, and that hurt so much." I choked embarrassingly through the tears. Shock completely dominated my senses and dissolved any thread of pride I may have had. "It hurt so deep." I twisted my head just enough to see the muscles in his jaw dancing. He was suffering too? Or . . . was he angry? It was impossible to tell. "I didn't do anything wrong, Greyson. It was all a mistake. I did go on a date with Ted, a long time ago. He has about a thousand girlfriends. I knew that. I went with him just because I am shallow, and I like wearing new clothes, and eating at restaurants, and letting my date pay for it . . . the food . . . not the clothes . . . that would be inappropriate . . ."

Greyson laughed softly at that. A refreshing sound amidst the turmoil and my anxiety. He wasn't angry . . .

He stopped his truck outside of my house. Untying my keys from where I had laced them into my shoelaces. He darted in and back out of my house with my purse in his hand.

He slid into the truck and sped down the road.

I twisted again, to reach gingerly with my right arm and touch Greyson's forearm. I had to explain . . .

"I didn't go kissing him in Las Vegas, Greyson. I only want to be kissed by you."

He cast me a look that was hard to decipher before turning his attention back to the road.

"Greyson?"

"What do you need?" His voice was tender.

"Greyson, it hurts when I sit this way." I gazed up at him.

He drove one handed as he lifted my fingers off his arm and righted my position on the seat. "Better?"

"Almost."

"We'll get you to InstaCare soon."

I sat back, pain slicing through my childish display of delirium. Leaning my head back against the headrest, I closed my eyes and focused on my breathing.

Miles sped under Greyson's tires.

Neither of us spoke.

I must have fallen asleep, because the next thing I knew, Greyson was helping me through the doors of the InstaCare. Injuring yourself early in the morning must be the best time because I was ushered right in and x-rays were taken.

While I waited for the doctor to tell me my results, the nurse brought Greyson back into the room to wait with me. I lay in my running clothes on the examining table, my beanie still on my head and my left arm in a sling. I made the nurse put my socks back onto my feet before I would let her bring in Greyson.

I was feeling more like myself. Thinking over the past hour, I felt so ashamed for my emotional display. What was I doing? Who did I think I was kidding by throwing myself all over this poor man? What a mess.

Greyson came in and sat in an orange, plastic chair. I needed to clear the air. "It seems like you are always coming to my rescue." His eyes were dark. He looked haggard and weary. "I'm sorry to take your time with my stupid clumsiness. I'm sorry for the grotesque emotional display that you just endured." I breathed deeply. "Thank you for your kindness and helping me. I just want you to know that I understand if you want nothing to do with me beyond this moment. I know you are incredibly busy. I can text someone to come and get me."

Greyson acted like he hadn't heard a word that I said. When he finally spoke, I had to strain to hear him, he spoke so low. He didn't meet my eyes but directed his gaze to a point on the floor. "I would never wish you to hurt yourself, but I wouldn't take back a moment."

My heart burned. I turned away. It was more emotion than I could deal with.

The doctor returned. As it turns out, I did a good number on myself. Three hairline fractures. One sprain. And a nice gash on my cheek. My remedies: one sling, crutches—as I see fit to use them, an ace bandage, and a butterfly bandage on my face . . . oh, and a bottle of Tylenol for the pain. Rest, rest, rest. The doctor gave me a note for two days of missed work. I was free to go.

Greyson stood, stepped beside me, and pulled another twig from my beanie. He lightly touched my shoulder. He and the nurse helped me into a wheelchair.

Greyson was my saving grace and took me by the school. I sat in the truck as he ran the note in and picked up the paperwork that I needed to account for my time off. A few more calls, a few more emails, and school would go on without me. Sadly.

Greyson escorted me into my house and settled me onto the couch. He wrapped me in a blanket.

A bowl of chicken noodle soup magically appeared at Greyson's hands. A tall glass of water, a bowl of black berries, and the remote control were also placed on the coffee table within easy reach.

Greyson touched my shoulder again. "Hey, I'll have Lori come by and check on you. Are you going to be okay?"

"I'm fine. I just feel so stupid. I'm so sorry for wasting half of your day."

Greyson brushed my words off like shooing a gnat.

"I wish I could stay, but I've got to get to work. I've got a man working single handed on a house that needs a full crew. I had better get there."

Resting in the warm blanket, I was perfect. "Thank you."

He stroked my head. My twig filled beanie was still planted on my head. "Do you want me to take off your beanie?"

"No. My curly hair does crazy things under a beanie. I'll take it off later. I don't want you to see me in any more of a shambles."

He bent toward me, hovered for a moment as if making a decision, and kissed me lightly on the beanie. "I'll come by after work."

"Thank you, again." It sounded so thin for the debt of kindness that I owed to him.

"No problem." He stood, grabbed his coat, and started for the kitchen door.

My heart caught.

"And Greyson?" I called over the back of the couch. "I really am sorry. About everything. About the text message from Ted. About everything . . ."

His reply was polite, like the kiss on my head. "I understand."

He opened the door. He paused. I wondered what he was thinking. Then he stepped out into the snow.

I slept the better part of the day.

Still in the beanie, and feeling the pain, I woke when Greyson, Lori, and Elizabeth walked into my house.

Lori bustled around in the kitchen. Greyson was with her, unloading sacks of groceries.

Elizabeth knelt on the floor in front of me on the couch. She touched my hand lightly. "Hi."

"Hi." I smiled weakly.

"Greyson told me what happened." She crossed her legs. "He feels like it is his fault that you fell. He feels like he ran you off the road."

"What?" I started. "No. Not at all. I tripped on a bush. It was all my fault. I promise."

"I think he just likes to worry sometimes. He takes things pretty serious."

She cast a glance toward the kitchen. Greyson and Lori were visiting, but their words were soft spoken, too quiet to be heard from this far away. I wondered what they were discussing. Elizabeth leaned forward. Speaking just above a whisper she said, "Like, he really took it hard when you two broke up."

"Broke up?" Was that what we were? And today I had thrown myself all over him. Ugh. I am such an idiot. No wonder the pitying glances and the pitiful kiss on the head. What must he think of me?

"He doesn't say too much about his feelings, you know, military and all . . ."

I nodded quietly, pondering her words.

She glanced carefully again. "But, I think he was really in love with you." Her eyes lighted with hope as she met mine. "I don't know if he can see it or not, but I know he still likes you. I think that text message really hurt him . . . a lot." She wrinkled her face up in a pitying grin, much like her brother's.

"Elizabeth, please understand. That message wasn't for me. It was a guy I had gone on one date with . . . months ago. I promise you I have never hidden any trips to Las Vegas from you, or you brother. I wouldn't." A wave of pain wracked my body. My face contorted and I steadied my breathing against it.

Elizabeth extended my glass of water to me. I took a sip as the pain subsided. She smiled, warm and genuine. Touching my arm, she leaned in. "I knew it. I knew it all along. When Greyson first read that message, I knew it couldn't be for you. You are too nice to do something like that, and he is just too stubborn to do the right thing sometimes."

Relief flooded. At least she believed me. She set the glass on the table for me.

"I never intended to hurt your brother."

"I know." Elizabeth reached an arm around me and gave me an awkward hospital-like hug. She leaned back. She told me something more. "See, Greyson was hurt more than he lets on when his engagement to Sarah ended. He thinks I don't know anything about it. He says I need to focus on my own priorities, but anyway, it was super difficult for him when they had to end things. I think he is overly sensitive because of it."

I was surprised by Elizabeth's openness. "Maybe he's just cautious?" I offered.

"Maybe? Who knows?" She grinned. Then her face lit up as though she were reliving a memory. "He did tell me some pretty funny stories about our mom making him ask girls to dances when he was in high school. He had a really horrible prom experience . . . it is so funny. You will have to ask him to tell you some time."

"Maybe I will, if I get the chance."

Lori and Greyson put food for all of us on the coffee table. As if on cue, Rick entered through the kitchen. With Greyson's help, I sat up. Lori sat beside me on the couch. Rick brought in a chair from the table for himself. Elizabeth sat beside me on the floor and Greyson sat directly across from me. I couldn't help it. My eyes kept finding his. We stared silently at one another for a few precious moments. I wish I knew what was going through his head.

Rick offered a blessing, and we ate one of Lori's scrumptious dinners of baked chicken, broccoli, and seasoned mashed potatoes with homemade gravy. Conversations rolled around the table. We laughed (well, I tried to laugh, it just hurt too much) at Rick's tales of growing up and the mischief he caused.

Studying the faces around me, my heart ached more deeply than I could have ever imagined. These were *my* friends. These were the people I loved, here in this special place. The Craig's had given me much more than a house, they had given me a circle of love. A lump formed in my throat.

Greyson.

That was one part of this new little family I was not sure that I would be able to keep.

The pain cut deeper than any wound.

I am alone for the night. I don't have it in me to take a shower. I'll do that tomorrow . . . hopefully.

Blast! I just realized that I should probably call my mom. Nah, I'll tell her all about it after I've healed.

Broken . . . Me

October 24th, Sunday

I didn't make it to church today. I did make it into the shower. I was so exhausted after my shower, I just crashed on my bed.

Lying there, staring at the ceiling, I wanted to read my copy of Mr. Craig's will. I was ready to understand all the circumstances that brought me here. Struggling to the closet with my crutches, I pulled down the file. Gratefully, it was not damaged in the downpour. Miracles.

Pressing the file open on the bed, I began. I read word for word Mr. Craig's will and his account of the events that involved my dad. I also found a receipt for a grave site memorial. Included was a photo of a headstone. My father's headstone. Mr. Craig had put a beautiful granite memorial on my father's grave. What a debt of gratitude I owe to the Craig family. My full heart burst. An overwhelming desire to see it flooded through me. This was my dad. I mean, I had two dads, but this was my dad.

A deep spiritual chord resonated. Gazing at the photo, I could see that a father that I had never seen, never known, never completed a puzzle with, or gone out for ice cream with—this father I had never known, had provided everything. Maybe it's kind of like our Heavenly Father.

Goodness, I am a weepy mess. Maybe it's the Tylenol? Maybe it's Greyson?

Speaking of . . . there was a soft knock at the front door. Greyson called up the stairs.

"Lindsey? Hey, it's Greyson. I have some lunch. Is it okay if I come up?"

Greyson was funny. He could have texted. He could have called. He always seemed to prefer real life interactions. "Sure. Come on up."

"Lindsey?" Greyson was at the top of the stairs. "Are you in your room?"

"Yep. Don't worry. I'm decent. Just push the door open." I wrestled with my body to sit up a little higher against the pillows.

Greyson looked amazing. Still dressed in his Sunday clothes, he was gorgeous. The great thing is, he doesn't know it. He is not obsessed with his looks. He just looks amazing.

I was instantly self-conscious of how disheveled I must have looked. I was clean, and I had brushed my teeth, but I didn't have one smidge of makeup on. I hadn't put any product on my untamed, slightly damp, curls. The sweats and old t-shirt from my freshman year in college completed my look. Oh, and let's not leave out the neon green fuzzy socks with pink flamingos on them . . .

And then I panicked.

The green fuzzy socks, and those cute pink flamingos, were sitting on top of my nightstand. I had failed to put them on my feet because I had wanted to read the will . . .

It was too late. Greyson was already in the room! My feet were fully exposed, resting on top of my mounded-up blankets. I was afraid to move.

Greyson grabbed the plush padded stool from the vanity with one hand and sat down beside me. "Lori sent you some soup."

He had no idea of my anguish.

He gently handed me a deep bowl, steaming with Lori's famous chicken and dumplings stew.

"Thank you." All the blood drained from my face. With my eyes wide, I determined to not make any motions towards my feet. I wouldn't even let my eyes pass that way. Maybe, Greyson wouldn't see them if I didn't point them out.

Greyson furnished a spoon and a napkin from his shirt pocket.

I smiled nervously.

"Are you okay?" Greyson was way too observant. I would have to play it cool. I sipped a few spoonfuls of delicious soup to prove my okay-ness while trying to push a corner of a blanket over my toes undetected.

I tried for a distraction. "Did Elizabeth come with you? She's welcome to come up."

"No, she's with Rick and Lori."

Agggghhh! He caught me!

Greyson caught my fidgeting and glanced toward my toes. I couldn't help it. I yelled, "No! Don't look!"

I tried to shield him, but my broken body and steaming bowl held me anchored to my spot.

Greyson started. "What? What's the matter?" He examined me, glancing over me from head to toe.

"No! Don't look!" I shouted again, which was completely unnecessary because Greyson was only inches away.

"Lindsey, what's wrong?" It worked. I diverted his attention back to my face.

"Please take this," I begged, extending the bowl to him as much as my body would allow. "Please."

"Of course, but what's going on?" Greyson lifted the bowl from my hands.

"Please," I begged again. "I know I am being irrational, but can you . . ."

I never finished my sentence. In his concern, Greyson quickly stood and placed the steaming bowl on the nightstand, next to my socks. Being the kind of man that he is, he walked to the foot of the bed and . . . well, I screamed. Then I did the most mature thing I could think of and buried my face into my hands.

I don't know what thoughts Greyson must have had. He never let on. As I sat, face in hands, he calmly pulled a blanket over my legs, feet and all. He didn't say a word.

I cautiously lifted my eyes, peeking out over my fingers.

Greyson sat back down on the stool and picked up the soup bowl from off of the nightstand.

I slowly found the courage to meet his eyes.

"Your deepest fear?" he asked.

I nodded, face still in hands. "I'm sorry. It's stupid, I know. I forgot to put on my socks."

"It's not stupid, and, for the record, there is nothing wrong with your feet."

"They are like troll feet with marbles for toes. They're hideous." I was emphatic. He had to know just how awful they were.

Greyson laughed. "No, Lindsey. They are not hideous. If you want to see hideous feet, go to boot camp and share a barracks with a bunch of smelly guys."

He caught me with that one. I couldn't help the laugh that flew out of my mouth. The image of a bunch of burly soldiers all standing at attention in their bare feet. Bare, calloused, hairy, smelly feet. Maybe there was hope for me?

He passed me the bowl. I took it. A smile passed between us. My breath returned to its normal rhythm. *He saw my feet,* I marveled. *He saw my feet, and he did not run screaming from the room.* Wow . . .

"Lindsey?"

"Uh huh."

"I came today because I was hoping we could talk." He leaned forward, his elbows on his thighs. He looked toward the floor, rubbed a hand across his short hair, and lifted his face.

We spoke in unison, each saying the other's name.

"You first," Greyson said.

"No. You go ahead," I insisted.

Bobbing his head, Greyson began, "Lindsey, I've been struggling." He paused. I didn't interrupt. He pulled in another deep breath. "Lindsey, I feel so . . ." He pushed his hands through his short hair. ". . . like an idiot." His eyes poured into mine, deep and troubled. "I've made a mess of things, and I hurt you. Something I never ever want to do." Sitting up, he continued. "I want to apologize for all the pain and humiliation I have caused you. I made assumptions, I accused you of something you didn't even do . . . I let my pride blind me . . . and I nearly killed you on the road two days ago."

I put up a finger. "No. Nope. You can't take credit for that one. That was all on me."

"I feel responsible. I can't help but think if it had been any other person to pass you on the road, you wouldn't have tripped."

"It was my two clumsy feet that caused my fall."

His eyes were troubled as he continued, "I want to tell you when I read that message on your phone, I thought I had been played. I stewed for days. I got your texts. I read every one of them, but I was blinded by hurt and pride. That's why I didn't respond."

I listened, my heart seizing as he spoke.

"The thing is, I'm an idiot. I never should have suspected you, or cast judgment on you for anything." He met my eyes. "The day you brought the cookies, Sunday."

I nodded.

"We were at Dave's. He let me rant for an hour. Then you know what he said to me?"

"What did he say?" I swallowed, my heart racing like a thousand stallions.

"He told me to get a grip and apologize to you because I was about to let the best thing that ever happened to me slip through my hands. Then I went home and found your note. You'll laugh at me when I tell you, but I broke down. While Elizabeth was in the house, I went out to my truck and I cried for an hour. I sobbed."

"Why didn't you call?" My heart ached for him. I hungered to reach for him, but that couldn't happen across this gigantor bowl of soup.

"At that point, I thought it was too late. Lindsey, I'm sorry."

It was too much. "Greyson, please stop. Don't torture yourself on my account. Please . . . okay? You did nothing wrong. Over and over you have rescued me from one calamity or another. I don't want to be the albatross around your neck, so to speak. I want to be with you. I want to be your cheering squad, not your burden. I loved working with you up the mountain. I love making meals with you. I would love to be a small part in Elizabeth's pallet bench project, if that ever gets finished . . . I . . ."

His face twitched and contorted as though he were biting back emotion.

I balanced the bowl of soup. Carefully sliding it onto the nightstand with one arm. Twisting, I pushed my legs over the edge of the bed (bare feet and all) to sit up.

"Greyson?"

He reached to steady me. He took my right hand in both his. "Lindsey, I need to tell you something."

I was strangely aware of my feet. Even though Greyson had already seen them, I was uncomfortable. Maybe it is just a habit, but I wanted them covered. I placed one foot inconspicuously over the other.

He studied our clasped hands for a moment. He must have caught my discomfort. He let go of my hand, then, kneeling, he lifted my neon green socks with the pink flamingos from the nightstand and carefully slipped them onto my feet one by one.

Color flushed to my cheeks. "Greyson . . . don't . . ."

He shook his head against my feeble protests. Looking up he said, "I need you to know . . ." He paused. He seemed to be struggling to find the right words. "Lindsey, there is no other way to put it. I love you. You have my heart . . ."

I cut him off as I reached an arm around his neck. The reach was awkward, but the message was clear. "I love you too," I whispered.

Closing my eyes, his lips found mine. All the pent-up emotions of the last three weeks poured into his kiss. Worlds spun. Time dissolved. Everything folded into this one moment. Drawing back, he clasped my hands and lifted them to his face. Kissing each one in turn. He met my eyes. Emotions surging, he grabbed me tight.

I winced involuntarily. Greyson quickly released me. "Lindsey, I'm so sorry. I'm hurting you."

I shook my head. "It's okay." I touched his face. I wished I could soften all the lines of worry. The rugged warmth swam under my fingers. Then, I grinned sheepishly. "Thank you for putting my pink flamingo socks on me."

"You're welcome." He smiled softly, kissed my fingers, and added, "Anytime."

I felt tired all of a sudden, but there was something more I wanted to ask. "Greyson . . ."

"What?" He helped me to move back to my position of leaning on the pillows against the headboard.

"Will you go to Las Vegas with me?"

"Las Vegas . . . wow. You don't waste any time." His smile was teasing.

My face flushed. "I didn't think about that," I said. "I want to go see my dad's grave, and I would really like you to go with me. We could go any time. It doesn't have to be soon."

He nodded. Then spying the photograph on the bed he asked, "Is that it?"

"Yes. I've never been there, but I would really like to go and see him . . . it."

Greyson handed me my soup. "I would love to go. You name the day."

Peaceful . . . Me

October 26th, Tuesday

Life is full of beautiful moments. Greyson, Elizabeth, and I left Cedar City right after school today. I winced and gritted my teeth a few times, but my parents have invited all of us down for dinner. I didn't want to miss it. I sat in the middle seat of Greyson's truck and held his hand. Elizabeth happily sat beside me. We sang all our favorite songs. Greyson sang three in Spanish.

All of the family was there—Susy, Annie, their husbands, and the little ones.

Mom and Dad welcomed Greyson and Elizabeth both with hugs. Mindy, Alice, and Michael all glommed onto Elizabeth and wanted to play. I hobbled along and did okay.

Mom steered the conversions around the dinner table. "Greyson, now do you think Lindsey is safe there alone in that big house? I just think it would be better if she were down here more often. Things keep happening that have me worried."

Ah Mom . . . I got myself into this mess.

"I wouldn't want her anywhere else." Greyson looked at me beaming. "I think the house is safe."

Susy nudged me softly under the table. When I looked her way, she nodded her approval of Greyson.

I smiled.

"So, Greyson," Dad asked, "Lindsey says you're a marine. Tell us a little about your military career."

Greyson humbly recounted his training and sights that he has seen across the years of his service. I listened in awe.

After dinner, Dad and the boys went out to the garage to look at Dad's new fishing pole. Susy and Annie rescued Elizabeth from the little ones. Elizabeth found me in the kitchen, leaning against the counter. She put her arm around my waist. "Thank you for inviting us to dinner. It has been so much fun," Elizabeth spoke to Mom.

Mom drank it up. "We'll have to get together again soon. Maybe we'll do something at Lindsey's house. Once you're healed that is." She smiled at me.

"I'd love that," I said.

Greyson and the boys walked back in. I could see from the light in Dad's face that he fully approved of Greyson.

Mom hugged us all before we left.

Elizabeth rode with her head on my shoulder all the way back home. Greyson spoke softly, rubbing the back of my hand with his thumb. "I love your family, Lindsey. They are wonderful people."

"Yeah, I kinda like them." I smiled.

"I kinda like you." He grinned.

I touched Greyson's face and kissed him once before he and Elizabeth drove off for the night.

I couldn't have asked for a better day . . . Me

October 29th, Friday

I did some research this week on how to build a bench from a pallet. It was a little overwhelming, but I made a plan. I texted Greyson:

> I'll meet you at your house tonight. I have a surprise for Elizabeth. I can't wait to see you.

Greyson replied:

> Lindsey, Thank you for your text. I love you.

My heart twirled.

Cooks' Experiment Night was all things pumpkin. Pumpkin biscuits, pumpkin stew, and pumpkin pie. I think I'm turning orange.

Tonight's questions were crazy enough. Elizabeth printed a set of would-you-rather scenarios. Greyson said he would rather sleep with a smelly sock on his nose than have the smell of garbage in his nose all day. Elizabeth said she would rather drink fishbowl water than pool water. And I said I would rather be a tree than live in a tree the rest of my life.

The doorbell rang and Elizabeth went to let Sharon in. As soon as Elizabeth was out of the room, I sprang into action . . . well, as much as I was able. Grabbing the question jar, I pulled out the paper strips and stuffed them in a cupboard. Greyson looked at me as though I had lost my mind. Unzipping my purse, I handed him a new set of questions, "Here stuff these in the jar."

He obeyed. "What have you got up your sleeve tonight?"

"You'll see." I stepped back, grabbed the washcloth and began wiping the counters. My pulse thumped. I caught my breath.

Sharon and Elizabeth stepped into the kitchen.

Sharon looked at me once. I gave a subtle nod. "Do I get a question?" she asked.

Elizabeth twisted the lid from the jar. "Yes, my friend," she said dramatically.

I waited.

Greyson raised an eyebrow at me.

Elizabeth read, "What do you need to make . . . a pallet bench?" She let the paper dangle in her hand, a look of consternation shaped her features. She looked at Greyson.

Sharon tried to hide a smirk as she played along, "Wow, that's a new one. Um . . . I guess I'd need a pallet and maybe a saw or something?"

Elizabeth cocked a hip. She squinted her eyes at her brother. "What are you doing?" She pulled another paper from the jar. She read it silently and set it on the counter. She pulled another and another. Each one read the exact same thing. "Okay, what's going on."

Sharon blew my cover. She pointed with her head and rolled her eyes in my direction.

Elizabeth looked my way, her eyes pointing. She pointed a finger at me.

"Oh boy," Greyson spun the suspense. "I think someone is in for a surprise."

I couldn't hold it in anymore. "Elizabeth," I exclaimed. "We're going to build a pallet bench tonight. Your pallet bench. And I bought you a few supplies to get the job done."

"No way . . . Are you serious? That pallet has been out there forever."

"Well, then we need to get started."

Greyson led the way to the garage. In the garage, I handed Elizabeth the gloves, a can of stain, a hammer, and the finishing nails that I bought her. Greyson plugged in the power tools and we all got started.

At ten o'clock, Sharon and Elizabeth retired to the basement for a late movie. Greyson pulled me into his arms. There in the garage, standing near the new pallet bench, we talked about marriage.

"Lindsey, I can't even think about not having you in my life." Greyson knew all the words to make me smile.

"Where would we live? My house or yours?" I asked.

"Why not both, for now?" he said.

"Mmmmm . . . that sounds good. I laid my head against his chest.

Yep, it's love . . . Me

November 4ᵗʰ, Thursday

Hello, diary. It's been a while.

Work, dating Greyson, and healing. That is what I have been doing, but today is special. Today something very precious occurred and I want to cover every detail. I want it written in stone, never to be forgotten through the annals of time.

Here it is for your reading enjoyment.

It was the last period of the day. Language arts. In the middle of my killer lesson on prepositional phrases, an office aide brought in a bouquet of gorgeous flowers, a mix of all kinds and colors. Very beautiful, especially on this cold fall day. I peeked at the card.

You inspire me.

My heart skipped. I lovingly set the bouquet on my already crowded desk. So sweet. I continued my lesson. I pointed to my example on the board.

"Prepositions usually go before a noun. A preposition expresses the relationship to another word in the sentence, or clause . . ."

Magically, another bouquet arrived. Absolutely beautiful. Pausing my lesson, I took the bouquet from the student aide.

"Miss J?" a voice from the back of the room called out. Clayton. I knew that voice.

"Yes," I absently responded, scooting a pile of papers with the back of my hand, I made a space on my desk for the second bouquet.

"So, a preposition is kind of like those flowers," Clayton said with a smirk.

I looked up, not sure where he was going with this.

"I'm thinking someone is expressing a relationship with you."

The class roared.

"Close, Clayton, but not quite." I tried to hide my smile as I read the card.

I want to be a forever part of your life.

My hands tingled. My butterflies stirred pools of elation. What was Greyson doing?

I had to get the students back on track.

"Okay, okay, everyone. Now, let's pull our focus back around. Start at the top. Work with your partner and complete one through ten. See if you can identify each of the prepositions in the examples."

The laughter simmered to the quiet murmurs of students working. I busied myself helping a team of students.

Less than a minute later, another aide was at the door.

"Miss Jones . . ." Clayton called out.

Still attempting to teach, I asked, "Yes?" without looking up.

"More prepositions are at the door."

All eyes left their work. A few elbows nudged one another. Laughs bubbled to the ceiling and out the door.

I was still swimming in the last delivery. I stood and collected the delivery. Hopeless to find any more room on my desk. I set it gently on the floor beside my desk. I read the note.

I struggle to find the words to tell you what I feel for you.

"Okay. Back to work," I directed. The students were quick to comply. My thoughts were tangled in Greyson.

Three minutes later, another bouquet was at the door.

Several voices chorused, "More prepositions!"

Good grief . . .

The longest minutes are the minutes without you.

I placed this bouquet with the previous one on the floor.

"What's going on, Miss Jones? You got a hot date or something?" Now Cassie was getting into the fun. Great . . .

Laughs.

"Or something, Cassie." I laughed. "Right now, you all have a hot date with prepositions. Let's get back to it." I guided the lesson forward the best that I could. I was absolutely more distracted than the students. What was Greyson up to? This was a little over the top.

Another bouquet arrived. I added it to the floor. Wow . . .

My deepest wish in this life is that I might be worthy of you.

"Someone's got a bad crush on Miss J. Come on, Miss J. Tell us about it." Clayton couldn't keep quiet.

Laughs.

"Tell us!"

"Yeah!"

"Thank you for that, Clayton. Now, I will tell you about the differences between prepositions and adverbs," I countered, determined to teach my lesson, but I didn't get very far because another bouquet was standing at the door. Literally. The bouquet was almost as big as the student aide doing the delivery. It was a bouquet with legs. This time it was two dozen red roses.

At this point, the class burst into cheers. I couldn't help the grin that lit up my face. I pulled the card from the holder.

The class chanted, "Read it! Read it!"

I read it silently:

I love you—Greyson

I set the card neatly on my desk, heart fluttering, tears threatening. I set the bouquet on my teaching cart right at the front of the class.

Four minutes before the end of the day, and deep in the heart of my lesson, a loud whoop went up from the class. I looked up just in time to watch Greyson step through the classroom door.

My heart caught in my chest. Elizabeth followed behind him. She stood quietly inside the door.

I took it all in. Greyson was in a button-up shirt (I love his button up shirts, so much more classy than a t-shirt), nice jeans, and a charcoal blazer.

Oh, and nice shoes. Yes, he looked good. His chiseled frame. His tight-clipped hair. His deep, swirling eyes that draw me in every time. Mostly, though, I saw his character, his honesty, his love.

Yes, I took in Greyson.

The world stopped, in a good way. Why was he here?

I was still teaching for four more minutes. I stared down the front row of students with a half-hearted attempt at my stern teacher face to restore some order. It worked to quiet three of them for about a millisecond.

Greyson stepped in front of me. He smiled. "Hi."

"Hi," I said back.

The class cheered and shouted, "Hi!"

Clayton called out. "Hey, are you the noun that sent the prepositions?"

Raucous laughter.

Kids can be so weird.

I blushed but smiled.

"Prepositions?" Greyson addressed Clayton. "Hmmm . . . I thought they were flowers."

Laughs and giggles.

I stood there, unable to talk, with flowers and roses that outnumbered the students. I had lost my class, my lesson had failed on everyone, except for Clayton who was putting in his own interpretation of prepositions. I would have to do a major reteach. And yet. Somehow it seemed okay. Very okay.

Then Greyson looked over the students. He held a finger to his lips. As if mesmerized by his signal, they all froze in their tracks and became silent. With eager faces, they watched and waited.

Greyson dropped to one knee. I think a girl on the third row fainted. Her friends helped her up.

I trembled.

Greyson looked back at me with eyes full of warmth, love, and light. "Lindsey," He winked at the class. "I mean, Miss Jones . . ."

A single voice from the back yelled. "Whoop! Whoop!" I bet you can guess who it was.

Greyson choked on a chuckle.

I was shaking as Greyson took my hand. His hand trembled, too.

I didn't mean for them to fall, but they fell. Those special happy tears, reserved for moments like this.

The room still waited, holding its breath.

With our eyes locked, Greyson spoke, "Lindsey, you are everything to me. Lindsey Jones, will you marry me?"

The students held their breath. Tears spilled off my face.

Greyson released my hand to open a silver velvet box with a sparkling ring inside.

Shaking, I answered with the only words that fit the moment . . . that fit my intense feelings for this man. "Yes. Yes, I will marry you."

Greyson slid the ring onto my hand. Then he gasped, jumped to his feet, and swept me into his arms.

The class broke into some wild dance party . . . with two of the students still tackling their prepositions . . .

Then Greyson asked me, "What time does class get out?"

"In two minutes."

"Perfect." He turned to the class. "Class dismissed."

The room was cleared of all students in about three seconds flat.

Elizabeth hugged us both in turn and raced off to get her things from her last class.

Greyson held my hand and gazed at the ring on my finger.

"Thank you," he smiled.

I smiled too. Then I kissed my fiancé.

Engaged to Greyson . . . Me

November 25th, Thanksgiving!

Hello, Posterity.

I am closing the pages of this diary, but not before I tell you that Greyson and I got married yesterday. When you know it's right, why wait? Right?

Remember the flowers? I wore them in my hair. It was beautiful. Everything was. The groom, the dress, the cake. Wonderful.

We had the reception right here at the ranch. Elizabeth wore a dress that belonged to her mother. Greyson wore one of his father's ties.

Annie, Susy, and their husbands all helped with the decorating. The house is bursting with white daisies, everywhere.

Dave and Jennifer came to the reception. Dave lifted Greyson right off the ground in a man hug when he walked through the door. He delicately hugged me as he wished us felicity. (We now have a monthly dinner date with them.)

Mom was on cloud nine. A few friends from St. George made it to the reception. She was fully in her element telling them all about the buckshot in the ceiling.

Sister Vandamm gave me a warm hug. She congratulated us both and gave us journals with new pens.

Rick and Lori hugged us both. Lori made us a patchwork quilt. She made one for Elizabeth, too.

Dad smiled and shook everyone's hands. Before the evening ended, he hugged me tight and said, "Lindsey, I'm so proud of you."

"Thanks, Dad."

Today is the first day of our honeymoon. We are on our way to Las Vegas. Will there be some sweet kissing? I guarantee it.

Tomorrow, we are going to see my dad's memorial. You see, I want to tell him thanks, too.

Oh, and, if you were wondering, Greyson still thinks my feet are cute.

Warmest regards, and best wishes for your happiness . . . Me

The End

About the Author

Sherrie Mackelprang earned her BA degree from Southern Utah University. *Fuzzy Socks and Midnight Clocks* is her second published work.

When she is not writing, Sherrie is typically found in her garden wearing closed-toe shoes, because she, like the heroine in *Fuzzy Socks*, is also ashamed of her feet.

Sherrie loves gardening, caramel popcorn, and eating her husband's egg foo young. She lives in Utah with her husband and their adopted cat.

AUTHORS WANTED

Whether you're an aspiring author looking to publish your first book or a seasoned author who's been published before, we want to hear from you.

Cedar Fort loves their authors and their stories! If you are interested in becoming a published Cedar Fort author please submit your manuscript to:

SUBMIT.CEDARFORT.COM

CEDAR FORT HAS PUBLISHED BOOKS IN THE FOLLOWING GENRES:

- LDS Nonfiction
- General Nonfiction
- Fiction
- Cookbooks
- Juvenile
- Children's
- Children's books with customizable characters

In harmony with our company values, we reserve the right to remove any profanity, violence, graphic, and/or sexual content in any book accepted for publication. We recommend you remove this type of content before submitting your book.